MW01282729

BILLION-DOLLAR RANSOM

For a preview of upcoming books and information about the author, visit JamesPatterson.com or find him on Facebook, X, Instagram, or Substack.

BILLION-DOLLAR RANSOM

A THRILLER

JAMES PATTERSON
AND DUANE SWIERCZYNSKI

Little, Brown and Company
New York Boston London

The characters and events in this book are fictitious. Any similarity to real persons, living or dead, is coincidental and not intended by the author.

Little, Brown and Company
Hachette Book Group
1290 Avenue of the Americas, New York, NY 10104
littlebrown.com

First Edition: September 2025

ISBN 9780316570039 (hc) / 9780316596770 (large print)
LCCN 2025932204

Printing 1, 2025

LSC-H

Printed in the United States of America

PROLOGUE

CHAPTER 1

Transcript of audio conversation (recovered from private Macao-based server)

ONE: Listen to my voice very closely. That is your only job right now. If you have any questions, please wait until the end of my short presentation. I will answer what is relevant.

[*No response.*]

ONE: Excellent. No names, even fictitious ones, will be used at any point during this operation. And that includes this briefing session, the only one we'll have as a group. All of you have been assigned code numbers. They will appear on your home screens. You may refer to me as One.

[*No response.*]

ONE: To set your minds at ease, please know that your voices have all been digitally scrambled. You may answer in the affirmative when I ask you a question directly. Do you understand, Two?

TWO: Stay silent until the question-and-answer portion of the program.

ONE: Well done. Let's hear from Three and Four. Understood?

THREE: Yes.

FOUR [*Under her breath*]: Seriously? [*Pause.*] Yes, One. Three and I understand.

ONE: How about you, Five?

FIVE: Yeah, I got you.

ONE: And, finally, Six?

SIX: Yes. I understand.

ONE: Goody. Now, some ground rules. First: Your numbered code names will stay with you throughout the mission. No trading numbers or changing them. They were assigned to each of you for a specific reason. If this is unclear, speak up now.

[*Pause.*]

ONE: Second rule: The plan must be followed *precisely*. Not a single change will be permitted. If you ignore a step, you will not be paid. If you improvise, you will not be paid. If you involve others, you will not be paid. If you perform a task a minute too early or a minute too late, you will not be paid. You are to perform your tasks at the precise minute—almost to the second. If this is unclear, speak up now.

[*Pause.*]

ONE: Final rule, and this is more of an expectation than a rule. It is possible, perhaps even likely, that one or more people will be killed at some point during our mission. You must not let this throw you. Some deaths are unavoidable and ultimately may serve the greater plan. If anyone has a problem with this, speak now and you will be relieved of your duties.

[*Pause.*]

ONE: Now for the pep talk. The one thing I want you to remember, above all else, is that you *deserve* this. You need to *internalize* that and truly *believe* it. You have earned this. Why? Because, like me, you've all come from nothing. And you are merely taking what is rightfully yours.

[*Pause.*]

ONE: When we have completed our mission, this group will have pulled off the most famous kidnapping in history. Nothing else comes close—not the Lindbergh child, not Patricia Campbell Hearst, not John Paul Getty the Third. *This* is the one they will study in books and films for decades to come. That will be for many reasons, not least of which is the size of the ransom. Which will be the largest ever: one billion dollars.

[*On the recording, there are a series of excited and astonished murmurs.*]

ONE: Upon successful execution of your part of the plan, you will be paid your share of that one-billion-dollar ransom within forty-eight hours. Then you have the rest of your lives to enjoy what is rightfully yours. If you follow the plan, no one will ever know you were involved. The money will be untraceable, and you will be able to spend it freely anywhere in the world. Are there any questions?

[*Pause.*]

ONE: Excellent. Now you may applaud.

[*There is a confused pause before One breaks out in a hearty laugh, which seems to give permission to the others. They join in the laughter and eventually erupt in a round of applause.*]

DAY ONE

CHAPTER 2

Wednesday, 3:14 p.m.

ELIZABETH "BOO" SCHRAEDER couldn't help but smile as she settled the tab at her favorite Beverly Hills salon.

The salon was arguably the most exclusive in LA. Their hair-extension work was unparalleled, and appointments with their stylists were among the most highly coveted on the West Coast. The real draw to potential customers, however, was the salon's clientele, a list of million-dollar names: Kim. Taylor. Chrissy. Zendaya. What you had done to your hair was not as important as who might be sitting in the next chair.

But Boo didn't patronize this salon for any of those reasons. She honestly just got a kick out of the place. The Style Circus, she called it when gossiping with friends back home in Arkansas. Only here could some of the world's most important faces be seen at their most unguarded and vulnerable. The sheer spectacle cracked Boo up, especially as she got a little wine-drunk in the early afternoon.

Now that her two-hour appointment was over, Boo emerged back into reality through the shaded private back entrance behind Burton Way, where her car—an onyx Bentley—would be waiting.

Boo had finally gotten used to the idea of having a driver. She'd resisted for months, but eventually Randolph had put his foot down. Yes, her husband understood that Boo was a woman fully capable of taking care of herself on the mean streets of Beverly Hills. "That's one of the many reasons I married you," he'd said. But Randolph also reminded her that being his wife came with all kinds of attention. Some of it was the kind of attention no one wants. And Randolph, as he liked to remind people, was a man with many enemies.

And Boo had to admit it was nice to be driven home after enjoying a glass (or three) of a 2017 Château Lafite while relaxing in the styling chair.

It helped that Boo genuinely liked her driver, Emily, the epitome of *chill.* LA's notorious traffic, which spiked the blood pressure of even the most seasoned drivers, didn't seem to faze Emily. She didn't waste time with small talk but was happy to engage in a chat. Not quite the same as talking smack with her besties from Fort Smith, Boo knew, but sometimes she was simply grateful for the companionship.

Emily climbed out of the driver's seat the moment she saw Boo. She smiled and moved to open the back door. "See anybody cool this afternoon?" the driver asked with a playful smirk. "Queen Bey, perhaps? She's playing at SoFi Stadium tonight."

Emily didn't see the hulking form crouched behind the Bentley. The form rose, quick as a shadow, a dark object dangling from his right gloved hand.

Boo shouted a warning. *"Behind you!"*

But it was too late.

The figure whipped a leather sap across the back of Emily's skull. Her body bounced off the side of the car and collapsed on the pavement. The attack lasted all of three seconds.

Boo spun around and grabbed the handle of the salon's back door. But it was locked. Guests had to be buzzed in, just like at the front entrance.

Deep down she'd known this, but she had to try anyway.

Before Boo could reach into her purse for her industrial-strength mace—an item that Randolph insisted she carry—the attacker had his burly arms around her upper torso, squeezing tight, letting her know he was in charge.

"Mrs. Schraeder, stay calm."

"Who the hell are you?"

"That doesn't matter. What matters is what I know about you," he said in a tone that was grave yet controlled. "For instance, I know you were army, Seventy-Fifth Ranger Regiment. You have training and know how to defend yourself."

"You want a demonstration, asshole?"

"That won't help you now, so please be cool. Last thing I want to do is hurt you."

Boo said, "Like you hurt my driver?"

"Your driver will be fine."

"I don't know. You hit her pretty hard."

"I needed the keys."

"Wait... all of this just so you can steal my Bentley? You're an idiot, whoever you are."

Boo tried to turn and get a closer look at the assailant. He was wearing some kind of sheer mask. The material resembled the mesh of a stocking, but the construction was something more advanced—it looked thin, yet it was substantial enough to twist and distort his features.

Boo's attacker placed his hand on her chin and, as gently as a doctor examining a patient, moved her head so she was facing forward. Then he whispered hot against her cheek: "That's not what this is."

Boo said, "You know someone is watching us, right? He's been watching this whole time. Guy in the green baseball cap, down at the end of the drive. I don't think you've thought this through."

"He'll be taken care of. Right after I take care of you."

"Take care of me how?"

"Don't worry. This won't hurt."

A harsh blast of wetness hit Boo's mouth and nostrils. It was like being slapped in the face by a wave from an ocean of chemicals. The spray seemed to instantly seal up her airway.

She tried to suck in a breath, but before that could happen and far quicker than she would have thought, her brain stopped recording.

CHAPTER 3

THE MAN IN the green cap standing at the end of the driveway had indeed been watching. He'd been there for a few minutes now and had witnessed pretty much *everything*:

The kidnapper hiding behind the Bentley.

The kidnapper bashing the back of the driver's skull with a leather sap.

The kidnapper grabbing the blonde and putting his mouth close to her ear as if he were telling her an important secret.

The kidnapper spraying a chemical into her pretty little face.

The blonde passing out instantly, like a puppet with its strings cut.

The kidnapper catching her full weight, then gently lifting her unconscious body and depositing it in the Bentley's trunk like he was putting away a doll in a fancy toy chest.

All in a matter of, what, thirty seconds? What a thrill to watch a total professional at work! The man in the green cap almost wished he knew the kidnapper's name for no other reason than that he was now an instant fan.

With his blond victim tucked away, the kidnapper took care of a few details. He felt for the unconscious driver's pulse. Once satisfied that she was alive, he dragged her to the back wall of the salon—presumably, Green Cap thought, so she'd be out of the way if someone came blasting down the drive. He scanned the asphalt to make sure the pretty blonde hadn't dropped anything, then climbed behind the wheel of the Bentley and peeled away.

The whole thing was great fun. Almost like a movie—ten out of ten, no notes. Green Cap wished he could rewind it and watch it again.

Alas, now it was his turn to work.

Green Cap pulled a burner phone from his jacket pocket. It was an old-fashioned flip phone with only one contact stored in its memory. He pressed the number. After exactly three rings, someone answered.

Following a moment of silence, Green Cap said: "One hundred percent."

The listener did not reply, nor was a response expected. The person simply hung up.

Green Cap began strolling toward Burton Way, looking like he didn't have a care in the world. And he didn't. Well, he wouldn't—after a few minor tasks. He pulled the battery out of the phone and deposited it in the first trash can he saw. This was improper battery disposal, but he didn't care. The world was already going to hell. One more cell phone battery wouldn't make a difference.

Without breaking his stride, Green Cap removed the SIM card from the phone and pocketed it. He snapped the body of the phone in half and tossed the broken pieces in two different trash cans. More fodder for the Great Pacific Garbage Patch.

He stopped to buy a small cup of piping-hot coffee from Starbucks, but this was not to drink. This was to drown and destroy the SIM card. Into the coffee it went—*plunk*—and then he tossed the entire cup into yet another trash can.

Green Cap reached an ATM four minutes after the driveway abduction of the blonde and his follow-up phone call. He pushed in his scratched-up debit card, entered his PIN (the day and month his divorce was finalized), and asked for the balance in his checking account. This morning the balance had been $789.43.

Now it was $25,789.43. He'd earned twenty-five grand for about five minutes' work.

Not bad at all!

Green Cap decided to celebrate with another purchase from Starbucks, this time a frothy latte he'd get to enjoy. And by God, he'd savor every swallow.

CHAPTER 4

THE KIDNAPPER PILOTED the Bentley west down Sunset toward the Pacific, weaving around other luxury cars, going a good fifteen to twenty miles above the speed limit. No one would stop him. Not in a Bentley. Traffic cops knew it wouldn't be worth the headache—they wouldn't stop him unless they saw a screaming old lady being dragged under the chassis. And maybe not even then.

Anyone who could afford a Bentley could easily afford a lawyer who'd make a moving violation disappear in an instant.

The kidnapper didn't keep the Bentley on Sunset very long. He made a sudden right on Linden Drive, tires screaming, executed a perfect K-turn, and reversed until he was trunk to trunk with a black Audi parked in a security-camera dead zone.

The kidnapper's code name was Two, and from this point on, his life would never be the same.

To be honest, this version was much more exciting.

He should have considered a life of crime *years* ago.

Two opened both trunks with simultaneous presses of the two key fobs. Both lids opened at the same time, like a beetle expanding its wings to take flight. Inside the trunk of the Audi was a soft oversize blanket. Two tucked the blanket around Boo Schraeder's unconscious body, wrapping her like a breakfast burrito, then moved her from the trunk of the Bentley to the trunk of the Audi.

Two removed a glove and pressed fingers to her carotid artery. Her pulse was slow but steady.

Her freshly coiffed hair was in disarray. Two fixed it as best he could, but he wasn't a stylist. Pretty far from it.

Trunk lids slammed shut, Two chucked the Bentley's key fob down a storm drain and climbed behind the wheel of the Audi. This would be his new ride.

For exactly 2.3 miles.

On a quiet side street near UCLA, Two repeated the routine, this time with a black BMW 7 Series. And several miles later, on the fringes of the Pacific Palisades, Two transferred his captive to still another black Audi. The cars were as clean as the plates on the front and rear bumpers.

The whole time, Boo Schraeder never stirred. The chemical he'd sprayed in her face was a potent one, a proprietary and long-acting form of halothane. Two had tried it on himself a few days ago. Probably the best sleep he'd had in over a year. He knew she'd enjoy the rest of the ride in ignorant bliss.

How she'd feel when she woke up, however, was another story.

CHAPTER 5

Wednesday, 3:14 p.m.

AT THE PRECISE moment Boo Schraeder was leaving her favorite Beverly Hills salon, a luxury charter bus made a right turn from Mulholland onto Roscomare Road.

Classes at the Curtis School had ended for the day, and the private motor coach was beginning its two-mile route to deposit a dozen children at their homes in Bel Air. The trip was short, but nonetheless, the bus was equipped with everything a child could possibly need for the journey—reclining seats, Wi-Fi, power outlets, and two private restrooms.

The driver glanced in the rearview at her young passengers, none of whom seemed to care about those amenities. All of them were bursting with the energy that only seven- and eight- and nine-year-olds have in the middle of the afternoon.

The driver? Please. She was eager to take a nap. Not that such a thing was likely. She had another gig this evening, ferrying adults around some studio lot until midnight. And then she'd be up again first thing to drive these same kids to school. If she was exhausted now, how would she feel at five a.m. tomorrow? She stifled a yawn, saw the speeding car, and stomped on the brakes at the last possible second.

The white BMW had blasted out of an obscured driveway. The car braked hard, and double screams of rubber on asphalt echoed through the canyon.

The driver yelled for the children to hold on. This vehicle was outfitted with every possible safety feature. The kids would be fine. But the driver was still paying off the loan for this luxury bus, and a wreck right now would be a financial nightmare.

Her first impulse was to scream something at the impatient moron who had almost crashed into a bus containing gradeschoolers. But the moron's passenger—a woman—was up and out of the car so quickly, the driver reconsidered.

Especially when she saw that the woman was wearing a skintight mask that warped her features, almost like a nylon stocking over a bank robber's face, and was holding some sort of device.

The driver lunged to lock the hinged loading doors, but the woman was already there, forcing them open with a gloved hand. *This seriously can't be happening. Not with the bus loaded with kids!* Whatever this was, this creepy bitch wasn't setting foot on her bus.

The driver pulled as hard as she could on the handle of the door mechanism. The masked woman forced her weapon through the gap anyway. *Oh, no, you don't,* the driver thought and pulled even harder, putting her entire body weight into it, trying to exert so much pressure that the weapon would drop from the woman's hands.

(That was the last thing the driver would remember. Later—during intense grilling by the FBI—the driver would learn she had been jabbed by two metal barbs and subjected to fifty thousand volts of electricity, at which point there was nothing she could have done to protect those kids. The electricity coursed through her system faster than her brain could commit anything to memory.)

The bus was under the kidnapper's control now.

CHAPTER 6

THE MASKED KIDNAPPER hurried onto the motor coach, trying hard to ignore the unconscious driver slumped over the wheel. There had been plenty of assurances there would be no long-term damage from this type of Taser, but still, she couldn't bring herself to look down at the poor woman. And this was no time to get emotional.

"Children?" the kidnapper said, loud enough to cut through their nervous chatter but in a relaxed, friendly tone meant to reassure them.

Her kidnapper code name was Four, and she knew this was the make-or-break moment of the mission. If she didn't keep these kids calm for the next thirty seconds, things could unravel *real* fast.

Four lowered the Taser to waist level. She prayed she wouldn't be forced to use it on one of the children. Using it on the driver had been bad enough.

"Everything's going to be okay," she said. "Please stay in your seats."

"Who are you?" one kid asked.

Outside, the kidnapper's partner backed the white BMW into an empty driveway. He killed the engine, stepped out of the car, glanced briefly at the nearest house, then tapped the key fob to open the trunk. The lid popped up, wobbled in the air, and steadied. The BMW driver jogged to the bus and went through its open doors.

His code name was Three.

Without a word, Three stepped up and hooked his hands under the arms of the unconscious bus driver. She needed to be out of the way. Keeping her head and neck supported, he quickly carried her off the bus and over to the trunk of the BMW.

Four didn't acknowledge Three or his activities. She trusted him to do his part as he always had throughout their marriage. No, she was keeping her eye on the children, waiting to see if any of them would try to make a break for it (unlikely) or use their phones to text moms and dads (entirely likely).

But any message they might try to send would fail to reach its destination. Four had a device clipped to her belt that briefly killed all cell phone and Wi-Fi signals in a quarter-mile radius. Nearby residents might wonder why their shows suddenly ceased streaming.

"Cal and Finney Schraeder," Four said, "please come with us right now."

The children turned in their seats to gawk at two kids in a middle row. They stood up, a boy and a girl who were undeniably related. Most people assumed, incorrectly, that they were twins.

"Are we being kidnapped?" asked Finney, who was eight years old and a little taller than her nine-year-old brother.

Four had wondered how the Schraeder kids would react to their abduction. Angry tantrums? Flowing tears? Stunned silence? She had been prepared for all three possibilities, but she hadn't counted on a direct question. The best response, she decided, was a direct answer.

"Yes," Four said. "You are being kidnapped. Now, please, come quickly."

Without another word and without resistance, the siblings began to move up the aisle. Perhaps, Four reasoned, their wealthy father or their ex-army stepmother had taught them how to react in this situation.

Which was smart, but also troubling. Because if they'd had a little family chat on what to do in the event of a kidnapping, the parents might also have taught them how to get the upper hand.

By the time the Schraeder children reached Four, her husband had stepped back onto the bus.

"The rest of you stay in your seats," Three said, raising his voice a bit too much. "The police will be here soon. Do *not* step off this bus!"

Four shot him a warning look. She knew her husband meant well, but she was worried he might have overdone it a little. She saw the children's startled expressions. This was all sinking in. People in masks taking their *friends*...

"It could be dangerous on the street," Four calmly explained to the children. "Cars drive awfully fast on this road. We don't want anyone to get hurt."

"What about Cal and Finney?" asked one voice from the back.

"Especially not Cal and Finney," Four replied.

CHAPTER 7

THE COLLEGE SOPHOMORE watching from the window waited until the two kids were seat-belted into the back of the white BMW and it had roared to life and peeled down the hill away from the motor coach.

Sophomore counted backward from twenty. No sirens. Excellent. She picked up the burner phone and called the only number in its memory.

"One hundred percent," she said.

The call ended without a verbal confirmation that the message had been received. This was expected, but Sophomore found it a little unnerving. What if she'd spoken too soon, before the listener had connected and heard the words? Well, too late now.

Sophomore peered outside and waited to see if any of the remaining children would try to step off the motor coach. Now she began counting down from sixty. Thirty seconds in, no kids came running out. They were good little listeners. After thirty more seconds, there was still nothing.

Countdown over, Sophomore set about covering her tracks (wiping down the doorknobs and windows) before she exited the house, which had been on the market for about a year now. The asking price was way too freakin' high—in *her* opinion, at least. But she supposed that worked to her mysterious employer's advantage.

Sophomore had punch-keyed into the home just a half hour before. She'd set up by the window of a second-floor bedroom and put down her backpack, which was a little heavier than usual; in addition to the usual notebook, pens, makeup bag, and a paperback copy of Faulkner's *Sanctuary,* it contained disinfecting wipes and a 30,000-megawatt laser.

Her task: Disabling every traffic and surveillance camera within range of the stopping point, which was marked on the asphalt with a spray-painted gray *X.* She'd steadily, carefully, taken aim and fired the laser at each camera, one by one, and the intense heat fried the pixels inside. Sophomore was grateful for all those archery lessons at summer camp back in New Jersey.

Within twenty minutes, the only operating street camera was the one that would record the two-minute abduction from the perfect angle. Again, all per her mysterious employer's instructions.

Sophomore's last job on her way out of the house was to avoid that lone functioning camera, which was why she left through the back and cut through the yard of the adjacent property. All of this had been scouted out in advance. There were no cameras, and the only neighbors were in Europe for the next few weeks. Sophomore made her way to the street where she'd parked the SUV that had been rented for her.

She didn't have to go through the hassle of returning the vehicle. All she had to do was park it at the designated spot on Hilgard Avenue and walk back to UCLA. She was almost sad to leave the SUV; it was nicer than any car she'd ever driven.

Sophomore refused to be the weak link in this operation and prided herself on handling the little details. She pulled disinfecting wipes from her pack and took a minute to clean the steering wheel, gearshift, and start button. She used a lint roller on the driver's seat to pick up any stray hairs that might have escaped from her baseball cap.

There. Perfect.

Hopefully.

She waited until she was back in her room on campus to check her account balance.

Like magic, there it was: She was twenty-five thousand dollars richer. For the moment. She needed to visit the bursar's office and catch up with her tuition payments. But there would be a *little* left over for recreational activities.

Sophomore checked the news on her personal cell phone, the one she'd left in her dorm. There was nothing yet, of course, but she set a Google alert to stay informed. She had to make sure the kids were okay. She didn't need that on her conscience as well.

CHAPTER 8

THREE AND FOUR made the getaway a kind of game for Cal and Finney, and they seemed perfectly happy to participate. Cal was assigned the role of timekeeper; Finney was the traffic cop.

"Now, Cal, you keep your eyes on the stopwatch," Four said. "And Finney, you check the streets for a white Audi. If you see the car before the minute is up, you get a point."

"And if she doesn't see the Audi before time's up?" Cal asked.

Well, there was zero chance of that. Three and Four had the route and switch cars plotted out perfectly. It should take only forty-five seconds to reach the next car. The goal was to keep the children busy so they wouldn't think about ways to run away or alert any passersby.

"Thirty seconds to go!"

"I see it! I see it!"

"No, dummy, that's a Rolls-Royce, not an Audi!"

"Look again," Four said.

"There it is!"

Three and Four and the kids changed vehicles three times in the next seven minutes.

The Schraeder children racked up multiple points, clearly excited to be winning so easily—and not thinking about where they were going. Four could practically read their minds: *What's bad about this? So far, being kidnapped is fun!*

CHAPTER 9

Wednesday, 3:14 p.m.

PARADISE CAME IN many forms. But the best versions of paradise—at least in Tyler Schraeder's opinion—were those private Edens that kept out the snakes.

Edens like this insanely exclusive Baja California resort not far from Cabo San Lucas on Mexico's East Cape. Spacious villas right on the beach, their kitchens stocked with gourmet food, each with a private pool and spa complete with sauna, mud bath, and jet bath. For Tyler, the resort's most attractive feature was its location—over a thousand miles from the nearest Hollywood studio. Tyler could do whatever he wanted with whomever he wanted, and no one would be photographing him, recording him, or even glancing in his direction.

In fact, since stepping off the private jet earlier this afternoon, Tyler and Cass hadn't had to deal with a single human being. Even the journey to their private cottage had been entirely automated. It was like everyone else on the planet had disappeared, and they enjoyed the place in peace and quiet for once.

Back on the studio lot in the real world, it was 3:14 p.m., but here on the Mexican coast of Baja California, time ceased to exist, along with all the rules.

"Bring that gorgeous ass over here," Cass said to Tyler with the come-hither smile she hoped would become her trademark on the big screen.

See, right there—in the real world, Cassandra Bart wouldn't risk uttering those six words in front of any human being, let alone to a camera. She wouldn't even risk *sexting* those words; that wasn't her brand. On-screen, she was an earnest and determined hero who would not stop until she saved the world. But here in paradise, she could say anything she wanted and just get her *freak* on.

Cassandra was twenty-six years old and for the past three years had been deftly climbing the action-movie ladder, first in a small but memorable role in a wildly successful franchise, then in a supporting role in a superhero tentpole, and finally in a starring role in an abysmal streamer action-comedy. That last one was a massive flop, but it had still worked in her favor—critics called her its only redeeming feature and hailed her as the next Margot Robbie. Now she was on the verge of breaking through in a big way. It was just a matter of finding the right starring vehicle.

Which had been Tyler's cue to step in and say: "I can help you with that."

A genetically gifted beauty like Cass intimidated most mortals, but Tyler Schraeder was not most mortals. He had all the benefits of a privileged upbringing plus a genetic advantage of his own—he favored his mother, an actress very popular in action movies of the 1980s and '90s. *You have your mother's cheekbones and her ruthlessness,* his father often told him. Well, back when he and his father were speaking to each other.

Tyler understood that Cassandra Bart, more than two decades his junior, had crashed into his life for reasons beyond his physical endowments and his incredible wealth. He'd turned a graduation present from his estranged father into a small production company on the Universal lot that had a knack for launching massive action franchises—the company had launched *plenty* over the years—and Cassandra was up for the lead in the next one.

Not that this was a casting-couch situation. Oh, no. The role was hers for the asking. But Cass was currently playing coy, wondering aloud if she should continue along the action-movie route. One forgettable summer tentpole, and suddenly no one considers you for prestige roles. That was her thinking, anyway. Tyler had suggested they go somewhere to discuss.

In depth.

Which was what they were doing now. Deep engagement without any annoying words getting in the way.

Tyler couldn't believe how thoroughly this woman was throwing herself into the unspoken discussion. Her body demonstrated her athleticism, playfulness, and invention. But the way she continued to lock eyes with him, almost daring him to comment—it was all too delicious.

Best notes meeting ever.

And then she earned herself an Oscar in his mind by somehow turning the most clichéd of phrases into something believable.

"Tyler," she whispered.

"Yes?"

She breathed in deep for a second, as if she couldn't believe she was actually going to say these words, then took the plunge: "I love you."

Tyler Schraeder knew better, but damn if he didn't completely buy her performance.

"Hell yeah, you do," he replied.

(Later, Tyler would blame Cass for distracting him at a crucial moment. Had he not been so overwhelmed by her multipronged assault on his senses, he surely would have heard the door to their private villa opening as well as the nearly silent footsteps across the hardwood all the way to their bed.)

A sharp *clack* roused them both from their passion.

"Do everything I say," said a man's voice, "or both of you die."

For Tyler, the initial shock was immediately replaced by entitled outrage. Serpents weren't allowed in this paradise—how had *this* one slithered in?

Even worse, the snake was clutching an AR-15, which Tyler recognized from countless film sets. But this was no set, and the semiautomatic weapon was no prop, and it was pointed at his midsection.

"No," Tyler said as if negotiating a deal, "this is *not* happening."

CHAPTER 10

"THIS IS *VERY much* happening, Tyler Schraeder," the gunman replied.

The producer flinched, which pleased the gunman. *Yeah, I know your name, rich boy.*

The most important weapon he had was not in his hands; it was the element of surprise. This would work only if he could keep the nude couple off balance for the next two minutes.

The gunman, whose code name was Five, had no doubt this spoiled prick would try something, if only to maintain the illusion of dominance. Question was, would he try right away or bide his time and size up his opponent?

Five decided it was best to proceed with clear instructions and wait for the producer to make his move.

"On your feet. Hands on top of your heads, fingers laced," Five commanded.

"Not gonna happen," Tyler said. "You and I are gonna talk

this through, because obviously, you're not thinking straight. I can get you whatever help you need."

"I won't ask again, *Tyler*."

The actress was already in full compliance mode. Cassandra Bart seemed to have made the transition from brazen hellcat to helpless victim without missing a beat. Then again, that's what people in her profession did. Maybe *she* would make the first move.

Five would have to watch her carefully.

"Look," Tyler said, "you hit the jackpot! I am a very wealthy man. And you're going to walk out of this room much richer than when you stepped into it, my friend."

Five just stared at him.

"But here's the thing," Tyler continued. "The longer you act all tough and the more you threaten to blow our brains out, the lighter your little payday gets. So do the smart thing. Drop the gun and you can name your price. But every second you hesit—"

Crack.

Tyler Schraeder was unable to finish his speech because Five smashed the butt of the AR-15 into the rich boy's handsome face.

"I'm sorry," Five said. "You were saying something about hesitating? How much has the price gone down now? Did I just lose a couple of thousand there, my *friend*?"

"You..." The naked producer struggled to stay on his feet. "You bwoke my fucking teef!"

"Yes, I did. Disobey me again and see what I break next." Five unhooked the bag from his shoulder and tossed it to the floor between the producer and the starlet.

"Inside the bag are jumpsuits. They're your sizes. Put them on."

"What is even happening?" asked Cassandra in a pitch-perfect blend of confusion and panic. "Please, I am seriously terrified, and I need to know what this is about—"

"Now!"

Maybe it was the blood pouring from Tyler's mouth or maybe it was the tone of the gunman's voice, but Cassandra Bart immediately dropped to her knees and unzipped the duffel bag.

The first jumpsuit she pulled out was too long. She held it out to Tyler without looking up at him; he snatched it out of her hand while also avoiding eye contact. As if they believed that looking at each other would confirm this nightmare was real.

This greatly amused Five. Just a few moments ago they had been all about athletic sex and cheap lies. Look at them now—bleeding, naked, afraid...and totally under his command. Being rich and powerful meant nothing when you had a gun aimed at your head and you were trying to pull on a stiff prison jumpsuit without falling over.

Tyler Schraeder looked up at Five, his chin covered in blood and a flicker of defiance in his hard eyes. Oh, yeah. Time to extinguish that too.

"Tell me, Cassandra," Five said, "will you still *love* him even without his perfect smile?"

CHAPTER 11

Wednesday, 3:30 p.m.

THE ESCALADE KEPT pace with the fourteen-year-old girl until she finally stopped and turned to glare at the woman behind the wheel.

"Shouldn't you be engaged in a deadly shoot-out down by the San Pedro docks or something?" the girl asked.

FBI special agent Nicole "Nicky" Gordon glared right back at the girl. "They canceled all the deadly shoot-outs for today. So I decided to give you a ride home instead."

"That was very kind of the international drug-dealing community," the girl replied. She remained a few feet from the Escalade.

"Come on, what are you waiting for?"

"Leave me alone, stalker!"

Nicky flinched, then cracked a wide smile. It was a silly game they'd played since...well, forever. "Will you get in already, you goofball?"

Nicky's daughter, Kaitlin, opened the door, flung her loaded backpack into the rear seat with expert aim and gracefully spun herself into the passenger seat. She was a natural athlete, like her mother. Though in terms in height, Kaitlin favored her father. When Nicky hugged her daughter these days, she had to be careful her forehead didn't slam into the kid's chin.

Nicky steered the Escalade away from the Girls Academic Leadership Academy—GALA—hoping to get ahead of traffic. But who was she kidding? This was LA. There was no getting ahead of anything, not at this hour. She checked the time on her dash—3:31 p.m. If the traffic gods smiled on her, they could make it to the Santa Monica Pier by four thirty or so. Although this appeared to be an impromptu *Hey, I was just in the neighborhood* pickup, Nicky had been planning it for a while now. She headed west on Olympic. So far, so good.

"How do you feel about dinner at the Old Maid?" Nicky asked as if it were the most casual of questions.

"Mom."

"Yes, honey?"

"Just tell me what's going on. I don't need a bribe."

Of course Kaitlin had immediately seen through the ruse. "The Old Maid" was their nickname for the Mermaid on the Pier, a favorite of Kaitlin's since she was a toddler. The early black-and-white Dennis Hopper movie *Night Tide* was largely shot in that location, which thrilled them both when they'd caught it late one night on cable. They had a running joke about killer mermaids swarming the place and pistol-packing Nicky saving the day.

"Nothing is going on," Nicky said.

"Didn't the FBI teach you special agents how to lie?"

Nicky fought hard to suppress a smile. "I'm not lying. Nothing's going on... *yet.*"

"Mm-hmm."

Nicky had been planning this conversation for weeks, but she still found herself at a loss for words. This wasn't how she'd imagined it playing out. And she very much needed to sell Kaitlin on this in the right way, because she couldn't do it without her daughter's support.

How would you feel about your mom becoming the first female director of the Federal Bureau of Investigation someday?

Granted, the position was an appointment of the highest level, subject to the political needs of the sitting president and requiring the support of the US Senate. But according to John Scoleri, her boss and mentor at the LA field office, there *was* a specific career path that could maximize her chances. "Take the right steps within the Bureau," John had told her, "put yourself at the center of a few high-profile cases, and you can get on a very short list."

Nicky Gordon had secretly dreamed of becoming director, but she'd never said it out loud. It spoke to Assistant Director Scoleri's powers of intuition that he'd figured it out. Maybe it was just a motivation tactic. But she knew this about him: He wasn't a bullshitter. If he said this was the way, he could back that up.

But this incredibly tempting career path came with a heavy price.

It meant starting on that track right freaking *now.* It meant hopping from one field office to another all across the country and dragging along her daughter (who absolutely adored GALA and her many friends at the school). It meant spending countless hours on high-profile cases and precious few hours with Kaitlin during the most challenging years of her adolescence. It meant putting herself in the public eye, which in these polarized times often blew back on family. And Kaitlin was Nicky's entire universe.

To do this, Nicky would need not only Kaitlin's approval but her total and enthusiastic buy-in. She could not go down this path alone.

So try putting all of *that* into words when you're weaving around Teslas and BMWs on Olympic Boulevard.

"Mom?"

"Okay, so there's this opportunity at work—"

Right at that moment, Nicky's cell, mounted on the dash, whirred with a message from the LA field office. Of course. Of course! Just saying the word *work* seemed to have conjured it into being.

"I'm sorry, sweetie," Nicky said as she tapped the screen. "Give me one sec."

"Great, keep me in suspense," Kaitlin said.

But Nicky was busy deciphering the short message, which was basically Bureau code for *All hands on deck, report to the office immediately.* These types of messages were reserved for serious incidents, like terrorist attacks or mass shootings or attempted coups. And this one promised to be shocking. Just the family name alone—the Schraeders.

The Old Maid would have to wait.

"What happened?" Kaitlin asked, reading the troubled look on her mother's face. "Some kind of national disaster?"

"More like three at once."

CHAPTER 12

Wednesday, 3:56 p.m.

NICKY ARRIVED IN Westwood and hurried through the lobby of the FBI's Los Angeles field office, which covered the Central District of California, trying to process the flurry of inter-agency updates beamed to her phone and the messages from her colleagues.

This was a crisis rapidly evolving on multiple fronts—three separate kidnappings within the same wealthy family, all executed at the same time. Nicky half expected to hear word of a fourth kidnapping when she stepped into her office on the sixth floor.

There she found her immediate superior, FBI assistant director John Scoleri, leaning against her desk, whipping through a stack of reports.

"Back so soon, Gordon?" he asked, not looking up from the pages.

"Very funny, Scoleri. Where do you need me?"

"This one's all yours."

"Which one? Schraeder's wife? His young kids?"

"Don't forget about the adult son and his starlet girlfriend down in Mexico."

Nicky and John had worked together long enough to speak in a kind of a shorthand that baffled other agents. Their brains tended to be on the same wavelength.

But right now, Nicky was struggling to read his mind.

"That's what I mean," Nicky said. "You want me working Beverly Hills? Bel Air? Or liaising with the PFM in Mexico City?"

Only now did John look up from the stack of reports, one of them, she saw, from the Policía Federal Ministerial.

"No," he said. "You're going to be heading up the whole thing. I'm putting you in charge of the task force on this one. Loop in the LAPD and the mayor's office. You pick your team. You call the shots. Just brief me enough to keep DC off my ass."

This stunned Nicky, but she composed herself. The smart move was to project the right blend of gratitude and confidence.

"Thank you."

"You may not be thanking me in a couple of hours."

Nicky shook her head. "No, Scoleri. I'm serious. You know what this means to me."

"And I'm serious when I tell you that this case is a goddamned hand grenade," John said. "Handle it carefully, bring everyone home safe, and it can make your career. Screw it up, and it'll blow you straight to hell."

"I'm not thinking about my career right now."

A wry smile grew on the assistant director's face. "Sure you are. And, hey, that's okay. It would be strange if you weren't."

John had clocked her ambitions from the first day they worked together. He liked to make jokes about him working for her someday, which Nicky dismissed. But those jokes also secretly thrilled her. If a longtime Bureau legend like John Scoleri had faith in her, she might actually head up her own field office in the not-too-distant future.

"With all that in mind," he said, "you sure you still want this?"

"Yes," Nicky said. "But I'm going to need you to set the tone. It must be crystal clear that I'm the one in charge. I don't want anyone reaching out to you behind my back or second-guessing me."

"You got it," John said. "I mean, you're the one who's been working all of our high-profile kidnapping cases lately. As far as I'm concerned, you're the expert."

"No one steps in, and that includes *you,*" Nicky continued. "Even if you think you're saving me from a mistake."

John nodded and showed her his palms in a *I'll keep my hands off* gesture. "You get those people back safe, the credit is all yours."

"And if I don't?"

John grinned but not in a particularly warm way. "I'm sure Kaitlin will be happy that you're retiring early."

CHAPTER 13

"OUR TASK FORCE will be led by Special Agent Nicole Gordon," John Scoleri said. "Gordon, this is now your meeting."

Nicky scanned the faces, both digital and in the flesh, of a dozen VIPs who had been summoned to the Sandbox.

The Sandbox was the FBI's ultra-secure meeting room in which leaders from all over the world could gather virtually; its state-of-the-art 4K video screens, flawless and encrypted ethernet connections, and communications capabilities protected by a next-level firewall offered visuals and security that rivaled an in-person meeting.

Despite all that technology, the Sandbox unnerved Nicky. In a traditional conference room, you could pull someone aside to stress a point in private. But the Sandbox's microphones were so incredibly sensitive, *everything* could be heard, even the smallest murmur of dissent. *Forget the Sandbox—it should be called the Fishbowl,* Nicky thought. And she was standing at the center of it.

One of the in-person faces was friendly. (Hello, LAPD chief of detectives Michael Hardy.) The rest, both in-person and virtual, not so much.

Some wore bored expressions, as if daring her to impress them. (Hello, Madam Mayor, beaming in from her own secure meeting room at city hall.) One person was clearly unhappy to be stuck in the Sandbox taking orders from an agent he'd long considered to be John Scoleri's lackey. (Hello, Captain Jeffrey Penney, head of the LAPD's SWAT team—here in person, sadly.) There were also a handful of bureaucrats and advisers not thrilled to be dragged away from their normal duties at the end of an already busy day—and for what? Rich-people problems?

But Nicky needed them all working as a team if she was going to crack this thing.

"You've all been briefed on the simultaneous kidnappings in Beverly Hills, Bel Air, and Mexico this afternoon," Nicky said. "Three different strikes executed with clockwork precision. Five different targets, all but one within the same family. Let me bring you up to speed on where the investigation stands."

She tapped her cell phone, and two of the Sandbox screens displayed live video feeds from the two LA crime scenes.

"We do have limited surveillance-camera footage from two of the scenes, Beverly Hills and Bel Air," Nicky continued. "We're actively tracking a potential witness in the Beverly Hills abduction and have agents going door to door in Bel Air."

Another tap brought up a screen with real-time transcriptions of dozens of phone calls.

"As of one hour ago, our tip line is active, and agents are

already sorting through the messages that have arrived. As of now, there have been no ransom demands. Which is not—"

"What about the kidnapping in Mexico?" the mayor asked, seeming impatient. "Have we had any sightings of either Tyler Schraeder or Cassandra Bart?"

Nicky wasn't surprised the mayor would focus on these two. Not only was the eldest Schraeder child the highest-profile member of the Schraeder family—aside from Papa Randolph, of course—and a well-known political donor, but he'd been abducted along with one of Hollywood's fastest-rising stars. This was the abduction that would receive the lion's share of media coverage. Naturally, it was also the part of the case that remained the most obscure.

"We have a small team on their way to Mexico City," Nicky said. "They should be landing shortly and liaising with local authorities."

"I understand they were taken from a private resort," the mayor continued. "Who reported them missing?"

"A massage therapist, who became concerned when Schraeder and Bart missed their midafternoon appointment," Nicky said. "She alerted the staff, who by then had heard about the other kidnappings."

"And we have absolutely no idea of their whereabouts?" the mayor said. "A high-end resort like that must have robust security systems."

Nicky knew the mayor wasn't going to like the answer she was about to get. Nicky didn't like it much either.

"This resort is known for its privacy," Nicky told her. "No cameras, no prying eyes, and a bare minimum of staff on-site."

"Tyler Schraeder didn't bring along his own security?" the mayor said.

"Apparently not." Nicky didn't bother to mention the obvious—the reason people went to an exclusive off-the-grid resort was specifically for the total seclusion from everyone, including security guys, many of whom loved to make a little extra cash from the press. But the mayor needed to vent her frustrations, and it was important to let her.

Now that they'd reached the low point, Nicky decided to share the ace she'd been keeping up her sleeve.

"I believe I know who is behind these kidnappings," Nicky said.

CHAPTER 14

WELL, *THAT* MADE everyone in the Sandbox sit up and pay attention. Even the mayor blinked in surprise.

"Do you have the name of this suspect?" the mayor asked, suddenly excited.

"No," Nicky admitted. "What I have is a *pattern*. I've been tracking a team of kidnappers here in Southern California. They've pulled off a series of small but successful abductions in Santa Barbara, San Diego, and Big Sur. The hallmarks are all the same: precision timing, no loose ends."

"So the kidnappers got a little taste of success," Mike Hardy said, "and they decided to try for a bigger fish."

"Not exactly," Nicky replied. "It's my belief that these earlier three kidnappings were simply *practice*."

Nicky tapped her cell phone repeatedly and brought up an almost dizzying array of crime scene photos.

"The first abduction was outside a salon on Figueroa Street in Santa Barbara. The vic was a model, the trophy wife of one of the city's richest men, and it happened so smoothly that nobody knew she was gone until the ransom demand was hand-delivered to the husband's office."

On the screen, a headshot of the victim that included the name of her modeling agency stamped in the lower right corner appeared.

"What happened to her?" the mayor asked.

"Quarter of a million dollars later," Nicky said, "she was safely returned to her home in Hope Ranch. She was unable to identify her abductor, who I've come to believe was a male working with a partner who was not present at the scene."

Another tap, and another photo appeared: a school bus in downtown San Diego surrounded by uniformed police, FBI, and dozens of terrified parents hugging their elementary-school-age children.

"Three months later, the twin daughters of a very successful comic-book artist were taken from their school bus. The children were returned safely, but not until the artist had been forced to essentially liquidate his own art collection to come up with the half-million ransom demand."

Jeff Penney asked, "Same male abductor?"

"No," Nicky replied. "The twins said they were taken by a man and a woman, possibly a couple, the twins said, based on how they spoke to each other."

"Then why do you think it's the same team of kidnappers?"

"I'll get to that," Before Jeff could interrupt again, Nicky tapped her cell phone.

A screen grab from a comedy show with a middle-aged

comic twisting his face into a display of faux agony appeared on a monitor.

"Six months ago, this comedian and his new bride, who is twenty-six years his junior, were taken from their remote cabin in Big Sur. Their families struggled to put together a million bucks to secure their release."

"I caught that guy's act once," Mike Hardy said. "He's famous for being a total dick to pretty much everybody."

The mayor shook her head in annoyance. If Mike Hardy weren't so incredibly good at his job, Nicky thought, he would have been fired a long time ago. He wasn't everyone's cup of tea.

"Were they released unharmed?" the mayor asked.

"Not this time. The comedian was severely beaten. He claimed that he'd been assaulted by a couple of gangbangers who were clearly working for someone else. He assumed they were hired by his former management, but that turned out to be a dead end."

The mayor didn't seem all that impressed with Nicky's theory. "Different people, different perps... I agree with Captain Penney. Why do you think these three cases are related?"

"For many reasons, Madam Mayor," Nicky said. "The smooth, well-practiced abductions. The escalation in ransom money as well as increasingly ambitious targets. And the ease with which they were able to secure the ransom money in all three cases suggests a group of individuals *extremely* familiar with our protocols."

Mike Hardy smirked. "You think they have a cop on their team."

"Or a former cop," Nicky said. "But the most important reason is that the three cases I've just presented seem to be dry runs for *exactly* what happened to the Schraeders this afternoon."

CHAPTER 15

Wednesday, 4:27 p.m.

FIVE WAS BORN in Tijuana.

And when he dreamed, he wandered the crowded streets of TJ, breathing in the aroma of grilled carne and chili peppers, lost in the pulsing music, and enjoying the stares from the curious girls up and down Avenida Revolución, who could sense he was *somebody*. And he was. His various business interests often took him away from his beloved TJ, and Five welcomed any opportunity to return.

Even if it *was* part of a massive kidnapping plot that could bring way too much attention to his hometown.

But there was no other way. Five felt safe here. He knew every inch of his little neighborhood, which was tucked away from the usual tourist snares. His home was fortified with all kinds of security features, both obvious and secret. Plus, Five knew the escape routes, the hiding places, the ways to avoid the cops...well, the cops who weren't paid off. Which was a very small number.

Those clandestine routes were good to know, especially when the Federales decided to do a showcase bust for American media.

Or when you had two famous people in the back of your truck, and you wanted to slip through the city undetected.

The radio in his Ford Bronco was tuned to a classic rock station in San Diego. Five was happy when reception finally improved; after winding his way up through Baja California, his speakers came alive with ZZ Top, Van Halen, Led Zeppelin, Santana—all that classic 1970s and '80s rock his papa used to listen to when disassembling cars in the garage.

The closer he was to home, the more relaxed he felt.

The more confident.

Five took a hard left onto the street where he grew up, and right away, he could see them: Men with guns. Four of them. Two keeping their eyes on the street; two training their gun sights on the house halfway up the block. Five's house. The one he'd grown up in and inherited after his mother passed away from the lung cancer that had ravaged her body and taken her from him much too soon.

Five nodded at the two shooters guarding the front. They nodded in response. Hard men who would never crack a smile in public. They were all tight with Five and had been since they were all kids.

One of the gunmen had the garage-door opener. As Five pulled forward, the door lifted.

"You two okay back there?" Five called over his shoulder.

There were no moans, no grumbles, no nothing. His captives were still unconscious from the knockout drugs.

Good.

Five pulled into the garage and watched as the door began to close behind him. That was triggered by one of the gunmen, who anticipated Five's every move. They were more than a working team. They were like brothers, with a connection thicker than blood. Sometimes it felt like they shared the same mind.

So, yeah, sure, the mysterious Mr. One didn't want Five to get anyone else involved in this kidnapping plot. He'd made that very clear:

If you improvise, you will not be paid. If you involve others, you will not be paid.

But Five didn't work without his brothers. You hired Five, you were hiring all of them.

CHAPTER 16

Wednesday, 5:13 p.m.

"OH, WOW, you have Mastermind!" Finney exclaimed.

"Of course we have Mastermind," Three said. "That happens to be our all-time favorite game. And no matter what my wife says, I am the master of all the minds!"

"I'll bet I can beat you," Finney replied.

"No one has ever beaten me at Mastermind," Three said.

Four responded to this with an eye roll. She knew the truth. Until a few days ago, Three had never heard of Mastermind. Shortly before the abduction, Three and Four received a list of Cal's and Finney's favorite board games. None of them required power or Wi-Fi; these were old-school board games like Clue, Monopoly, and, yes, Mastermind.

Three and Four were given no instructions, just the list, typed on a plain index card and mailed in a crisp white envelope, but they'd understood what to do. They'd gone out that night, purchased every single one, and brought them to their hideaway in suburban Garden City, California, just outside of Pasadena.

Three and Four *still* didn't know how they'd ended up on One's radar. But they were the couple best suited for the task at hand. Or so he had claimed.

And right now, the task at hand was keeping Cal and Finney happily distracted. They were smart kids and needed to stay fully engaged.

"Set up your pegs," Finney said. "I'll guess first."

"Never in a million years, my friend," Three replied.

"I'll guess it in five moves!"

Cal nodded. "You don't understand," he told Three. "She's really, really good."

"Did you know," Finney said, "that Mastermind was invented by an Israeli communications expert as a way to practice code-breaking?"

"Is that right," Three said, staring at the game board as if it had suddenly transformed into a difficult math problem. Four knew that Three was very bad at math. He had no idea how to play the game. The box had made it look simple—little colored pegs on a plastic board with holes in it. How hard could it be?

"While you all master each other's minds," Four said, "I'll get dinner started."

"What are we having?" Cal asked.

"Flatbread pepperoni pizzas."

Finney looked concerned. "I don't know how much kidnapping research you did, but I happen to be a vegetarian."

"She is," Cal confirmed.

"Don't worry," Four said. "We did our research. I'm making one without pepperoni and with plenty of mushrooms and green peppers."

"That's my favorite!" Finney exclaimed.

Four smiled. "I know."

Truthfully, someone else had done the research (and, yes, the children's dietary habits were fully detailed). But Three and Four had had to choose the hideaway location. The only rule One had insisted on was that no one could help them or be in contact with them at any point.

That meant no babysitters, no spotters, no nothing. If One discovered they had secret coconspirators, he'd warned, two things would happen: They would never see a dime of the ransom, and they would be turned over to the authorities within the hour.

It's not as if they would be in a position to point a finger at One; nobody knew his name or had any way to identify him.

Finding the hideaway had been left up to them, and that was a whole other challenge. Cal and Finney were white. Three and Four were not. There were certain neighborhoods where that would attract attention. And they wanted zero attention. So that shrank the map of possibilities.

Luckily, Four was a part-time real estate agent, one of her many side hustles over the past seven years, so she'd searched for an ideal neighborhood with a house that had been on the market for a while. Which was difficult these days; LA's housing market was so tight, it practically squeaked.

But Four had kept searching—she always worked best

under pressure—and found this modest town house in Garden City, which had been a multiracial town since its founding. The private garage on the ground level was a bonus. As was the well-equipped kitchen, which was far nicer than the one they had at home.

As she opened the oven, Four was startled to find Cal watching her from the doorway.

"Can I ask you a question?"

"Sure," Four replied.

"Why are you doing this? Kidnapping is a serious felony."

"What we're doing," Four said very carefully, "has nothing to do with the two of you. You and your sister will be safe and well cared for. You have my word on that."

"I'm not worried about us," Cal said.

"You're not?"

"I'm a good judge of character," Cal replied. "And like I said, you and your husband seem like very nice people."

"Why, thank you."

"But clearly you didn't do *all* your kidnapping research, because my father is *not* a very nice person. And he's not going to like that you did this."

From the other room, Four heard a cry of disbelief from her husband, followed by a bit of gloating from Finney Schraeder.

"Guessed it in *three* moves!"

"Are you cheating?"

"Ha-ha-ha! Who's the Mastermind *now*?"

CHAPTER 17

Wednesday, 5:21 p.m.

"SO WHAT NOW?" Boo Schraeder asked.

"What do you mean, what now?" Two said.

Boo looked up at him with impatience on her pretty face, and Two resisted the urge to smile.

Must have been a real shock to roll out of a Beverly Hills salon and wind up handcuffed to a chair in an unfinished room with no windows, spartan furniture, and soundproofed walls and ceiling. The overall effect was not unlike a backroom massage parlor in a bad part of town. The minimal lighting covered up a whole lot of ugly.

Two's eyes had adjusted to the near darkness. Boo's had not. He could feel her straining to read his expression.

"I mean, how long are you planning on keeping me here? Wherever this is."

"I have no plans," Two said. "I'm just a guy waiting for a phone call."

"You're more than that," Boo said. "You're also a guy who knocks women unconscious and handcuffs them to chairs. What kind of pervert are you?"

"I'm not going to touch you. Not unless you cause me trouble."

"And what happens when you get that call you're waiting for?"

"Then I do what they tell me."

"What do you think they'll tell you to do?"

Two shrugged.

Boo sighed, more in boredom than frustration, Two thought. *Aw, too bad, rich girl.* The fewer details he shared, the better. The best policy was to simply parrot back what she already knew. Right now, Mrs. Schraeder here was desperate to gain some kind of edge or insight into her predicament. Her type of brat assumed there was *always* an answer to life's problems. Two knew better. Sometimes life handed you a raw deal, and you had no choice but to accept it. She'd learn that soon enough.

"Did you pick this location or did your boss?" she asked.

"Does that matter?"

"I'm trying to get a sense of how much you or your boss have thought this through. Do you even know who I am? I mean *really,* beyond my résumé, which you can probably find on LinkedIn."

"You are Boo Schraeder, the fifth wife of billionaire Randolph Schraeder."

"Ah, can't help but notice the emphasis on the word *billionaire*. So this isn't political. This is only about money."

Two shrugged.

"Well, you or your boss made a slight miscalculation there. Do you know anything about fifth wives, my tall friend?"

"I've never been married," Two said, then immediately regretted saying it. Granted, it was nothing major. A little over two billion people on this planet were single. But she had gotten him to give away something personal. The first crack in the wall.

"I'll bet no woman was ever able to get inside your skull," she replied. "That drives us nuts. It's driving me nuts, and I've known you for only a few hours. And I spent most of that time unconscious."

Two couldn't help it—he laughed.

"*There* you are," Boo said. "I was beginning to think I'd been abducted by a cyborg. So here's the thing with fifth wives: Every fifth wife knows she's ultimately going to be replaced by a sixth wife. It's practically a law of nature."

"I didn't know that."

"You also probably didn't know that Mr. Schraeder is divorcing me. Hell, it's impossible for you to have known that. I just found out myself."

"I'm very sorry to hear that."

"I'll bet you are. But thank you. And honestly, it breaks my heart a little, even if I did know that wife number six was somewhere on the horizon. I know what everyone thought. Close friends, total strangers, the press—"

"What did they think?"

"That I married Randy for the money."

Two stared at her, trying to figure out where she was going with this. He noted the use of the cute nickname "Randy." Did anyone really address that old tycoon by anything other than "Randolph"? Or, more likely, "Mr. Schraeder, sir"? Even in the bedroom?

"Didn't you?" he asked.

Boo smiled and shook her head. "No. I married Randy for the *possibilities*. He is one of the last freethinkers in this country and being in his orbit is intoxicating. The more time you spend with him, the more you start to think the world has no limits."

"Except when it comes to marriage."

"Except for that, yes," Boo said quietly. "He has a restless heart to go along with that big restless mind."

Two's captive seemed genuinely sad, which surprised him. This was not what he had expected. Nor had he expected to say the two words that came tumbling out of his mouth now: "I'm sorry."

Boo looked up at him with glistening eyes. "I'll be okay," she said with a smile. "I mean, if I don't die here, handcuffed to a metal chair."

Two was quiet.

"No response, huh?" Boo asked. "Well, we're going to have to grapple with that eventuality sooner or later, because if this is about money, I don't think you or your boss will ever see a dime. In fact, if you kill me, you'll save Randy a lot of legal fees and paperwork."

"I don't know about that," Two said. "If wife number five

ends up dead, that might put a damper on your husband wooing wife number six."

Now it was Boo's turn to laugh—warm and infectious. Two couldn't help but smile.

"So we're in agreement," Boo said. "Killing me would be bad for everyone. Especially me. It would ruin my chance at a fresh start."

"I can see that," Two said. "I'm all about fresh starts myself."

Boo's eyes widened. "*This* is your idea of a fresh start?"

After a perfect moment of comic silence, both cracked up. It was like they were old college friends catching up over dinner and cocktails and enjoying some in-jokes instead of two strangers who were stuck together in the middle of a vast and complex kidnapping scheme.

"Like I said," Two told her, "I'm just a guy waiting for a phone call."

CHAPTER 18

Wednesday, 5:24 p.m.

"AGENT GORDON? I think we have the kidnappers' demands."

Nicky looked up from the flurry of field reports arrayed on her laptop. She was confused. Why was Hope Alonso, a twenty-eight-year-old junior agent who served as Nicky's personal assistant, giving her this news?

"Let's hear it," Nicky said.

"We haven't played it yet," said Hope. Nicky found the junior agent to be timid but super-observant. She reminded Nicky of her younger self. She too had been wide-eyed, quiet, taking in as much as she could without getting in the way. Until the day she realized that staying quiet in the back of the room practically guaranteed you'd remain in the back of the room.

"*Played* it? What do you mean?"

Hope handed Nicky an old-school cassette tape. Affixed to

it was a narrow white label with one neatly typed word: SCHRAEDERS.

Nicky hadn't held a cassette tape since grade school, when a shy boy she barely knew made her a mix of his favorite songs.

"Where did this come from?" Nicky asked. "And do we even have a machine that can play this thing?"

"An unhoused person hand-delivered it to the reception desk," Hope said. "The Schraeder name immediately raised a red flag, and that person has been held for questioning."

"Who is it?"

"White male, approximately fifty years old, no identification. Says somebody paid him two hundred fifty dollars to bring this to the lobby. We're waiting on prints."

Nicky nodded. Her immediate impulse was to march downstairs and question the deliveryman, then trace his steps back to the mastermind behind this triple kidnapping. But that wasn't her job now; Nicky needed to stay on the sixth floor and focus on the big picture.

"Tell Agent Rodriguez I'd like him to question the deliveryman."

"Right away," Hope said. "As for a player, I have Nancy down in the AV room looking for a working device. She'll bring it to the main conference room as soon as she finds it."

"Good. Call everyone back into the Sandbox—and contact the mayor's office so we can patch her in."

"Right away, Agent Gordon."

This was what her boss and mentor would have done. Still, delegating felt strange to Nicky. Why was it that the more power you had to wield, the more impotent you felt?

Nicky stared at the cassette, wondering if it offered any clues beyond the message encoded in ferric oxide powder on magnetic plastic. The brand was Maxell and the tape could record sixty minutes of material. The cassette itself was clear with no fancy design elements, very unlike the garish Day-Glo Memorex cassette that kid in grade school had given her.

Nicky idly wondered if she still had that mix tape somewhere in storage at her parents' house. The songs had actually been pretty good, she recalled.

But this wasn't a third-grader with a crush. These were kidnappers who had pulled off an audacious and meticulously timed series of abductions in three different locations. Why deliver your first message with a piece of decades-old technology?

Ah, but that was the point, wasn't it? Turn back the clock to when tracking people was a lot more complicated. Before traceable IP addresses. Before high-definition cameras recording in every conceivable location. But what did it ultimately mean? Was it merely about staying under the FBI's radar, or were they making a larger point?

Nicky was lost in some theories when Hope Alonso gave three quick knocks on the door frame.

"They're ready for you, Agent Gordon."

CHAPTER 19

"NO ONE HAS listened to this tape yet?" the mayor asked from the 4K screen.

Nicky said, "We're all about to hear it for the first time."

"So how do we know it's legit?" asked Jeff Penney, the SWAT leader. "This could be somebody's idea of a sick joke."

Mike Hardy laughed. "You're right. This is all just an elaborate prank on you, Penney."

"Don't do that, Hardy," Jeff said. "This could easily be some jerk trying to cash in on a bad situation."

"Except that nobody outside this building knows what happened a few hours ago," Mike said. Then, with a smirk, he added: "Unless *you're* talking to the press."

Nicky had to bite her lower lip to stop from smiling as the LAPD's SWAT team leader's face turned a furious shade of red. Mike loved to push things to the edge and see what happened. And what had happened now was that Jeff looked like a tick about to pop.

"The kidnappings happened *two hours ago,*" Jeff said. "Shit, I was hearing rumors before I set foot in this building. Word spreads like greased lightning in this town!"

"Enough of that, Captain Penney," said the mayor. "Agent Gordon? Let us hear the tape."

Nicky pressed play. The first thing she noticed was the ambient hiss on the tape. This message, whatever it might be, had been recorded on a device with a primitive microphone.

But the voice itself sounded as if it had been digitally distorted. Either that or the speaker was underwater.

"We have the Schraeders," the mysterious voice said, so garbled it was almost unintelligible.

Nicky flinched. Deep in her bones, she knew this was the real deal. This was not someone playing a joke. This person meant every word.

"Elizabeth, aka Boo, thirty-four years old, last seen wearing a pale blue L'Agence blouse and white jeans. Calvin, aka Cal, nine years old, last seen wearing a red Burberry polo shirt and dark trousers. Finnegan, aka Finney, eight years old, last seen wearing a light top and a plaid Dolce and Gabbana skirt. Tyler, forty-eight years old, and Cassandra Bart, twenty-six years old, were both unclothed at the time of the abduction. All five were taken at three fifteen p.m. Pacific daylight time."

"Shit," Jeff said. "Nobody except the kidnappers could possibly know all that detail."

Mike didn't give him so much as an *I told you so* glance. Like Nicky, he was troubled by what he was hearing. Not the details so much as the tone.

The voice continued:

"We removed the Schraeders from their ordinary lives with great care. If you want them safely returned to their ordinary lives, you must act with equal care."

Here it comes. Nicky braced herself for the follow-up punch. She'd been in these situations dozens of times. The ransom demands varied in terms of price, but they all featured the same elements: The personal details no one except the kidnappers could possibly know. The threat that unless the authorities followed the kidnappers' instructions to the letter, the victims would be killed.

Next would come a series of complicated directions that would push the task force to the edge of its capabilities and then, finally, the ransom demand itself.

But the tape contained nothing but hiss.

After ten seconds, Jeff cleared his throat. "Is that it?"

"Shhh," the mayor said from the screen.

Another ten seconds of ambient noise.

Then thirty more.

Around the sixty-second mark, Mike Hardy leaned over the conference table and murmured to Nicky: "That can't be all."

But this was the Sandbox; every other participant could hear him.

Nicky couldn't believe it either. This wasn't a ransom demand. It was simply a prelude. A table setting. But to what end? What did these kidnappers want, ultimately?

After more interminable silence...

"Should we fast-forward this damn thing?" Jeff Penney asked. "I mean, what the hell is their point?"

"No," Nicky said impulsively.

After three full minutes of silence, the mayor sighed. "That's enough. These bastards are toying with—"

"Congratulations," said the voice on the tape. "If you are listening to these words, you demonstrated a degree of patience. You're going to need that to bring the Schraeders home safely."

The mayor was right, Nicky thought. The bastards *were* toying with them. But the kidnappers were also teaching them all how to behave, much like you teach dogs to behave by not letting them enter the house until you give the verbal cue.

Sit. Stay. Stay...

Then:

Come.

"Tell Randolph Schraeder to meet with his money manager right away. If he wants to see his family members alive again, he'll need to gather one billion dollars."

Everyone in the Sandbox looked at each other. Did they just hear that right?

CHAPTER 20

"HOLD ON," said the mayor of Los Angeles. "I know the voice on that tape was intentionally distorted, but did he seriously just ask for a ransom of a *billion* dollars? With a *b*?"

"That's right, Madam Mayor," Mike Hardy said. "One billion is what I heard. I'm not sure I have that much in my checking account right now, but I can take a look."

"Agent Gordon?" the mayor asked as if seeking a second opinion on a medical diagnosis: *Are we sure it's cancer? Couldn't it just be a cold?*

"Detective Hardy is correct. That's what I heard too."

"What I'm saying is," the mayor continued, "are these people serious?"

The idea of a billion dollars was mind-boggling to most people, but Nicky was sure the mayor grasped exactly how much that was, considering that the budget of the City of Los Angeles was close to thirteen billion.

"We have to assume they are," Nicky said.

"Does it need to be in cash? Is it even possible to place that much cash in a bag?" the mayor said. "Or would it be several bags? Help me visualize this in terms of physical money."

"A million dollars in hundred-dollar bills—the largest denomination currently circulated by the US government—weighs approximately forty-two pounds," Nicky said. "Roughly as much as a four-year-old child."

"What's the total weight for a billion dollars?"

"One billion," Nicky said, "equals one thousand million."

The mayor took a moment to contemplate the math. "These kidnappers are asking for the equivalent of the weight of *a thousand toddlers* in cash?"

"Yes," Nicky replied.

The room fell silent as everyone—including Nicky—tried to imagine gathering that much money in one place. The transportation logistics alone were enough to blow their collective mind.

"How do you know they'll want cash?" Jeff finally asked.

"He did say dollars," Mike said.

"That's just a monetary unit," Jeff replied, "not a specific request."

"I'm not sure about that."

"Captain Penney's right," Nicky said. "Could be in cash. Could be in jewels or gold. Or it could be in crypto or maybe a wire deposit to an offshore account. Whatever it is, they're going to want something utterly untraceable."

"Like Starbucks gift cards," Mike said, trying to lighten the mood, which a small part of Nicky appreciated. But she couldn't let that show. In any group, there was always one person who could get away with jokes like that. She had never been that person. Mike, however, was.

The mayor, looking like she was trying to put a brave face on a brutal case of food poisoning, said, "I'm going to meet with Randolph Schraeder immediately. He must be going out of his mind with worry."

Nicky knew the reason the mayor wanted to insert herself into this investigation: Randolph Schraeder was a mercurial billionaire and a significant political donor. He contributed to candidates on both the Left *and* the Right, boasting to reporters that he liked to "stir the shit pot now and again."

Most recently, Schraeder had put a considerable amount of money behind the current mayor of Los Angeles. She owed her job to him and was gearing up for a bitter reelection fight. She could not afford to alienate him right now. Rather than telling him the ugly truth, Madam Mayor would focus on keeping Randolph Schraeder happy with hollow promises, which was a mistake—they'd miss a key opportunity.

"Madam Mayor, may I make a suggestion?" Nicky said, knowing they might have only one shot at a face-to-face meeting with the reclusive billionaire. "Call Mr. Schraeder right away and let him know that we have the full resources of the FBI and the LAPD handling this and that we will bring his family home safe. But let me and Chief Hardy visit him so we can assess the situation in person."

"You think the kidnappers have inside help," Jeff said.

"It's a very strong possibility."

"Did they have inside help with those cases in Santa Barbara and San Diego?" he asked. "Is this part of their pattern?"

"No," Nicky admitted, "but this is a unique situation. As I said earlier, I believe those were practice runs. This is the main event. They'd want every possible advantage."

The mayor furrowed her brow. "I doubt he'll see you. Randolph is...ornery. He has his own way of doing things. I'm actually not even positive he'd meet with *me* right now."

"I can be very persuasive," Nicky said.

"I can vouch for that," Mike added with a smirk that Nicky caught but prayed no one else did. *Come on, Hardy. Not now.*

The mayor was still uncertain about letting them go, possibly due to her concerns about the case, but more likely due to her concerns about her reelection. Nicky knew the mayor was doing the political math now, and Being There in Person was always far more politically rewarding than Phoning In My Condolences.

"What if I go with you?" the mayor suggested.

Nicky steeled herself. She had to thread a fine needle of flattery and practicality.

"If you're there, all of Mr. Schraeder's attention will be on you," she said. "But Hardy and I are just a couple of nobody cops. It will keep his mind focused on his family."

As the mayor thought it over, the conference room's door opened a few inches, and a junior agent dared to insert his head into the gap. When he saw a dozen high-powered faces staring back at him, the junior agent flinched.

"What is it, Agent Duffield?" Nicky asked.

"Sorry to interrupt, but I think we found the SUV."

CHAPTER 21

WHAT SUV? NICKY wanted to ask. There were at least a half dozen vehicles involved in this case, and she struggled to figure out what this SUV was and why it was important. If it was important.

But she didn't dare ask that question in front of the mayor. Nicky told the group she'd be right back. Mike Hardy followed close behind her.

The moment they were both outside the Sandbox, Mike took her arm and whispered in her ear: "I'll go back inside and get the mayor on board. Give me ten minutes. Then we'll head up to Bel Air to meet with Old Man Schraeder."

Nicky nodded.

As Agent Duffield led her down the hall to the tactical operations center, the junior agent brought her up to speed.

"We've been checking the surveillance cameras all along

Roscomare, which is where Cal and Finney Schraeder were abducted from their school bus. All the cameras had been disabled except for one. From that camera, we were able to track an SUV leaving the scene a short time later and trace it to Westwood, on Hilgard Avenue near the UCLA campus. LAPD is on the scene and about to enter the vehicle."

"So it could be nothing," Nicky said. "Just someone leaving their house?"

"This happened exactly one minute before the first responders arrived. The timing seemed suspicious."

Timing, Nicky thought, *was everything with this group of kidnappers.*

On the screen in the operations center, they watched a live feed of a leafy stretch of Hilgard where over a dozen uniforms were approaching the SUV as if the trunk might contain a suitcase nuke. Nicky was 99 percent sure they'd find nothing inside. Even if this vehicle was connected to the kidnappers, they wouldn't have gone through all this meticulous planning only to leave a clue behind in a cup holder.

Nicky watched anyway.

After a quick visual check inside and beneath the chassis of the SUV, the LAPD began hauling the vehicle up onto a flatbed. From here it would be transported to the closest LAPD garage, where a vehicle-forensics team would examine every inch before virtually and then physically taking the SUV apart in the hope of finding a useful shred of evidence.

Nicky doubted they would. Her gut was telling her this vehicle *was* part of the kidnappers' plan, and that plan was to keep sending the task force on wild-goose chases. Like this one.

"Agent Gordon!" boomed a voice from the hall. Nicky turned just as Michael Hardy poked his head into the tactical operations center.

"We have the green light to visit the old man."

CHAPTER 22

"ADMIT IT, MOM. You ditched me to catch an Uber home earlier because you're on that big kidnapping case, the billionaire dude and pretty much his whole family."

"What I am *on,*" Nicky said carefully, "is speakerphone. Because I'm in the car with Chief Hardy."

"Oh, sorry," Kaitlin said, and she sounded like she meant it. "Hey, Mike."

"What's going on, Special K?"

"And you know that I don't discuss active investigations over the phone," Nicky continued, "*especially* with my teenage daughter."

"But *I'll* tell you everything," Mike said. "Every last salacious detail. Names, dates, locations, you got it. Whaddya want to know?"

"Spill the tea, Mike!" Kaitlin said.

"Hardy," Nicky warned.

"Oops!" Mike said. "Your mom outranks me on this one. Sorry, K."

Nicky rolled her eyes but secretly loved how well her daughter and Mike got along. She'd been unsure how her daughter would feel when her "friend" from the LAPD came over for dinner that first time six months ago. Kaitlin's father had been a cop too, an incredibly gifted detective with the Robbery-Homicide Division, and Nicky had fallen for his big investigative brain. But eight years ago, the same brain caught a random shot from a fleeing bank robber, and her husband died before EMTs could arrive on the scene.

Kaitlin had been six. She said she remembered him, but dimly, like pieces of a dream. Kaitlin also swore she'd marry the opposite of a cop someday. "You mean a criminal?" Nicky had joked. "No," Kaitlin responded. "Someone who doesn't have to carry a gun to work."

"You doing okay, kiddo?" Mike asked now.

"Well, I was just about to shoot up some heroin with a needle I found in the alley out back, but don't worry, I ran the tip under *really* hot water."

"The kid's got street smarts," Mike said to Nicky. "You have to admire that."

"Then I thought I'd send some nudes to random middle-aged men on the internet."

"Be sure to eat some dinner while you do all that," Nicky said. "There's roasted chicken, couscous, and some salad makings in the fridge."

"Mike, don't listen to her," Kaitlin said. "She's trying to make you think she's all domestic. The fridge has nothing in it but a bottle of vodka, some ketchup packets, and a wilted stalk of celery."

"The makings of a Bloody Mary? That's it, I'm putting her up for Mother of the Year."

The banter between Kaitlin and Mike usually amused Nicky, but occasionally it drove her up the wall. Especially when neither of them seemed to grasp the gravity of the situation.

Or maybe they completely understood, and this was their way of dealing with the stress.

"Meanwhile," Nicky said, "here in the *real world,* I'm going to be back late tonight."

"Because you're working that huge kidnapping case involving the billionaire and his family. Got it."

Mike said, "Don't worry, I'll tell you all about it, K."

"No, he won't."

"If Mike wants to crash here later, it's cool," Kaitlin said. "I know it's a long drive back to Pasadena."

"I appreciate that, K."

Nicky wrapped up the call: "Okay. Dinner. Homework. Only a *little* heroin. It's a school night, after all."

"And save those Bloody Mary ingredients for me, K. I have a feeling I'm going to need one in the morning."

"Love you," Nicky said.

"Love you more," Kaitlin replied, then quickly disconnected. She also loved having the last word.

Nicky guided her car along the curves of Sunset Boulevard. When traffic slowed, as it always did, she put on her lights and drove in the turning lane until it was time to take a left up into the hills of Bel Air.

"Have you ever met Schraeder?" Nicky asked.

"Nope. I've only seen him on TV," Mike replied.

"I don't watch much cable news. What's he like?"

"He's paranoid about his privacy, but he also *really* likes being on TV—go figure. He'll patch in from some undisclosed location and try to scare the American public into hoarding supplies and buying crypto and never trusting the government."

"And by *the government,* he means..."

Mike Hardy smirked. "Oh, yeah. He freakin' can't stand the FBI."

"Good to know."

"If it makes you feel any better, he thinks most politicians are bottom-feeders and parasites."

"That doesn't make me feel any better, because that means you and I report to those bottom-feeders and parasites."

Mike squeezed his eyes shut, nodded, and smiled in that way he had that put her completely at ease, like he was saying, *We both know this is ridiculous, but this is the hand we've been dealt, so let's have fun.* Nicky appreciated it.

"Just keep in mind," he said, "that we're not dealing with a rational human being here."

"What do you mean?"

"The guy lives in a ten-billion-dollar bubble," Mike said. "Even worse, he's a self-made billionaire, a man who started out with nothing in a small town in Nebraska. Which means he believes his decision-making skills are right up there with Warren Buffett's and Jesus's. To him, there isn't an obstacle in the world that money can't overcome."

"Except maybe this one," she said.

"So how do you want to play this? I've got some ideas if you're interested."

"Clearly you have more experience with ornery billionaires than I do."

"It's not the money thing. It's the politics. Like I said, the old boy doesn't mind local cops too much, but he hates the feds. And he's probably not too fond of lady cops. No offense."

"Offense? Please. It's a badge of honor."

"So let me glad-hand him while you twist the screws."

"Boy hero and castrating bitch. Got it."

"Boy?" Mike asked with a smile. "You think I look young enough to be called a boy?"

"Nah. I was just being a castrating bitch."

CHAPTER 23

Wednesday, 6:34 p.m.

THE SCHRAEDER HOME was not a house so much as a compound—a 105,000-square-foot mega-mansion that Randolph Schraeder had bought for $141 million.

Nicky had looked up the address earlier, while she waited for her car to be brought up from the garage at 11000 Wilshire. Twenty-one bedrooms and two full bathrooms for each of those bedrooms. Nicky's entire *apartment complex* wasn't nearly that large. Though Nicky was proud that her apartment had two bathrooms, even if one was reserved for the occasional guest and their cat, Rocky. Kaitlin called it the "cathroom."

After an outer-gate security check and a front-door weapons and identification check, an assistant finally granted them access to a parlor as spacious as a bus terminal. The assistant left them alone there, but Nicky had no doubt they were being watched. Most likely recorded as well.

"It's a little smaller than I expected," Mike said with a gleam in his eye.

A new slender and severe assistant appeared. Nicky noted that she didn't make eye contact with either of them. Perhaps that was how the reclusive billionaire liked it.

She simply said: "Mr. Schraeder will see you now."

Nicky and Mike followed her down a hall lined with framed art. It resembled a mini-museum dedicated to pure wholesome Americana: farmhouses, Depression-era kids fishing, amber waves of grain, all that. A vision of this country that had probably never existed.

Abruptly, the assistant pivoted on a heel and led them into a nearly lightless empty room. Nicky looked around, trying to force her eyes to adjust to the darkness.

"This can't be right," Mike said. "Hey, we're here to see Mr.—"

But the assistant had already left and closed the door behind her.

CHAPTER 24

AS HER EYES adjusted, Nicky realized the room wasn't *completely* empty.

A mammoth 4K screen was mounted on one of the walls. It flickered to life, and once the area was bathed in digital light, Nicky saw that they had been ushered into a deluxe screening room with movie-theater-style seats and, in a whimsical touch, a street-cart popcorn machine.

"What the hell is this?" Nicky asked, her voice almost a whisper.

"Maybe Schraeder's going to show us his greatest media hits from Fox News and MSNBC."

Randolph Schraeder's face appeared on the screen as if he were beaming into one of those cable channels.

"No, I'm not, Detective Hardy."

Schraeder's media setup had been carefully composed to emphasize his strengths (his piercing avian glare; his wide bony shoulders) and deemphasize his weaknesses—namely, that he was old and frail.

Although the billionaire seemed to dominate the frame, Nicky noticed he was trembling slightly, his forehead beaded with perspiration, and he was not making much eye contact. Was this due to a medical condition? Or was he truly terrified for his family and in a state of shock?

"Thank you for agreeing to meet with us, Mr. Schraeder," Nicky said. "I'm Special Agent Gordon, and I am heading up the task force to safely bring your family back h—"

"I know all about you, Agent Gordon. Here's what I don't know. What are you doing to find my wife and two young children?"

Nicky noticed he didn't include his older son, as if Tyler were not his concern.

"At this moment," Nicky said, "you're in the position to help us the most. If we may ask you a few questions about your two young children, your wife, *and* your older son—"

"You misunderstand the situation, Detective," Schraeder said. "Your little task force means nothing to me. I am taking charge of this investigation, and I will personally handle all negotiations with the perpetrators."

Mike decided to tag himself in, catching Nicky by surprise.

"Respectfully, Mr. Schraeder, that would be unwise. You will have the resources of the LAPD and the LA field office of the FBI at your disposal. *Use us.* We will be working around the clock to bring your family home. But to make that happen as quickly as possible, we're going to need your cooperation."

Schraeder flat-out ignored the chief of detectives. He was

attempting to hijack the investigation through sheer bluster, which was a mistake.

"My investigatory team will be led by James Haller and Virgil Tighe, the CEO and CFO, respectively, of the security firm Capital. I expect you will give them your full cooperation."

The room lights came up. Sitting several rows of seats behind Mike and Nicky were two men with one empty spot between them. They had been watching the whole time. At least they hadn't helped themselves to popcorn while they enjoyed the awkward show.

Nicky was well aware of Capital and its reputation. Hollywood loved the company, and its stock prices were riding an all-time high. Capital managed to project an image of high-end private security and investigation unheard of since the glory days of the Pinkertons. The name alone intimidated.

But Nicky knew it was all glitter and smoke. Half of Capital's so-called operatives wouldn't make it past the FBI's initial screening interview.

Mike was the first to cross the room and extend a hand. "Mike Hardy, chief of detectives. LAPD."

The first man stared at Mike's hand as if it were toxic. "James Haller. Capital."

"Yeah, I just heard that."

"We're going to need the ransom tape as well as any ancillary materials, like the packaging it arrived in and camera feeds."

"You're going to have to talk to Ms. Gordon about that. You were listening when she mentioned *she* was heading up the task force, right?"

Haller slid a bone-white business card out of his jacket pocket and extended it to Mike. "You can have the materials sent here."

"And you can discuss that with Ms. Gordon, who is standing right over there."

Virgil Tighe was a touch friendlier, if only by comparison. He locked eyes with Nicky and leaned forward.

"Agent Gordon? Virgil Tighe." His surname sounded like *tiger* minus the *r.*

"Good to meet you, Mr. Tighe."

"We'd like the ransom cassette, naturally. But I'd also like to hear more about the previous Santa Barbara kidnapping. I understand you believe that case is related to this one?"

Nicky felt the ground shift beneath her. These were not details Randolph Schraeder should have known. Then again, most targets of a kidnapping-for-hire didn't have the financial power that Schraeder had. And he'd apparently used it to buy himself a mole in Nicky's own task force. Her mind spun through the faces in the Sandbox. Who was feeding Schraeder this intel?

She turned away from Tighe to face the screen. "Mr. Schraeder, believe me when I tell you this is not a good idea. You're going to risk putting the people you love in grave danger."

Randolph Schraeder finally locked eyes with Nicky and flashed a smile that caught her by surprise. It wasn't cruel or sneering; he was genuinely raw with emotion.

"Do *you* love my wife and children with all your heart and soul? Or is this just another case for you, one you eagerly accepted because you saw it as the fast track to heading up your own field office someday?"

"When the stakes are personal, it is very easy to make an error of judgment," Nicky said, ignoring the dig. "You're far too smart a man not to realize that."

"Really, Agent Gordon," Schraeder said. "So if kidnappers took your daughter, Kaitlin, would you happily cede control to a third party who was only in it for the paycheck? Or would you do anything in your power—and I mean *anything*—to guarantee her safe return?"

CHAPTER 25

Wednesday, 7:17 p.m.

WHEN MIKE AND Nicky left the Schraeder estate, it was already dark. Even though FBI headquarters was in nearby Westwood, traffic was a slog, and they found themselves idling at way too many lights.

"That was a low blow, mentioning Kaitlin like that," Mike Hardy said. "I should have warned you that Schraeder fights dirty."

"I also think Schraeder has a mole somewhere on the task force."

"Yeah, I heard Tighe ask you about the Santa Barbara job. Those two aren't smart enough to have put it together that quickly."

"Who do you think it is?"

"No idea. Another mystery to solve."

"We went there for answers and came back with more problems," Nicky said. "Yay us."

"I'll be honest, I don't think it's all bad," Mike replied.

"Maybe we can tap into some of Capital's resources. Get them to do the scut work for us. They can afford to throw endless bodies at this thing."

"That works only if we have open lines of communication," Nicky said. "Haller and Tighe will play everything super-close to the vest, if for no other reason than to make themselves seem important to their rich client."

"You forget how impossibly charming I can be when I really turn it on."

"Are you turning it on now?"

Mike gave her his best boyish smile and raised his eyebrows suggestively.

"Great," Nicky said. "Use that on Haller. Meanwhile, I'll become besties with Tighe."

"Ah, not Haller! That guy has a stick so far up his ass, I doubt he's able to bend over and tie his shoes."

"But you're impossibly charming," Nicky reminded him.

Mike grumbled, which was what he did whenever Nicky scored a point.

They were in constant contact with the command center all the way back to Westwood, but the day's biggest break in the case didn't come until they stepped onto the elevator in the garage, at which point both of their phones lit up with urgent updates.

The ride upstairs took only about twelve seconds, but to both of them, it felt like a dozen years.

The moment they stepped onto the sixth floor, a voice shouted from across the room: "Agent Gordon! You need to come over here and check this out."

Nicky wound her way through the bodies crowding the Sandbox to face the main screen. Mike struggled to keep up with her.

Hope Alonso, the junior agent who was Nicky's assistant, was speeding through the footage from the lone security feed that had captured the brazen daylight abduction of Boo Schraeder. Nicky had already watched it dozens of times.

"Is there something we missed?" Nicky asked.

"Yes," Hope said. "It's something everybody missed, because almost no one knew about it." The assistant froze the playback just as Boo fell unconscious into the arms of her kidnapper. Then she tapped on the track pad, expanding the image of an area just above the back door leading to the salon.

Nicky saw it: a black plastic circle no bigger than a half-dollar fixed to the wall above the door. "A spy cam?" she asked. "Why didn't the owner of the salon tell us about this?"

"The cam wasn't placed there by the owner," Hope said. "It was put there by the jealous husband of one of the customers. He suspected she was having an affair and that the boyfriend routinely picked her up after her hair appointments. The husband wanted to catch her in the act."

"*Was* she having an affair?" Mike asked with a devilish gleam in his eye.

"Husband didn't say," Hope replied. "But when the news broke about Boo Schraeder, he remembered his spy cam, which uploads the previous twelve hours of recording before auto-erasing. He emailed the file to us."

"No doubt looking for a little reward money to ease his possibly betrayed heart," Mike said.

"Bring up the video," Nicky said.

A few taps brought up the feed from the spy cam. The lens wasn't well positioned to capture the kidnapper's face. Basically, all you could see were the tops of his and Boo Schraeder's heads as they struggled.

But the view farther down the driveway revealed something shocking.

A witness.

CHAPTER 26

THERE HE WAS, standing just twenty feet away, watching the abduction as if it were a not-so-interesting piece of street theater.

The witness was a slender man on the tall side wearing a green cap. This wasn't your typical bystander. He was clearly watching every detail yet doing absolutely nothing about it. A professional gawker.

Even after Boo was deposited into the trunk of her own car and driven off, the witness in the green cap didn't seem troubled. He made a brief phone call, then strolled away seemingly in no hurry.

"Okay, we need to find this douchebag in the stupid green baseball cap," Mike said.

"Let's spread the clearest versions of these images far and wide," Nicky said. "What do we have on him so far?"

"No facial recognition yet," Hope said. "He's too far away from the spy cam. We've got digital forensics trying to sharpen it up a little."

Nicky squinted. "Is that a cell phone in his hand?"

"We think it's a burner, and we have agents scouring the streets nearby to see if we can locate it."

"Or pieces of it, anyway," Mike said. "Not that it will lead us anywhere." He noticed Nicky was lost in thought.

"What is it, Nicky?"

Nicky pointed to the man in the green cap. "If the kidnappers had someone watching the abduction of Boo Schraeder..."

Mike followed her instantly. "Then someone was probably watching when they took the kids off that school bus. Damn it!"

CHAPTER 27

Wednesday, 10:11 p.m.

JUST AFTER TEN o'clock Nicky decided she was willing to accept defeat, at least temporarily. There was nothing more she could do in the office, and she needed *some* modicum of rest before returning in a few hours. Plus, she had to lay eyes on Kaitlin, even if it was only to make sure she was fast asleep in her bed. Long ago Nicky had sworn that no matter where her career took her, she would do her best not to let a single day pass without seeing her daughter.

"Give you a lift?" Mike asked.

"My SUV is right downstairs," Nicky replied.

"Give *me* a lift, then?"

Nicky smiled and shook her head. "You're absolutely shameless, Detective Hardy."

"I'm just trying to be efficient. Why travel all the way to separate homes when you know the two of us will end up texting about the case all night long?"

"I need sleep," Nicky said.

"What a coincidence! So do I."

In the end Nicky relented, and not just because of Mike's self-serving (and shaky) logic. She simply enjoyed being around him. Usually their meetups were squeezed into the spare moments between their cases, which, until today, had rarely coincided.

Right now, Nicky felt spoiled by having been with him all evening. And she liked the idea of this particular "date"—no matter how crazy it might be—not ending. Could they figure out a way to be a family someday? Kaitlin seemed to genuinely like him, which was supremely important. Nicky had spent way too much time building her bond with her daughter to have an outsider upend everything. Maybe Mike was the missing piece they hadn't known they needed. Maybe there was a life outside all... *this*.

Still, there were priorities.

"I mean it," Nicky said. "Just sleep."

"I'm too exhausted for anything else."

"And not too much talking."

"I'll barely say a word."

Something occurred to Nicky. "Wait. You should message Haller. And I'll message Tighe. Maybe they can help us search for the man in the green cap."

"You're thinking this is the part where, if we appear to cooperate, they'll do us a solid down the line?"

"Not *appear* to cooperate. Why not *actually* cooperate? Tell 'em what we found. If they use it to find Boo Schraeder, great. They're welcome to the glory."

"Texting him now."

By the time they reached Nicky's modest house in Koreatown, her mental gears were working overtime. "Rubin," she said to herself.

"Is that a name," Mike asked, "or are you saying you want a midnight snack?"

"No, Rubin Padilla. From the Santa Barbara job."

"Seeing as my jurisdiction is the City of Angels, you're going to have to walk me through this one, honey."

"Rubin Padilla was the one piece that wouldn't fit. People identified him as a witness to the abduction of the trophy wife, but when we brought him in, he claimed to have seen nothing. When I sent a junior agent back to him a few weeks later with some follow-up questions, he was evasive. You know the drill—we moved on to other cases, and a long-shot witness like Padilla wasn't exactly a top priority. But I'm thinking that if this is the same kidnapping team and they're in the habit of using spotters to confirm a grab, Padilla would be in a position to tell us something."

"So you're going to feed him to Tighe as a goodwill gesture?"

"Like you said, Capital has the bodies to throw at this thing, so why not let them scoop him up?"

"You're a genius."

"You're buttering me up."

"Both can be true, Agent Gordon."

DAY TWO

CHAPTER 28

Thursday, 6:03 a.m.

AT FIRST, RUBIN Padilla thought it was a scam.

Had to be.

It was a lot of money for doing practically nothing. Couldn't be anything but some kind of con game—and Rubin was expert at spotting those.

At the time, he was barely scraping together an existence in Oxnard, and his former cellmate Ramiro insisted (metaphorical hand on an imaginary Bible) that it was legit. Just be on such-and-such a corner in Santa Barbara at such-and-such a time, wait for something to happen, then call a number on a burner when it did. That was it.

Had to be a scam.

But sure enough, seconds after he confirmed that, yes, some rich bitch had been snatched right in front of her hair salon on Figueroa Street, the money had appeared in his account.

Twenty-five grand in less than a minute!

By the time the sun set, Rubin had hightailed it out of Oxnard to the one place he knew he could lie low and make that money last—Sin City. He waited for the other shoe to drop.

It didn't.

A few days later, Julia caught wind of his good luck and showed up at his place in Vegas. She wasn't interested in him when he was broke, but now she was cozying up to him? But Rubin didn't care. Julia was hot. Ramiro's loss was his gain. (Never mind that ladies usually fell for Rubin. Hell, even that sweet-looking FBI agent who'd shown up a few weeks later wanting to ask some questions seemed really into him.)

The money was enough to cover, among other things, a few months' rent on a Spanish-style bungalow just south of the Strip on Whispering Palms Drive. Rubin put the rest of his windfall to work. He was good with cards, especially in the less glitzy joints up on Fremont Street. *Bet modestly and leave early*—that was his mantra. He was even better at scamming out-of-town tourists, which, unlike poker, was a sure thing.

Soon, life settled into routine. Sleep till noon. Have Julia cook something to fill his belly. Hit Fremont Street by three for either poker or conning middle-aged soccer moms from the Midwest out of their vacation money. Come home by dawn with more than he'd left with. Play some Fallout, get drunk, get high, get naked with Julia, sleep till noon the next day, and start all over again.

Meanwhile, his tidy little stack of cash hidden in the crawl space above his bedroom continued to grow. If Julia knew about his hiding place, she didn't let on or touch a single dollar.

That's how things had been going for more than a year now. But today was different. Today when Rubin woke up, Julia was gone, no food was prepared, and she didn't respond to his texts. That wasn't like her. And up on Fremont Street, Rubin felt like he was being watched by people instead of the other way around. He ended up losing money at the tables too. Was his whole night jinxed?

But when Rubin saw the same two faces watching him in two different casinos, he knew the other shoe had finally dropped.

Somewhere around four a.m., Rubin slipped out of a side exit and weaved his way through the Fremont Street crowds until he was sure he wasn't being followed, then he boosted a car from the valet lot at the Plaza and raced all the way down I-15.

He texted Julia their code for "Get the eff out of town": Fly. Maybe she had already. Maybe she was why Rubin was being followed.

When he pulled onto Whispering Palms Drive, the sun was just starting to come up. He half expected to see black-and-whites parked on his front lawn.

But there was no one. There was still no sign of Julia either—the house was empty. Rubin didn't care about her, but he was ready to throw up at the idea that she'd stolen his money and made a run for it. Maybe all the way back to Ramiro.

Rubin pulled over his gaming chair, stood on it, pushed aside the panel, and shimmied up into the crawl space.

The money was still there—all of it, as far as he could tell—packed inside a Nike Cortez box. His relief was so profound, he couldn't help but laugh out loud. The worry had all been about nothing.

And then came the pounding at his front door.

"Rubin Padilla! We need you to open up *right now*!"

CHAPTER 29

Thursday, 6:32 a.m.

RUBIN FROZE. Who had come for him? Did casino security somehow follow him all the way back here? And if so, for what? Rubin hadn't even pulled off a score that night—the vibes had been way off.

He could grab the shoebox and run for it, but he had no idea what he'd be facing outside. Could be one guy out there. Could be two. Could be twenty. It would be way too easy for a bunch of cops or gangsters to light him up as he tried to scurry toward the airport.

No. The best strategy would be to wait it out, like a bad run of cards. No matter how loud the people at his door knocked and shouted. And yep, they were at it again, calling for him by first and last name. At least two different voices.

"Rubin Padilla! We need to speak with you urgently."

"Open this door!"

They didn't announce themselves as LVPD, so they had to be casino security or some other kind of private law. In any case, they had no legal right to enter or they would have done it already.

Then it occurred to Rubin that maybe Julia's disappearance was not a coincidence.

Maybe she'd decided that Rubin's lucky streak was coming to an end, and she'd have a better time if she went back to Ramiro. She claimed to hate Tijuana, but maybe he'd set up something sweet for himself down there and she wanted to be part of it.

Maybe she'd told Ramiro about them being together, and Ramiro decided he couldn't live on the same planet with someone who had been screwing his beloved Julia—even if that someone was his former cellmate.

Rubin was a *thousand percent* sure this was the case when his front door was blasted off its hinges and he heard multiple people's footsteps below him.

One by one they shouted "Clear!" as they checked out each room. *Huh. These weren't Ramiro's usual TJ foot soldiers.*

Rubin listened hard and tried to count voices, mostly to figure out how screwed he was. He gave up after he realized there were at least three or four different guys down there looking through his shit.

While they searched, Rubin used his foot to slowly, *slowwwwwly,* slide the ceiling panel back into place, praying none of the people downstairs would look up and see it happening. He sucked in a breath and closed his eyes and played dead.

Julia, Rubin thought, *if I ever lay eyes on you again, I'm going to make you suffer for this. I don't care how hot you are.*

Below him, the footsteps fell silent. They couldn't have given up this fast, could they? Rubin pressed his ear against the floor of the crawl space.

And Ramiro, you slimy snake, I'm coming for you next. Forget about Julia. Brothers don't sic the police or whoever these guys are on each other.

Rubin's neck muscles strained as he resisted the urge to take another breath. If these guys went quiet, that probably meant they were listening. He sure as hell wasn't going to give himself away. He'd hold his breath all night long if he had to—

But a loud *ka-chak* sound from right below Rubin's prone body forced his hand. He gasped. His whole body twitched. Instinctively, he reached out for the Nike box full of his winnings.

Before he could touch it, however, the ceiling beneath him exploded. Everything went dark, and Rubin Padilla didn't have to play dead anymore.

CHAPTER 30

Thursday, 6:39 a.m.

"NICKY."

"Hmm?"

"*Kill it,* Nicky."

Nicky rolled over, mumbling something she intended to be a coherent sentence.

"Nicky," Mike said, "I swear, if you don't shoot it, I will."

She struggled to swim up from the murky depths of unconsciousness.

"It's on *your* side of the bed, honey."

The alarm clock. Yes. The damned thing deserved to be shot because it was loud. *So loud,* each sonic *beep* like a steel spike into her frontal lobe. Never mind that Nicky had intentionally selected the most annoying tone at the loudest setting to rouse her out of dead sleep. This infernal device deserved a bullet. The next bullet would be for herself.

Somehow, her hand found the off button, and they both roused themselves from her bed like middle-aged zombies. Nicky was used to her own solo frenzied morning routine, so it was a bit awkward to do this dance with Mike Hardy.

Somehow, they made it work, arriving downstairs together just before seven. Was Kaitlin up already? She'd been sound asleep when Nicky got home last night. Nicky hoped she wouldn't be faced with the unpleasant task of waking a surly teenager.

As it turned out, Kaitlin was not only awake but frantically moving between the stovetop and the kitchen island and the fridge to the hum of a pop song on her portable speaker.

"Whoa, what is this, Special K?" Mike asked.

Kaitlin was clearly bursting with pride but tried hard to cover it up with the stern expression of a schoolteacher: "Well, since we seem to be running a hotel of *sin* here—"

"Hey," Nicky said. "Watch it."

"Whatever," Kaitlin said. "Anyway, in keeping with the hotel idea, I've prepared breakfast. Mom, you have your usual boring options of overnight oats, fresh fruit, and hot tea. And Mike, I understand you're fond of those horrible frozen breakfast sandwiches that will probably kill you long before your time, so I came up with a healthier version: a turkey sausage patty with scrambled egg whites on a whole-wheat English muffin."

"I'm touched, K," Mike said. "You don't want me to die!"

"Not yet, anyway."

Despite the bantering tone, Nicky knew that Mike really *was* touched, and Kaitlin did care about him. And while Nicky had no idea what she and Mike Hardy were to each other (and this was not the time to clarify), it felt good having her daughter's approval.

"This looks amazing," Mike said. "But what about you, kid? What are you having?"

"Well, I was so busy preparing this spread, I kind of forgot about myself. I'll have a Pop-Tart on the way to school."

"You will not," Nicky said. "Have some oatmeal, at least."

"Too late! Scarlet just texted, and she's almost here, so I gotta scoot! You two have fun with your wildly complicated kidnapping case. Me and Scarlet and Callie might catch a movie later or maybe not."

"Keep me posted on your whereabouts," Nicky called out.

"Yes, Agent Gordon!" Kaitlin said as she left.

Mike smirked. "She does that to you too?"

"Yeah, you're both annoying. Congratulations."

Her abrupt exit made Nicky and Mike realize they'd better pack up their own breakfasts and try to eat on the way to Westwood. Their phones were already blowing up with overnight updates.

And then came a message Nicky hadn't expected.

A text from Virgil Tighe at Capital.

CHAPTER 31

Thursday, 7:05 a.m.

VIRGIL TIGHE HAD refused to enter Rubin Padilla's bungalow until his four-man team of Capital operatives had completely cleared it and declared it safe from any hidden threats. He'd thanked them for their swift work.

And then he'd started cracking skulls.

"Will someone tell me why *this man,* our best possible witness in this kidnapping plot, is dead?"

Capital operative Neal Perry—the man who'd unloaded a shotgun into the ceiling of the Rubin Padilla's bedroom—responded to his boss while watching the blood drip down from the massive hole in the ceiling.

"We knew the suspect was on the premises, Mr. Tighe, and we gave repeated verbal warnings, as you heard on the comms."

"Yeah, go on."

"We heard movement in the crawl space above the bedroom,

and I believed our team to be at imminent risk. I chose to neutralize that risk."

Virgil Tighe did not respond to Perry's statement, not even with a nod or a grunt. He strolled away and began inspecting the ex-con's little Vegas hidey-hole.

The place was filled with the usual lowlife accoutrements—video-game consoles, 4K HDTV, empty vape cartridges, fast-food containers, booze bottles. Virgil didn't care about any of that. He was looking for the items that *didn't* belong.

Like the glossy brochure from a certain Beverly Hills beauty salon tucked between a couple of shoot-'em-up video games. This would be the same salon where Boo Schraeder was last seen one day ago. He alerted another Capital op—Steve Rollie—to make an extensive digital record of the discovery and upload it to their servers.

Virgil made his way to the bathroom, which was surprisingly clean, and found some high-end makeup and a box of tampons in a wicker basket beneath the sink. "Padilla had, or has, a woman living here with him," Virgil announced to no operative in particular, knowing they'd all be paying close attention.

"I want you to pull this place apart until you know who she is," he said. "And then I want you to determine her current location. Right away, people! This is where we go on the offensive."

"What do you want us to do with Padilla?" Rollie asked.

"Finish our work as quickly as possible, then alert the Las Vegas police. He's their mess to clean up. The man is of no use to us now."

Virgil reached out and grabbed Perry's shoulder as he tried to walk past. "Your penance is dealing with the LVPD when they arrive," the boss said. "Give them the usual, Perry, and keep them off our backs."

"Understood, Mr. Tighe."

Virgil clapped Perry's shoulder. "Good man."

Then he went out the broken front door to the street. He pulled his personal cell from his jacket pocket. Only two people on the planet—Virgil Tighe and James Haller—had access to the top contact in his list.

The billionaire answered right away. "Mr. Tighe."

"I have promising news, Mr. Schraeder. I believe we have located potential conspirators involved in the kidnapping plot against your family."

"You're not going to hand them over to the Feebs, are you?" *Feebs*—Schraeder's right-wing-news-friendly nickname for the FBI.

"Of course not," Virgil said. "But, sir, you should be aware that—"

"I want you to squeeze those sons of bitches you found until they burst," Randolph Schraeder said. "Do you understand me? No cops. No Feebs. They can have all the bleeding-heart lawyers they want... *after* my family is safe."

Virgil Tighe swallowed. There was no easy way to deliver disappointing news, so he just said it plainly. "One of those suspects is gone, and the other is dead."

"What? Who killed him?"

"The suspect was cornered and quickly became a threat. Our men had no choice but to neutralize that threat. But there is plenty of evidence tying him and the woman he was living with to your wife's abduction. And we *will* locate the female suspect very soon."

Schraeder was silent, no doubt processing this stream of intel. He had made it very clear to Capital that he wanted to be notified of every single development, no matter how inconsequential it might seem.

"You'd better," Schraeder said, then disconnected.

Virgil let the insult linger for a moment, then pushed it away. He was about to head back to his car when another thought occurred to him. This time he used his Capital cell phone to send a text: Nicky, we located Rubin Padilla in Las Vegas but he resisted our operatives...

CHAPTER 32

Thursday, 8:49 a.m.

"I CAN'T BELIEVE this. They fucking killed him!"

"What?" Mike Hardy asked. "Who?"

"Rubin Padilla was killed by Capital's goons. Virgil Tighe just texted me. Seems almost proud, like we should be high-fiving him or something."

Mike grunted and shook his head. "Damn it. I'm sorry, Nicky. I shouldn't have pushed you into feeding Padilla to Tighe and those Capital meatheads."

"Nobody pushes me into anything," Nicky said, vaguely annoyed Mike was trying to take ownership of this screwup.

No, this was all hers.

As soon as they parked beneath 11000 Wilshire, Nicky began the exhausting daisy-chain process of contacting Randolph Schraeder. The main number brought you to the LA assistant, who then forwarded you to an assistant in the Nebraska office, who sent you to an assortment of assistants and advisers.

She needed to clarify things before more people died. Capital had to stand the hell down. And only the cranky billionaire could make that happen.

She had run the entire gauntlet, and the Nebraska adviser told Nicky he was "very confident" Mr. Schraeder would want to speak with her. She waited through a small eternity of "patriotic" hold music.

"Come on, Schraeder, pick up."

But the adviser returned and said, "I'm sorry, Agent Gordon. Mr. Schraeder isn't available right now. Would you care to leave a message?"

Nicky very badly wanted to say *Yes, tell him this: Randolph, your self-sabotaging anti-government bias and your blind reliance on hollow mercenaries like Capital might very well get your family killed, you stupid ass.*

But no—as long as Nicky was the head of this task force, she was forced to take the high road.

"Please have him contact me as soon as possible. There's been a major break in the case."

Next she tried James Haller at Capital, but received the same runaround from his phalanx of assistants and underlings.

Nicky found herself pacing the length of corridor between her office and the Sandbox like a caged predator looking for something to lash out against. But she wasn't angry. She was *processing*. Physical movement helped.

The hunt for the spotter at the salon abduction, the man in

the green cap, had stalled. Chunks of a burner phone were found, but they'd been destroyed beyond recovery, and there was no way to connect them to the unknown man anyway. Facial recognition so far was a dead end.

Rubin Padilla had been casually brushed off the chessboard.

There was no sign of a spotter at the abduction of the Schraeder children.

On top of everything else, there were zero leads out of Mexico, so they had no hard evidence in the Tyler Schraeder and Cassandra Bart abduction. The authorities there seemed to have other priorities.

And it wasn't even nine a.m.

Mike clocked Nicky's restlessness but stood up and chased after her only when she started blazing a trail to the elevators.

"Hey! Hold up! Where are you going?"

"They want to hide behind assistants, fine. I'll show up at their front door."

"Nicky, what are you talking about?"

"I'm headed to Capital and not leaving until they agree to stay out of our way."

"Listen to me," Mike implored, "you're the head of this task force. You go over there, you don't seem any more important than one of their assistants. It's beneath you."

"I'm not going to fight with their assistants," Nicky said. "I'm going to have a heart-to-heart with Haller and make him understand that unless we work together—"

Nicky's cell phone buzzed. She glanced at the screen.

"Who is it?" Mike asked.

"Someone who just saved me a trip."

CHAPTER 33

"NICKY, CALM DOWN. Please."

"You can address me, Mr. Tighe, as Ms. Gordon or Agent Gordon," Nicky said.

"Apologies. I thought we were beyond formalities. Look, I know you're upset, and I don't blame you. But listen to me, *I was there* when Rubin Padilla was shot."

"And you just let it *happen*?"

"The man was trying to escape with a boxful of money, but he decided to ambush our operatives on his way out. We stopped him before that could happen. I wasn't about to risk one of our operatives' lives on that scumbag."

"Padilla was our best witness. I shouldn't have to explain this to you, but dead witnesses are useless."

"If he was such a vital witness, why didn't you bring him in yesterday afternoon, *Agent Gordon*? Or did you think it would be amusing to have us do your scut work?"

Nicky took a deep breath and tried to channel her inner

John Scoleri, who was legendary for the way he suffered fools and assholes all day long with grace and intelligence. He'd gladly suffer a thousand insults if it meant solving the case at hand. Maybe that was why his clearance rate was so impressive. Maybe that was also why he'd be trapped here in the LA field office until he retired.

"I don't want to do this with you, Virgil," Nicky said, intentionally using his first name and speaking in a soft, conciliatory tone. "There's too much at stake. Wouldn't you agree?"

"I would."

"I should have given you more about Rubin Padilla before sending you after him. We will be more transparent as we proceed."

"I'm very glad to hear that."

"And that works both ways, right?"

There was a pause, as if the Capital man were too proud to promise anything. But it turned out that wasn't the case at all.

"Listen, Haller would skin me alive if he knew I was telling you this..."

"I'm listening."

"Because this aspect of the case is supersensitive to Randolph Schraeder. He doesn't want to even hear about it, let alone deal with it."

"At some point you're going to have to just say it out loud."

Virgil sighed. "The older son. Tyler Schraeder. No offense to the current wife and those little kids, but Tyler's the big catch, and the kidnappers know it. Yet he's the one part of the case we can't even bring up to Randolph. And we're kind of stumbling in the dark here."

"So you'd like us to take the lead on that one."

"I know it would make the mayor very happy. Tyler Schraeder, like his father, is a generous donor to her campaign."

"I don't care about that," Nicky said, which was the truth. But she agreed with Virgil that Tyler was the real score. She suspected that the trophy wife and kids were almost beside the point.

"So here it is, me cooperating. I have a good source in the Mexican police who tells me Tyler and that actress, Cass Bart, are most likely being held in Tijuana. Forget the resort town and start looking there."

"I appreciate that," Nicky said, and she did. But she was already anticipating the headaches that would come along with liaising with TJ police. As a rule, they were corrupt. And quite possibly in the pocket of the kidnappers. This tip could be misinformation that added to the fog obscuring their movements.

"And since we're in this new era of cooperation," Nicky added, "maybe you can tell your mole or moles on my task force to stand down for their own good. Because once we find them, they're gone."

"I don't have a problem with that," Virgil said. "We hire a lot of ex-feds."

CHAPTER 34

"MS. GORDON, COME quick!"

It was Hope Alonso, the junior agent whose ability to hyperfocus was like a superpower. Nicky was still impressed by how she'd spotted the spy cam over the back door of the salon. And now she was teeing up more video footage in the Sandbox.

"What do you have up there?"

"You know how there was only one functioning camera on Roscomare Road when the two kidnappers took the Schraeder children? And we couldn't see any spotters, unlike the Boo Schraeder abduction?"

"Yeah?"

"I think I found the spotter," Hope said.

The digital detective work wasn't conclusive, but it was impressive. Hope had seen a pale figure behind the picture windows of the closest house. The figure was almost as wispy as a ghost and could easily be mistaken for a splash of sunlight on the window. Except for...

"What is that? Is that a backpack over that figure's shoulder?"

Hope beamed. "Okay, you see it too! I'm already having digital forensics try to sharpen the image, but for now, just go with me a sec..."

She tapped keys to bring up another video feed in a new window.

"This is Linda Flora Drive, the street that runs parallel to Roscomare Road. I pulled up footage from their traffic cams around the same time when the school bus was stopped over on Roscomare. And look at this."

On the surveillance feed was a slender young woman in a pale blue raincoat with a buff-colored backpack slung over her shoulder. She moved quickly but not as if she were fleeing. More like she was late for class.

"Do we know who she is? Does she live in that house?"

"No ID yet," Hope said, "but she does not live there—the owners moved, and it's been on the market for a while. And if we rewind a few seconds"—she did—"you'll see that the possible spotter came from the back of the adjoining yard. No reason to do so unless she came over from the house on Roscomare."

"Oh, that is good work," Nicky said. "Please tell me we can trace her movements from this point."

Mike Hardy had joined them and was studying both video feeds intensely.

"We can trace her a short distance," Hope said. "She walks down the hill a bit and climbs into an SUV. Looks like it's the same SUV we tracked earlier and found abandoned on Hilgard Avenue."

"Would that be our second spotter?" Hardy asks. "The Girl in the Pale Blue Raincoat joining our Jerkbag in the Green Cap?"

"Maybe," Nicky replied.

"Yeah, something's bothering me about them."

"Go ahead."

"These kidnappers are smart. They've overlooked no details so far. They disable every single camera in the area except the one they want us to see."

"Right. And?"

"And somehow they miss a spy cam in one location and don't realize the getaway path for the second spotter is lined with functional cameras?" Mike said.

"Maybe we weren't supposed to see the figure in the picture window," Nicky replied. "I think we all would have missed her if it hadn't been for Hope."

"No offense to you, Alonso," Mike said with a smile, "but I can't help thinking that they're still playing with us. Sending us on a manhunt for these two people as a distraction."

Nicky nodded. "It's the green ball cap and the blue raincoat that are bothering you, right?"

"Very distinctive fashion choices, wouldn't you agree?" Hardy said. "You wouldn't catch me dead in a green cap in this town. People might mistake me for an Eagles fan."

Nicky had to admit that Mike had a point. She was also thinking about Virgil Tighe's tip about Tijuana.

Maybe this was phase two of the kidnappers' plot: Let the

members of the task force believe they were making excellent progress on a number of fronts while the kidnappers' actual movements were obscured.

"That doesn't change the fact that we need to find these two right away," Nicky said.

Mike nodded. "I call dibs on Green Cap."

CHAPTER 35

Thursday, 12:35 p.m.

THE REALITY OF the situation dawned on the children right around lunchtime.

It was easy to pretend that last night was nothing more than a sleepover full of games and food and jokes, followed by a surprise breakfast of cereals that were outright banned in the Schraeder household.

Cal hadn't known such a thing as Cap'n Crunch's Crunch Berries existed, let alone the Cap'n Crunch's Oops! All Berries variation.

But once the sugar high wore off, Cal and Finney began to feel different. They were wearing the same clothes they had put on for school yesterday. And now for lunch, they were staring at packaged deli meats, Kraft singles, and white bread, none of which were allowed at home. According to their father, processed food was poison, Finney said.

Four watched Cal carefully. The boy was struggling to put on a brave face, most likely for his little sister's benefit. But Four could see his hands trembling as he spread a dollop of mayonnaise on the thin slice of bread in his hand.

Call it Mom Radar. She could always tell when something was off with her own child, and apparently, this skill transferred to other children too. The longer this whole ordeal wore on, the worse things were going to get for these children. And Four wasn't sure she could bear it.

"How are you doing there, Cal?"

"Fine."

Cal was absolutely not fine. And he refused to make eye contact.

"Look, I know how strange this all seems. I promise, you and Finney are going to be okay."

Cal finally looked at Four, and his eyes almost took her breath away. They projected sadness, fear, and anger all at once.

"You don't know that."

"I swear on my—" Four caught herself. "I swear nothing will happen to you."

Finney looked up from her cheese sandwich and watched their exchange intently.

"You can't swear or promise anything because you're not in charge," Cal said. "You're taking orders from somebody, right? That's how kidnapping works. But if you are in charge, why don't you let us go?"

"It's not as simple as that, Cal."

"Somebody could just call your cell phone and order you to

kill us," Cal said. "Isn't that right? You have to do whatever they say."

"Cal, *no*."

"Maybe they already told you to kill us. Maybe there's poison in the mayonnaise! I notice you and the other guy aren't eating the same food as us."

Finney glanced down at her sandwich, studying the bite mark she'd just made.

Four and her husband—who was currently upstairs taking a shower—weren't eating the same food as the children because neither of them had been able to choke down anything other than black coffee since this whole crazy thing began yesterday. Probably even before that. Four couldn't remember her last hot meal.

And yes, Cal was right: Four and Three were ultimately not in charge. Despite the circumstances, though, she'd sworn to do everything in her power to keep these children as safe, comfortable, and mentally healthy as possible.

Four took a clean spoon, dipped it into the mayonnaise jar, widened her eyes playfully, then scooped up a big mouthful and ate it as if it were vanilla ice cream. She almost gagged, and her stomach was already in knots. But the wide-eyed surprise from both kids made it worthwhile.

"See?" Four said after she swallowed. "No poison."

Finney giggled. Even Cal cracked a smile.

"Cal, honey, I know you're afraid. You want to know how I know? Because I have a daughter who's a little older than you, and sometimes she gets afraid too."

"You do?" Cal asked. "So where is she?"

Leave it to a child to innocently hit the heart of the situation. *Yes, Four, where is your daughter? And why aren't you with her right now, when she needs you the most?*

"My daughter is with my baby sister, her aunt," Four explained, "while her daddy and I are looking after you two goofballs."

But this last attempt at humor didn't work. Finney solemnly placed her sandwich back on her plate. "Why does your daughter get afraid?"

"She's sick a lot," Four said quietly.

"Sick from what?" Cal said.

From what? Four thought. *That's the million-dollar question, isn't it.* If she knew the answer to that question, they might not be sitting here in this strange house with these innocent children.

"Nothing for you to worry about," Four said, which was the truth in a twisted way. Her family problems were nothing to the Schraeder family. "But can I tell you something? I get scared too."

Cal looked at Four, truly perplexed. "Why do *you* get scared? You're a grown-up."

"Sometimes it can be very scary to be a grown-up. Because you're the one in charge, and so many things depend on what you do or don't... do."

No. She couldn't do this. Not in front of these kids, who continued to look at her with wide eyes. She muttered something along the lines of *Finish your lunch,* rushed into the guest bathroom just off the living room, and closed the door behind her.

Four knew this violated the letter of the plan—and One took his plans very seriously; they were to follow them under pain of death. The children were never to be left alone. But she thought it would have been far worse to openly weep in front of them.

CHAPTER 36

THERE WAS A gentle *knock-knock-knock* on the bathroom door. "Honey, you okay?"

Four wiped her eyes, then stared at herself in the bathroom mirror. It helped to think of herself as a number, not a name. She was Four. Outside the door was Three, checking on his partner. Three and Four were employed by One to do a job. That was all that mattered inside this house; nothing else.

She opened the door and saw Three's eyes were wide with panic. "Hey, I thought we agreed never to leave them alone?"

"Are they still here?"

"Yeah, of course. They're finishing their sandwiches. But—"

"Then what are you worrying about?" She could tell Three wasn't buying her cool-as-ice act. Not for a second. He knew her far too well. He also knew when to back off and not pressure her, and this was one of those times.

"Have we heard anything from One?" she asked.

"Do you honestly think I'd keep that to myself?" Three

replied. "No, not a word. And I don't think we'll hear anything for a while. That's a *lot* of money to pull together."

Four understood, but that didn't stop her from hoping that the text message would come soon, the promised money would be deposited, and they could all go back to where they belonged. These two kids to their billionaire father; Three and Four to their daughter's hospital room.

But they both silently wondered about the other possible ending. One they had fooled themselves into believing could never happen—that even someone as cold and calculating as One could never actually contemplate it.

What if the family didn't pay the money? What would happen then?

What would Three and Four be forced to do?

"Well," Four said, "since we're in this for the long haul, let's distract them with an afternoon of fun and games."

For the next couple of hours, they stuck to the list of board games they'd been supplied with. But soon, the delights of Mastermind and even the Settlers of Catan faded, and the Schraeder children were restless. That's when Three revealed what he had in his back pocket. Literally.

"You kids ever play Robbery-Homicide Division?"

"Three," his wife cautioned. "No."

"C'mon. It's just a video game. Mostly driving."

"I've *always* wanted to play that game," Finney said in a tone of awestruck reverence. "My friend Katie's older brother has it."

Four shook her head. "This is exactly the kind of thing we agreed not to do."

"Who's gonna tell?" Three asked. "You kids aren't going to rat us out, are you?"

"Considering we've been kidnapped," Cal said, "playing a mature-seventeen-plus-rated game is probably the least of our worries."

"You see?" Three said.

Four sighed. Her husband was addicted to these damn games. He had a handheld console on him at all times to while away the long hours at the hospital (and Four wasn't crazy about her husband encouraging their daughter to play too). Soon, Three, Cal, and Finney were taking turns executing a complicated getaway from a downtown Los Angeles bank. Four refused to take a turn on principle.

"You're *really* good at this!" Finney exclaimed after Three showed her how to use the 110 exchange through Chinatown to avoid the LAPD.

Four knew she shouldn't say anything, but she couldn't help it. "He *should* be good at this. He used to be a criminal."

Three shot her a piercing look. "I was just a kid. Barely a teenager. I did a lot of stupid things back then."

Cal turned to face Three. "This might not be your brightest moment either."

CHAPTER 37

Thursday, 1:03 p.m.

"YOU DON'T SEEM like an idiot," Boo Schraeder said suddenly in the near dark of the room.

"Uh, thank you?" Two replied.

He had stayed awake almost all night, a skill that could be credited to his former career. He was used to entering a kind of low-power mode in which he was consciously aware of his surroundings while his body recharged. If anything happened, he could come back online in a half a second.

Two's pretty captive *had* slept—or at least, she had appeared to manage a few hours of slumber. He had to admit, he enjoyed watching her. The sound of her breathing was reassuring. The only interruption had been a single bathroom break for his captive, which both handled with quiet grace. No sudden moves, no awkwardness. She was fully compliant, even when it came time to cuff her to the bed frame again. ("Ooh, kinky," she'd joked.)

"I'm lying here," Boo said, "wondering how you, a human being of above-average intelligence, ended up in this position. I mean, kidnapping must be the dumbest crime ever."

"I don't know, Mrs. Schraeder. Everything seems to have gone according to plan so far."

"Oh, it will unravel. These kinds of complicated plots always do. I'm a bit of a true-crime junkie, so I've read more than my fair share of kidnapping stories. You want to know how they end? Let me give you a sneak preview. You'll end up either dead or spending the rest of your life in a room just like this one."

"I'm not so sure about that," Two said. "I know a lot of crime stories too."

"Then you know you're doomed."

"Aren't we all, ultimately?" Even though the room was dim, he could see her amused smile.

"Let me assure you," she said, "I'm not prying into the details of your precious little plot. I'm genuinely curious how you ended up in this line of work."

Two considered her question. Despite her protestations, she was plainly fishing for useful information. But she'd happened to touch on something he'd been pondering for a while now. Especially over the past twenty-four hours.

"Sometimes," he said, "you just have to play the hand you're dealt."

Boo let out a laugh that was almost a bark. "Oh, not the old poker metaphor! That's *such* an alpha-male thing to say. You can't possibly believe that."

"Sure I believe it. Not everyone is lucky enough to marry the mega-rich, like you."

"Ouch."

"And I'm not sorry."

"So you believe your entire life hinges on a random draw of cards? That there's zero free choice or skill involved? I don't know. Maybe you *are* an idiot."

"Skill doesn't matter when the game is rigged," Two said. "If this world were even *remotely* fucking fair—"

Boo wasn't smiling anymore. "What happened?"

"It doesn't matter."

"Of course it does. Denying it only makes it worse."

"Let's just drop it, okay? Are you hungry?"

Boo did not reply. She stared off into the darkness, lost in her own thoughts.

"Mrs. Schraeder?"

Two didn't like this. He stood up from his chair and slowly approached the bed, stretching the stiffness out of his muscles as he moved.

"You're right, by the way," she said quietly. "About the unfairness of life."

Two could make out the tears on her cheeks, and they were plain in her voice too. Maybe this was part of a game, another way to throw him off balance. But somehow, Two didn't think so. His bullshit detector was a highly sensitive instrument, and the needle wasn't twitching even slightly.

"I tried my best to be a good wife," she said. "But I was either too much or not enough."

And before he knew what he was doing—before he could even weigh the pros and cons of this crazy-stupid impulse—the kidnapper found himself kissing his abductee.

The same beautiful woman who, if it came down to it, he had agreed to kill.

CHAPTER 38

Thursday, 1:05 p.m.

FIVE HAD LIVED on high alert since he was a kid.

Down in TJ, it was practically a requirement. If someone decided to mess with you, you needed to know long before he made the first move. Then you could prepare your defense or maybe even a preemptive strike. Either way, the guy would learn pretty quick that you were not one to be messed with.

Tyler Schraeder was definitely about to mess with Five.

Ever since Five had shown Tyler and Cass to their locked room, Tyler had been exhibiting *all* the signs: The sudden heat in his eyes. The change in breathing. The tension in his muscles, even though he clearly assumed he was projecting the opposite — cool, utter calm.

Yeah, there was no doubt Rich Kid Tyler had all kinds of action-movie nonsense rattling around in his skull.

Five double-locked the door behind them and prepared himself.

From the dossier that One had provided, Five knew that Tyler Schraeder had extensive martial arts training. Krav Maga. Brazilian jujitsu. Kickboxing. Wing Chun. And so on. If it was trendy for even a Hollywood minute, Tyler had studied it. He didn't want to be one of those stuffed-shirt producers. He liked to play around with the actors and the stunt guys.

But as far as anyone knew, Tyler Schraeder had never been in an *actual* fight.

This became painfully clear to Five when Tyler threw the first punch, which was intended to be devastating. The guy probably thought he was following his version of street rules: Hit first and hit hard enough to end the fight then and there.

Problem was, Tyler was focused on the strength of the punch rather than the stealth of it. The blow was ridiculously telegraphed, to the point where Tyler should have said: *Hey, I'm going to try to hit you really, really hard.* That might have actually surprised Five.

Instead, Five pivoted a few inches, and Tyler's fist sailed harmlessly past his face. The momentum carried him forward and he stumbled over his own feet. Five had all the time in the world to select his own move. He opted to deliver a jab powerful enough to crack a rib. Which, judging from the sound of the blow when he landed it, did just that.

Tyler fell to his knees, already wheezing.

"You really want to do this, rich boy?"

A beast-like growl came out of Tyler's throat, and he hurled himself at Five.

Tyler Schraeder did have a size and weight advantage. And

Five *was* momentarily caught by surprise; he'd expected some of that fancy Hollywood martial arts nonsense from Tyler, not a full-on NFL-style blitz.

Tyler tackled Five hard enough that when he hit the wall behind him, the framed art hanging there rattled. Then Tyler locked his hands around Five's neck and squeezed, probably imagining that he could strangle him or snap his spine or some other dumb action-movie nonsense.

Didn't he realize that Five had been picked on by kids much older, heavier, and meaner than him? Did Tyler think he would be this easy?

Clearly he did, because he had no defense for when Five jackhammered his forehead into the rich boy's perfect nose.

And, oh, how he screamed.

What did Five enjoy most—the agony, the gore, or the idea that Tyler's handsome looks would be ruined forever if he didn't get major reconstructive surgery? Five decided he enjoyed all of it equally.

Tyler deflated and dropped to the ground; his trembling fingers touched his face as if he could put it back together again—if only it didn't hurt so damn much.

"You'd better be careful," Five said. "You're seriously cutting down on your own hostage value. I think they pay less for an abductee with a missing tooth and a broken nose."

Rich boy rolled over, spat blood, and in a mumble began to suggest that Five should have carnal relations with himself.

Five kicked Tyler in the stomach before he could finish the thought. *This guy, man. He doesn't give up.* "Pretty sure your value would go down even more if you were dead," Five said.

To be honest, Five was wishing for that. As much as he'd like his share of the treasure, it would be supremely satisfying to watch the life drain from this spoiled asshole's face, his eyes all wide, with his girlfriend's terrified screams the last thing he heard on this earth.

Hell, he might kill him even if the money *did* come through. One would be pissed, but so what?

Then Tyler Schraeder said something that genuinely surprised Five.

He turned over, snuffling blood and trembling, rested on his elbows, gave Five his most defiant sneer yet, and said, "Here's what you don't get. The last thing my father would ever do is pay a ransom for me."

CHAPTER 39

"STOP IT!" CASS shouted. "You're going to kill him!"

All this time, Cassandra Bart had been watching the fight scene play out as if they were on a stage. As if she weren't sure if this was real or not. Maybe she was clinging to the hope that this was some kind of reality show. Or an extreme screen test.

Five smirked. "Maybe. Maybe not. But *you* have nothing to worry about, honey. You, I like."

Tyler spat out another thick wad of blood and struggled to catch his breath. Five could see the defiance building up again. What a stubborn son of a bitch! Five almost respected him for it. But still, he needed to extinguish that tiny flame of resistance for good. He didn't want to have to worry about this prick, especially if the ransom money was slow in arriving.

Five grabbed a fistful of the man's hair and pulled back hard, exposing his neck. He was tempted to punch him in his Adam's apple. Oh, man, did Five long to do that, let him struggle to breathe until he simply couldn't.

But instead he grabbed Tyler's left ear and twisted it almost ninety degrees.

"I'm begging you!" Cass said. "Don't!"

Five gave her an icy glare, then raised a finger. And then he turned his attention back to her boyfriend.

"Saw this TV show once," Five said, "about some rich kid just like you who was kidnapped. He grew up in an oil-money family. Grandpa was a stubborn fuck, though. Refused to pay the ransom. He thought the grandkid was, like, faking it and shit. The kidnappers were Mafia or something. I'm talking about the old-school kind, from Italy."

"That *rich kid* was John Paul Getty the Third," Tyler said through gritted teeth. "And you know what happened to the gangsters who kidnapped him? They went to prison for life, just like you're gonna, you stupid f—"

Five gave another painful twist to his ear: *Not your turn to speak.*

"When the grandpa refused to pay, the Mafia took the rich boy and cut off his ear. Mailed it to Grandpa. Said, 'Pay up, or we'll send more pieces in the mail until there's nothing left.'"

Another hard turn of the ear, to the point where even Five wondered if he'd taken it too far. "Let me tell you a little secret, rich boy. I might cut off your ear for fun."

Before Tyler could react, Five kneed him in the face. Blood spurted everywhere.

Five straightened up and realized he had a lot of this guy's blood on his clothes, which annoyed him. He dragged Tyler across the room by his arms, then reached into his jacket pocket and found a few zip ties. He tossed them to the actress. "Tie his wrists to the bed nice and tight."

She didn't even attempt to catch them. They landed at her feet.

"I'm gonna change my clothes. Don't bother trying to bust open the door. It's reinforced."

Cassandra didn't move.

"Hey, honey? His wrists aren't going to tie themselves, you feel me?"

CHAPTER 40

Thursday, 1:12 p.m.

"I THINK I may know why Old Man Randy is so eager to sideline us," Mike Hardy said.

He extended a manila file folder to Nicky. She opened it and saw that it was stuffed with printouts of insurance documents from a certain high-end company often used by wealthy Southern Californians. Nicky had dealt with them before. And she saw the name of the client: Randolph Schraeder.

"Where did you get this?"

"Intercepted it from your financial-crimes guy on my way over here," Mike said. "Some big dude named Lindbergh. He seemed super-proud of himself."

"So why didn't you let Ross deliver them?"

"I wanted you to think I was important and useful."

Oh, Mike was loving this. She used to wonder what it would

be like if Mike came to work at the Bureau or if Nicky joined the LAPD. Now she was finding out, and she was delighted to realize she didn't mind it one bit.

But right now she had to keep her head focused.

"So Schraeder has K and R insurance," Nicky said, flipping pages.

"A metric ton of it," Hardy said. "Lindbergh said this specific kidnapping and ransom policy covers practically the full billion."

"Now why would he carry such a huge policy unless..."

"He thought he'd need it someday? I was thinking the same thing."

Nicky continued to scan the documents and let out a low whistle. "If I'm reading this right, the yearly tab for the kidnapping insurance is something like zero point zero four of the total policy, and that's just for Randolph. Factor in the other family members and..."

Mike stared at her. "If you're asking me to do arithmetic, I'm about to disappoint you. Just ask Father O'Neil at Sacred Heart. He flunked me. And I deserved it."

But Nicky was running the numbers in her head. "This would cost Schraeder something like thirty or forty million annually. That's a hefty price tag."

Now it was Mike's turn to whistle. "And where does Capital fit into this? Don't insurance companies have their own investigators?"

"I don't know, Hardy. I could have asked my financial-crimes specialist if you hadn't ambushed him."

"Oops."

"And why didn't Schraeder or those Capital guys mention the policy?"

"I think this means old Randy just became our number one suspect."

Nicky reached for the phone. "I'm calling Ross Lindbergh."

CHAPTER 41

THE FINANCIAL-CRIMES GUY, Agent Ross Lindbergh, looked nothing like the stereotypical accountant.

Ross had the build of a college linebacker—which he had been, at the University of Texas at Austin. But Ross said he enjoyed the stats of the game more than the game itself, so when he was recruited by the Bureau, he practically begged to join the numbers team.

And to Nicky Gordon's mind, Ross was *the* key member of her task force. Kidnapping, at its core, was a financial crime. More extreme than mugging someone at knifepoint or threatening a bank teller with a grenade, but the motive was the same: money. Nicky needed someone who could ignore the abduction drama and literally follow the money. That was Ross Lindbergh.

"This whole thing is happening at an interesting time for the Schraeder Organization," Ross said.

"Tell me why it's interesting," Nicky said.

"There's been some fighting over the family investment business. Oldest kid, Tyler, wants full control. He says his father should be declared non compos mentis."

"Does Tyler truly believe his father is not in his right mind?"

"It's unclear. Tyler points to his father's comments in his numerous media appearances, but that won't be enough to sway a judge. I mean, everybody goes on cable news and says outlandish things these days."

"And what does Randolph have to say about it?"

"Randolph is refusing to surrender control and is trying to have his son removed from the board. Says he has to wait his turn like the rest of his children. With an emphasis on the word *children*."

Nicky could see this from either side. If Randolph *was* behind these abductions, it would be far too easy to have Tyler removed from the board—permanently—and blame the kidnappers for his death. Cold-blooded? Absolutely. But not out of the realm of possibility. Especially with billions at stake.

From Tyler's point of view, it would be equally simple to have himself, his father's wife, and his half siblings abducted. He had intimate knowledge of the family and their behavior. If his father bungled any part of the ransom delivery, it would erode the firm's confidence in his leadership, and it would be even worse if a member of the family ended up dead. Nicky made a mental note to check on the relationship between Tyler and stepmom number four.

"Can I tell you what's bothering me about this?" Ross asked.

"That it's looking like an inside job?" Nicky replied.

"Yes, but on top of that, it's the billion-dollar ransom. That's a staggering figure, and it'll require a monumental effort to gather it, not to mention deliver it. Have the kidnappers given any instructions yet?"

"Not yet. But Schraeder's men at Capital say he's already working on it."

"Kidnappers only ask for what they think they can receive," Ross said. "So whoever they are, they have enough information about Randolph Schraeder's assets to know exactly how much he can liquidate in a given amount of time."

"Which is why I'm wondering if it's Schraeder himself," Nicky said, "or his son."

"Or someone in the investment firm. I'd like to take a closer look at the other board members and see if anything jumps out."

"Great thinking," Nicky said. "Do it."

"One more thing, Ms. Gordon—let me know as soon as the kidnappers give the ransom instructions."

"You'll know the minute I share it with the rest of the task force."

"No, what I mean is, the type of payment they request might give us a clue as to their identities. How much in cash, how much in diamonds."

Smart man, Nicky thought. He wasn't thinking about just the handoff of the ransom. He was thinking about eventual prosecution. "You'll know as soon as I do."

CHAPTER 42

"ARE YOU PEOPLE out of your minds?" James Haller shouted over the speakerphone. "I guess I can be glad that you called *me* with this bullshit instead of Mr. Schraeder."

"Come on, Haller," Nicky said. "The optics are pretty damning."

"The only thing Mr. Schraeder cares about is the safe return of his family. And that includes his older son. Implying anything else would be slander."

"If we didn't follow up on this," Nicky said patiently, "we wouldn't be doing our jobs."

"Here we go, typical FBI horseshit," Haller said, his voice growing even louder. "You want to know who set up that K and R insurance policy? *I did.* Personally. When you have a client as powerful and high profile as Mr. Schraeder, you have to cover all bases. He didn't want me to do it, but I insisted."

"You talked him into spending forty million bucks a year," Mike said, "just to... what did you say? 'Cover all bases'? Come on."

"Who is this? Is this Hardy?"

"Yeah, this is Chief of Detectives Hardy, with a take-home of a hundred and forty K per year."

"You just proved my point," Haller said. He made a strange noise that could have been interpreted as a laugh. "You and Nicky Gordon should stick to what the citizens pay you for. Namely, hunting down criminals for eventual prosecution. But when it comes to Mr. Schraeder's personal and financial business, including the safe return of his family, leave it to the professionals. Anything else?"

"Don't worry, Haller," Nicky said. "We will absolutely find the mastermind behind these kidnappings. No matter how hidden—or well protected—they may be."

"Is that supposed to mean something, Agent Gordon?"

"Thank you for your time," she said, then hung up.

Nicky and Mike stared at each other for a moment, then broke into grins. It was a tension reliever, the only one they had.

"What an asshole," Mike said.

"True, but for now we're going to stick close to Haller and the rest of them. Because if Schraeder is the one behind his own family's abductions, he must have had help. And Capital feels like the ideal partner in crime."

They stood up and were preparing to leave the Sandbox when something occurred to Nicky. "You hear what he said about Tyler?"

"Yeah. Kind of hard to miss."

"Father of the Year," Nicky replied.

But as she spoke those words, she couldn't help thinking of Kaitlin. Nicky could imagine absolutely *no* circumstance or situation that would ever drive that kind of wedge between her and her daughter. But if something like that ever did happen, Nicky knew she'd spend the rest of her days trying to fix it and begging Kaitlin for forgiveness.

So what could have happened between Schraeder and his son to cause that rift? And were they both so incredibly stubborn that they refused to even entertain the idea of trying to repair the damage?

Then the answer occurred to her, almost like an intrusive thought from her subconscious: *Ambition.*

Schraeder had been too busy building an empire to give his oldest child what he needed. Nothing mattered to the old man as much as the pursuit of the next goal.

Then Nicky realized something, with more than a chill.

And what am I *doing right now instead of being with Kaitlin?*

CHAPTER 43

Thursday, 1:15 p.m.

"YOUR LIPS ARE very soft," Boo said after she pulled back from the embrace. "You know, for a ruthless and dangerously violent kidnapper."

"Don't worry," Two said. "This is only a side hustle."

"Is that what I am?" Boo asked with a devilish smile. "Your side hustle?"

"I don't exactly know *who* you are, let alone *what* you are, other than the most strangely pleasant surprise."

"Finish your thought."

"What do you mean?"

"You said I was the most strangely pleasant surprise, but you didn't give it a modifier. I'm the most strangely pleasant surprise... of the day? The week? Or maybe the month?"

"The past couple of months, easily."

"Clearly you're not a full-time kidnapper," Boo said. "Otherwise you'd be meeting all kinds of abductees. Some of whom might also be kissable and surprising."

Two laughed. "Let's just say I'm glad I was assigned to you."

The moment Two spoke the words, he realized his tactical error.

"Interesting. *Assigned* to *me*," Boo said, working it out. "As opposed to someone else. Presumably someone else in my family. Which most likely means other members of my family have been abducted."

"That's not what I said."

"Of course you didn't. But I was able to figure it out anyway. So who else? C'mon. You might as well tell me. What difference could it possibly make?"

"I know nothing about any other abduction," Two said, which was mostly the truth. The other parts of the plan were hidden from him, but he had checked the news. The Schraeder kidnappings dominated headlines and airwaves. "My sole focus is you."

"I assume Randy is safe," Boo said. "Because you need somebody to gather the money and pay the ransom. How much are they asking for?"

Two shrugged. He could have told her the truth—maybe she would have been impressed. But he'd already said too much, and he vowed to keep all details to himself from now on. He would stop this line of questioning by any means necessary.

"I wonder if you all would be foolish enough to go after Randy's older son, Tyler," Boo continued. "Because Randy can't stand him, and the feeling is mutual."

Two reached out with his index finger and slowly traced the line of her jaw.

"What are you doing?"

"Trying to distract you."

"That feels nice, but it's not going to work. Because...oh God. You people wouldn't be so cruel as to kidnap my younger stepchildren, would you?"

His finger rounded her perfect chin. Nearly perfect. There was the faint trace of a scar running on a diagonal. Perhaps a minor injury from her time in the military. But no, it was too faint for that. Something from childhood?

"Where did you get this scar?"

"Double points for attempting a double distraction," Boo said. "But it's not going to work."

"No?"

"Do you think I'm that easy?"

"I don't know. I'd like to find out."

Two kissed her again, deeper and longer, to the point where he wasn't sure where he stopped and she began. Only her very intentional rattle of the handcuffs snapped him out of his reverie. And it reminded him of why they were stuck in this room together.

When the time comes, Two, will you have it in you to execute your orders?

Boo's soft voice broke into his thoughts. "Are you trying to make love to your captive?"

"Probably not a good idea, right?"

She smiled. "You really *are* new at this, aren't you?"

CHAPTER 44

Thursday, 1:22 p.m.

MIKE HARDY CAME storming into the Sandbox. "Remember that nonsense Schraeder and Haller were both slinging?" he said. "About how all Schraeder cared about was getting his family back?"

Nicky nodded.

"Well, it might be true that he wants his kids back. But I'm not sure that applies to his wife. I have it on good authority that ol' Randy is in the process of getting himself unhitched for the *fifth* time."

"Why? Has Boo Schraeder aged out of trophy-wife status?" Nicky leaned back in her chair. "How good an authority is this? Please don't tell me you're reading TMZ."

"I'm buddies with a guy from law school who travels in the same circles as Schraeder's money manager."

"Does Boo have a prenup?"

"Yeah, but it's downright miserly. I suppose Schraeder or his lawyers learned from their past mistakes." Mike drummed his fingers on the table. "What do we know about Mrs. Fifth Wife?"

"They met on TV," Nicky said. "It was a segment on a cable show about the army's abortion policy. Randolph Schraeder was firmly against the policy, and they invited a female active service member to debate him."

"Which would be the woman who became Mrs. Fifth Wife."

"Exactly. They really got into it too! Boo tore him apart. The clip went viral for a couple of days. And it went viral again when the news broke that Randy proposed to her."

Mike rolled his eyes. "Because he's the kind of guy who just loves a strong woman, right?"

Nicky smiled. "Just like you, Detective."

"Me? Nah. I'm drawn to the gold-digger types who are just in it for my fat police pension."

"I'm not sure Boo Schraeder is a gold digger."

"You're going to have to show me your math on that one."

"She's forty years younger, true," said Nicky. "But close friends say she's super-down-to-earth and not afraid of a messy fight when it comes to defending her family or the Schraeder name. Apparently, she's also a good stepmom to Cal and Finney."

"Speaking of, where is Mrs. Fourth Wife?" Mike asked. "Should we be looking at her?"

"I understand she's been on a rotation tour of spa resorts and rehab clinics ever since the divorce," Nicky said. "But we should have someone contact her anyway."

"That's more your world than mine," Mike reminded her.

CHAPTER 45

Thursday, 2:45 p.m.

WHAT DOES A billion dollars look like?

Virgil Tighe was curious about that. And he was on his way to Randolph Schraeder's place in Omaha, Nebraska, to find out.

Virgil had taken this flight countless times over the past year, a private jet from Burbank to Omaha. The flight ate up three hours, maybe a little less if the pilot pushed it. He wished the old man stayed in his Bel Air castle more often.

Not that Schraeder's Omaha spread wasn't impressive, but it was more of a small town than a mansion. As a young man, he'd inherited a dilapidated A-frame built at the turn of the century that was still underwater to the local savings and loan.

Schraeder's uncanny knack for savvy investments turned that around. The first thing he took over after he started making money was, naturally, that savings and loan. Then he bought the land all around that sad A-frame, then the next parcels of land, then the next, and so on until Randolph Schraeder owned a sizable chunk of Sarpy County and found himself clubbing with Warren Buffett. The original family house, now essentially a museum, was surrounded by buildings in a variety of architectural styles. WELCOME TO SCHRAEDERTOWN, POPULATION ONE GIANT EGO.

One of the company drivers met Virgil at the private airfield and sped him to Randolph's "work shed," a euphemism for a brutalist structure the size of a small airplane hangar.

Virgil Tighe had seen many crazy things in his career, but nothing compared to the sight waiting for him inside the work shed.

"Virgil! Get on over here and help me think."

The interior of the work shed was lined with folding tables, each of them supporting tall piles of cash bound with paper wrappers. Each table was manned by an armed guard—personnel vetted and hired by Capital, naturally. A few of the tables held gold bars. Fewer still had a variety of jewelry in Ziploc baggies. The place looked like it contained the life savings of the head of one of Mexico's more successful cartels.

And still, it was only a *fraction* of Randolph Schraeder's fortune.

"Looks like you've got the situation well in hand" was all Virgil could say. He knew his boss had been pulling from his investments all over Omaha, which was where most of his money was tied up.

"Eh," Schraeder muttered, "I don't think we're even ninety

percent of the way yet. And I'm still waiting for the duffel bags to arrive. Can you believe that? It's easier to gather all this folding money than a pile of goddamned duffel bags."

"I'll make a call, Mr. Schraeder."

"Don't bother. They're on their way. No, I need your brain for something else."

This was the primary reason Schraeder had hired Capital: spare brains. Logistics bored him, even logistics involving the return of his abducted family. If something bored him, he delegated it.

"Anything," Virgil said.

"What's your best guess on the payment instructions? I mean, should I be thinking about higher denominations in fewer bags? Or will the drop-off involve some kind of shipping container? Your expert guidance, please."

His expert guidance, huh? All Virgil could think was *There's no way any kidnapper would want all this fucking cash.*

But Virgil swallowed. He'd known this question was coming, and he'd spent much of the flight crafting the best possible answer, one that would reassure his mega-wealthy client but also not sound like total bullshit.

"The best thing to do," Virgil told his boss, "is what you're doing. Stay flexible and prepare for all possibilities. Most kidnappers like to keep their targets scrambling. But here's the mistake these guys made: They chose you as a target. And you're way ahead of the game."

It was flattery, yes, but also true. Schraeder didn't waste time on emotions. The moment he'd understood the situation, he began gathering the cash, knowing that time was the only commodity that truly mattered in this predicament.

"And remember," Virgil told his boss, "this is for show. Because there is no scenario in which these sons of bitches get away with part of your fortune. We guarantee it. And we guarantee you'll be with your children and the beautiful Mrs. Schraeder very soon."

Old Man Schraeder looked out over the tables of cash, seemingly lost in thought. Virgil knew better. Schraeder was not one for idle reflection. He was calculating... something. Virgil was steeling himself for another logistics question, so he was surprised when Schraeder said, "You have no idea how much I love her."

Virgil had to pretend he wasn't stunned. "Of that, I have zero doubt."

"I was on the verge of divorcing her," the old man said. "Yeah, nobody knew but my lawyer. But you want to know something, Virgil? Success is a lousy teacher."

"Sir?"

"It seduces people into thinking they can't lose. And I very much do *not* want to lose my wife."

CHAPTER 46

Thursday, 2:47 p.m.

IAN COUGHLIN DIDN'T consider himself a criminal.

He was a *watcher.* Big difference.

Like right now. What he was doing was not a crime. Anyone was allowed to stroll around Fashion Square in Sherman Oaks and do a little window-shopping and people-watching. No laws against that—yet. And so what if he liked to focus on the high-end stores (Bloomingdale's and Coach and L'Occitane) and the people who frequented them? The human eye was designed to be drawn to pretty things.

Besides, Ian Coughlin was not simply an observer; he liked to consider himself a storyteller. When he found attractive human beings inside a shop (Swarovski or Apple or Kiehl's) surrounded by pretty things, he liked to make up little stories about them.

Take this attractive human being—late thirties, ash-blond

hair, pumps, lips with filler, no wedding ring. She had money and liked to treat herself, but that was not why she was shopping alone this afternoon. She had the look of the lonely, someone tired of swiping right on the dating apps and spending quiet nights at home with her cat. If only she could find a partner…

That was a good story, right?

Sometimes those stories could be turned into profit. Wasn't that what Hollywood was all about? Once Ian Coughlin had a fairly complete idea in his mind, he could enjoy the story himself and follow it through to its natural conclusion—if the risk profile was low. Or, if the tale was a little more complex, he could sell it to an organized band of people who specialized in follow-home robberies.

So, sure, Ian *associated* with criminals. But when you think about it, every American business was rooted in a crime at some level.

But this one here looked like a story Ian could handle himself. This woman didn't pay too much attention to her surroundings. Ian suspected she considered people like himself unworthy of notice, which worked to his advantage. Once she finished making her purchase (nice bracelet, by the way), he'd shadow her to her vehicle in the adjacent multilevel parking lot and then decide which way the story should end.

But wait.

Someone else was watching too.

Ian could feel it at the back of his neck.

Not the useless mall security. He'd stopped fearing them years ago and now saw them as comic relief. It wasn't the woman either—she had no clue Ian had been trailing her for the past twenty minutes.

There was someone else.

Waiting.

Eyes on him.

Ian ran through his mental Rolodex as he quickly scanned this level of the mall. Was one of those follow-home robbery gangs dissatisfied with a story he'd sold them? Were they here to force him to cough up another one for free?

Well, whoever it was, Ian Coughlin wasn't going to walk into their trap.

He spun on his heel and made a beeline for the parking structure. Time to head back to his piece-of-shit Honda Accord and drive to his even worse apartment in Van Nuys. He'd try again another day. Maybe at the Sherman Oaks Galleria this time. It had been a minute since—

"Wait!"

Nope, not turning around, not falling for it.

"Ian, please! Wait!"

Now he couldn't resist, because the voice was young, and female, and pleading, and whoever she was, she knew his name. Ian turned.

The lonely thirty-whatever woman with the ash-blond hair and the pumps was running toward him.

CHAPTER 47

WHAT THE HELL was this? How did she know his name? Ian had selected her at random!

Then — movement out of the corner of his eye. A man about his age, suburban-dad type, with the body to match. He was also closing in and pulling an automatic pistol from a clip holster on his khakis.

So was the woman with the ash-blond hair and the pumps. She was clearly his partner. And not in a matrimonial-bliss kind of way.

Goddamn it, this was a police sting!

Ian Coughlin pumped his legs and begged the universe for forgiveness. He'd been too cocky; success had come too quick and the universe was trying to restore some balance. There was no such thing as easy money. And now he would have to fight for his freedom.

Well, fine, Universe, we'll play it your way.

Once he was behind the wheel of his piece-of-shit Honda,

Ian sucked in air and hit the gas pedal. He'd watched many LA car chases on TV over the years (they were the best and cheapest form of local entertainment) and knew the mistakes to avoid. For one: Never, *ever,* take the stupid freeway. Stick to local roads, make frequent and confusing turns, and pray you stay out of sight of the police helicopters, because once they locked onto you, it was all over.

He zoomed south on Hazeltine, then hung a hard left onto twisty Valleyheart Drive. So far, no sign of Officers Ash Blond and Suburban Dad. No pursuing vehicles. Good.

As Ian made a right turn onto Woodman, a new plan was forming. He'd lose them up in the hills of Benedict Canyon. He could drive those streets coked out of his mind. In fact, he had. Multiple times.

Oh, what a story this will make! Now let's give it the ending it deserves.

But as he sped up to make the yellow light at Moorpark, the universe decided to write one of its own.

All at once, the ground began to shudder as if someone had grabbed the Earth and was shaking it like a snow globe.

Before Ian knew it, his piece-of-shit Honda Accord was plowing through wooden rails and into a cactus-shaped neon sign with the words CACTUS TAQUERIA and BEST TACOS on the trunk. Shattered glass tubing rained down on his hood like hail.

Ian went for his door handle, but he was already surrounded by three black-and-white prowl cars. Including the one that had T-boned him.

Minutes later, in the back seat of his car, arresting officers recovered a green baseball cap.

CHAPTER 48

Thursday, 3:58 p.m.

BY THE TIME Mike Hardy arrived at the Van Nuys station, the man in the green ball cap had been cooling off in interview two for about forty-five minutes. Though *cooling off* wasn't quite the right term. Ever since his arrest, their witness had been working himself into a hot and angry lather, a performance worthy of any local improv theater.

"What am I even doing here? What, now it's a crime to go to the mall? At the very least, this is entrapment!"

All sound and fury, right up until the moment Mike stepped into the room with a manila folder in his hand. He used his foot to close the door behind him.

"How's it going, Ian? Been a while."

"Oh, man," Ian said, visibly deflating. "Why are *you* here? I thought you were promoted or given a medal or something."

"I thought the same about you. Clearly, you've been keeping yourself busy and moving up in the world of crime."

"Crime? Come on. I was just doing some shopping."

"Time is short, Ian. I'm not here to play games with you. I know you're part of this kidnapping plot. I didn't want to believe it, but there you were, in your green baseball cap."

Mike Hardy did know Ian Coughlin pretty well. Before his promotion to captain, Mike had headed up an LAPD task force dealing with follow-home robberies—thieves who looked for victims with expensive jewelry or vehicles, then literally followed them home to see what else they owned. It was thought there was some kind of criminal mastermind behind these robberies; in the span of a single month, there had been more than forty follow-home robberies on LA's west side.

But after months of investigation, Mike Hardy and his task force realized there was no mastermind. It was simply an idea that had gone viral in the underworld, and soon you had small-time opportunists like Ian Coughlin here offering to spot potential victims for strong-arm gangs.

"I'm no kidnapper," Ian said. "Wouldn't know the first thing about it."

"And I believe you. The Ian Coughlin I remember was this frightened little creep who liked to find victims for real criminals."

Ian shrugged. "Yeah, I'm just a frightened little creep. May I leave?"

Mike Hardy smiled, then opened his manila folder. He plucked out a printout and placed it on the table in front of Ian.

More printouts—black-and-white stills from a surveillance camera—followed in quick succession.

"There you are, watching an abduction take place behind a Beverly Hills salon. We have other cameras placing you at the scene, like this one." Another printout. "And this one"—another printout—"where you're just standing by with your thumb up your ass while some thug grabbed a woman, drugged her into unconsciousness, then placed her in the trunk of her own vehicle."

"Uh-huh."

"You did absolutely nothing to stop him."

"LA is a strange place," Ian said. "For all I knew, they were practicing a scene for a TV show or something."

"You had a phone in your hand. You didn't even call for help."

"Like I said, it was none of my business. I didn't want some assistant director chewing me out for ruining a take."

"Except you *did* make a call. I have to presume that you were up to your old tricks, playing the spotter, only now you're doing it for a band of kidnappers."

"You said it yourself. I'm no kidnapper."

"But you're working for one."

The witness frowned. "I didn't know that at the time."

Finally. The crack in the armor Mike had been waiting for. Maybe Ian was smart enough to realize that at this very moment, he was the lone suspect dangling on the hook for these brazen crimes. Whatever he was paid, it wasn't enough for him to take the fall for this.

"Look, I know you're not a bad guy," Mike said, softening his tone a little. "Just tell me what happened."

Ian appeared to be weighing his options. Mike knew this was a face-saving move. There were no other options.

"They came to me anonymously," Ian finally said. "At first I thought it was a scam. I mean, all that money for doing nothing?"

"Nothing being what, exactly?"

"Standing on such-and-such a corner, waiting for something to happen, then calling a number when it actually happened. Then I was supposed to say three words: 'One hundred percent.' That was it."

"Back up a minute," Mike said. "How did they come to you? Who's your contact?"

"It doesn't work like that. They reached out to me anonymously."

"And you just trusted them? What, do you fall for every internet phishing scam too? Come on, Ian."

"Well, phishing scams don't usually drop five large into your bank account."

Mike Hardy considered this. "And you just gave them your account number?"

"They already had it. They knew all about me. Another reason I took them seriously."

"Then give me the number they called you from."

"There wasn't any number! When they texted, the contact was completely anonymous. I did what they wanted, and I got paid."

"And you have no idea where the money came from."

"Like they'd give me a receipt? Come on, Hardy. You want to track some routing numbers, have fun."

Ian had an answer for everything. That was concerning. The last time Mike and Ian had done this dance, this little twerp had cracked quickly under pressure. What if the task force had gone through all this trouble to corner this creep—and he was no use at all?

CHAPTER 49

IAN COUGHLIN HAD one card to play—and he wasn't going to use it until he received *exactly* what he wanted. If what he suspected was true, his life literally depended on him getting it.

He swore and vowed to repeat this to himself until the end of time: *There is no such thing as easy money.*

"Listen, like I said, it was completely anonymous. But I might have heard a name. One I wasn't supposed to hear."

"Go on."

"No, Hardy. You and I know how this works. I want something in return."

"That all depends on the name."

Here was the tricky part. Ian Coughlin suspected that *cops* were behind this whole triple kidnapping.

It was the only thing that made sense. Only two types of people knew to reach out to Ian in the first place: cops and career criminals. The follow-home robbers in his circle were nowhere near ambitious enough to pull off something like this; they were either junkies looking for a quick score or gang members looking for bragging rights.

That left one other option: the cops.

Ian's first thought when the original text showed up on his phone was *This is Entrapment with a capital* E.

I mean, who else would make such a ludicrous proposal? Twenty-five grand for watching a back alley in Beverly Hills?

But the mystery texter had offered to send a small good-faith payment. Only five grand, but at the time, Ian was flat broke (after months of being watched by Hardy's stupid task force), and even if it *was* the LAPD messing with him, he really needed the rent money.

"Ian?" Mike said now. "You still with me? Just give me a name and we'll take it from there."

This was the problem, though. Since Ian was convinced cops were somehow involved in this whole crazy scheme, the question was: Was Hardy one of those cops? Ian didn't think so, otherwise Hardy wouldn't look so frustrated.

"Ian? Come on, man! Innocent lives are on the line. You're about sixty seconds away from being completely useless to me."

Ian stared up at his interrogator. "But can I trust you? Because you're probably not going to like the name in my head."

"Let me be the judge of that."

Ian stared at him. Then: "Tim Dowd."

Mike stared right back at him. "Nice try. I know Sergeant Dowd."

"Yeah," Ian said, not breaking eye contact, as if he were trying to tell him something by telepathy. "I *know* you do."

Mike Hardy stood there looking like a stupid ox, and Ian was relieved. This could have gone a very different way. He could have spoken Dowd's name and taken a bullet to the face for knowing too much.

"Look, Hardy, I know how this sounds, but I'm completely serious. I don't think I was supposed to know his real name. Everyone uses code numbers."

"What was your secret code number?"

"I didn't have a secret code number. I was just a spotter."

"So how did you hear that name?"

"Here's how it worked. The guy in charge is called One. That's the only thing I know about him, other than that he's a him. And everyone is terrified of him. But One let me listen in during some calls with Two, so I'd be up to speed and know what to look for."

"You recognize One's voice?"

"No, but I recognized Two's voice. It was Dowd. That asshole grilled me for hours once—I'd know his voice anywhere. He's got this tough-guy-actor voice, like he thinks he's a cop in a TV show or something."

The way Hardy was pacing the room, like he was wrestling with the idea, confirmed for Ian that his suspicions were correct: Cops were involved in this thing. Hopefully none of them were *this* cop.

"Sit tight, Ian," Mike said, then left the room with his manila folder.

Like Ian had a choice? But he'd made the only move he had.

Something told him when all this was over, One was going to clear the game board. He didn't know how many spotters there were, but he was pretty sure none of them would live to spend much of their money.

After all, there could be only one One.

CHAPTER 50

Thursday, 4:21 p.m.

TIM DOWD HAD a decent place in a bad neighborhood. The SWAT team was currently surrounding it.

Dowd lived in a rented bungalow in Atwater Village. Somebody in command was going through the real estate records looking for specs, but it didn't matter now. The SWAT team was about to enter regardless.

After Jeff Penney announced their presence and gave Dowd ample time to respond—the former police sergeant should know the routine—Jeff ordered the team to breach the doors.

Bam! Bam!

Two enforcers—thick steel battering rams with handles—blasted open the front and back doors. The team fanned out through the bungalow, guns at shoulder level, prepared for any response from a former cop who knew every trick in the book.

Bedroom one—clear.

Bedroom two—clear.

Closet—clear.

Bathroom—clear.

Sitting room—clear.

Crawl space—full of insulation and dust and spiders, but clear.

In under five minutes, Penney's tough, efficient squad made a thorough sweep and determined one thing with dead certainty: There was no trace of Tim Dowd in this house.

Penney entered and did his own sweep, looking for anything his team might have missed. He was known in certain circles as the "crime scene whisperer"; he found tiny details that often made all the difference. Halfway through this sweep his cell went off. He answered. "Penney."

"Any sign of Boo Schraeder?" Mike asked.

"There's no sign of nothing," Jeff replied. "Hell, I don't think Dowd's been here in a while. Mail's piling up in the box, stuff in the fridge is past its sell-by date."

"Shit."

"You knew the man best. Any idea where he might be?"

"If I had any clue," Mike said, fighting to keep the annoyance out of his voice, "I would already have shared it with you and the entire task force."

"Take a minute and think. Vacation pads? A sibling somewhere with a big house?"

"I'm telling you, Penney, I have no idea."

Jeff walked around the bungalow, taking in details of this former cop's sad little life. Why anyone would want to live in this neighborhood—with homeless people camping out on your front lawn and junkies puking in your hedges—was beyond him. Maybe Tim Dowd had spent so much time in squalor, he'd gotten used to it. Jeff Penney had a three-bedroom, three-bathroom mini-manse way up in Santa Clarita, far from this misery.

"Looks like there are two possibilities, Hardy. Either your buddy found some little hiding place that he kept a secret from everybody or your witness is fucking with you."

"Yeah," Mike allowed. "Let me get back to you."

"Go on and do that. But the clock is ticking for poor Boo Schraeder."

CHAPTER 51

Thursday, 5:07 p.m.

NICKY WAS HALFWAY home when Mike Hardy called with the update. She wasn't heading home for the night, of course—just long enough to put eyes on Kaitlin and make sure she had something nutritious in her belly before she and her friends went off to the movies. They were seeing some South Korean thriller called *Shut In* that, Nicky had noted, was rated R and playing late, but Kaitlin had rolled her eyes and told her to stop being so old-fashioned. "Callie's mom is taking us. And you know there are things, like, a billion times worse on YouTube, right?"

So when Mike Hardy's name appeared on her dashboard display, Nicky hoped it was good news. Her fantasy: He'd tell her that Boo Schraeder had been found at Tim Dowd's house and that Dowd was currently spilling all the details about his coconspirators.

Mike crushed that fantasy immediately.

"No sign of him or Boo," he said. "I'm not saying Dowd's in the clear, but I don't know. Something about this just doesn't fit."

"Sounds like your witness screwed us," Nicky said.

"Well, he's going to be the sorry one when he's facing obstruction-of-justice charges."

"Maybe that was his real job all along. Obstructing justice."

"I don't follow."

"Think about it," Nicky said. "Why would the kidnappers need—or risk—a spotter? If they didn't trust the man who abducted Boo Schraeder, why would they have involved him? Your witness in the green cap was just window dressing. They *meant* for us to see him."

"But don't forget, we have that footage by accident," Mike said. "Hell, it was a miracle we recognized Coughlin. That's not exactly serving it up for us on a plate."

"Yet those pieces fell into place quickly. You found Coughlin easily so he could tell us a former cop was involved in the plot."

"What does that get him?"

"It's not what it gets him—it's what it gets the kidnappers. Maybe the point is to distract us. Sow doubt. Show us how incompetent we are. Demonstrate how easy it is to waste our time."

"Or all of the above," Mike said. "Shit."

"Look, I'm going to make sure Kaitlin eats something other than frozen french fries, then I'll be back at Westwood. See you there?"

"No place I'd rather be," Mike said.

"Liar."

CHAPTER 52

Thursday, 5:13 p.m.

WORD SPREAD THROUGH the ranks of the Tijuana police like a brushfire on a parched hillside: The FBI and PFM were looking for some rich American movie producer and an actress who'd been abducted from a private resort down on the peninsula but were possibly being held on the border. Tijuana made a lot of sense. You could literally walk to the United States from here, and the city was about as lawless as you could get.

As this news traveled, many of the officers snapped into action. Not official action—the smart ones were working out their own angles. Stealing from kidnappers (who were most likely American) felt like a much safer bet than ripping off the cartel. Some of these cops' colleagues had attempted that recently, raiding a cartel warehouse full of fentanyl near the border only to end up decapitated and stacked like cordwood as a gentle message from the syndicate: *Steal from anyone you like, just not the cartel.* The smart ones understood.

Two of the smart ones were now walking down a quiet, dusty street just off the North Zone, taking in the neighborhood as the sun began to dip behind the hills. Nobody reacted, but everyone on the block noticed.

The two police officers took their time getting to their destination, a semidetached two-story house right in the middle of the block.

The two guards standing on the second-floor balcony flicked away their cigarettes. One muttered something about seeing trouble.

"Yeah, you do," the taller of the two cops called up from the street. "Why don't you tell Little Rami to come on out here and talk to us."

Little Rami. No one had called Five that since he was a baby. Five's men outside hoped he was too busy with the guests to hear such disrespect. The very grown-up Ramiro would lose his damn mind.

"Not home," said one of the guards, slowly removing the Glock from his leg holster, an action that was obscured by the balcony wall. The other guard prepared his weapon, which was also out of sight.

"Well," said the shorter of the cops, "we'll just go inside and wait for him."

"Door's locked," replied a guard.

"Come on down and open it."

"Nah, not gonna do that. Why don't you come back later?"

"We want to go in now."

"Too bad."

"Tell Little Rami we'd like to be compensated for the inconvenience."

"Like we told you, Ramiro's not here."

The conversation was Mexican Kabuki. Both sides knew how this would most likely end, but first, they needed to see how committed the other side was. Nothing was preventing the smart cops from breaking into Ramiro's house except bullets. Nothing was preventing the guards from blowing the heads off these stupid pigs except the noise and the cleanup hassle.

After a moment of heavy silence, it became clear that neither side was willing to back down, so it was now a matter of who would draw first.

The smart cops didn't have to discuss their plan—they'd done this many times. The short one would provide cover fire while his partner went through the front door. If that meant taking the guards out, who cared? Idiots should have just opened the damn door.

But the smart cops didn't realize that Little Rami had fortified his home a while back, and hidden behind the balcony wall was a tactical gun-in-a-box.

If you looked at the balcony floor (not that any outsiders could), you'd see only a tread-plated toolbox, standard equipment on the back of a pickup truck. But inside that box was a foot switch that controlled a Russian PK assault rifle with a four-hundred-round ammo can. When activated with said foot switch, the gun would protrude from a long horizontal rainspout at the bottom of the balcony wall and spray bullets at whoever was unlucky enough to be knocking at your front door.

Before the short smart cop could even raise his service weapon, one of the guards stomped on the foot switch.

CHAPTER 53

"WHAT THE HELL is wrong with you?"

Five ran outside as soon as he heard the gun-in-a-box blasting, echoing up and down the block and off the nearby mesas. The PK was empty and wheezing. Two shredded cops was about the last thing Five wanted to see. He quickly scanned the block, looking for witnesses. He caught no faces, but he did see a few hastily pulled window shades. Good. This was none of their business.

Now he had to deal with these two idiots.

"Are you *trying* to make this plan go to shit? Do you want the goddamned Federales rolling up here with a tank?"

The guards had been proud of themselves right up to the moment Five came storming outside. He knew the guards had been itching to use that stupid thing ever since he'd purchased it last summer, and they'd tested it out up in the hills. They wanted Five to buy another one for his pickup. You know, just in case.

"We're sorry, Ramiro. They weren't going away."

"It's your job to *make them* go away!"

"They were the stubborn type. They were going to cause trouble for us."

"And look at this freaking mess! If someone drives by right now—"

But then Five collected himself and remembered that these weren't hired guns. These were his brothers; they went way back. They could be knuckleheads, but when the knuckleheads were your loyal friends, you forgave them. Always, without question.

"Okay. Fine. Matteo, go find their car and bring it back here. Ernie, put them in the trunk. Make it all disappear. And get someone to spray the blood off the street. It looks like you were slaughtering cattle out here."

Ernie couldn't resist. "No cattle, Ramiro. *Pigs.*"

Five didn't want to smile in front of them, but after he turned his back, he couldn't resist. Pigs. That *was* funny.

And ultimately, he knew it didn't matter. This was no big deal. Cops died all the time in Tijuana.

But he also had his guests to worry about. Surely they'd heard the gunfire. This would fill them with either dread (not a bad thing) or hope (not ideal).

Five moved swiftly down the hall, removed the twin padlocks from the door, made his way down the stairs, and used another set of keys on the triple dead bolts. Inside this room, his guests were still zip-tied to different parts of the bed.

"Were those fireworks?" Cassandra Bart said, playing the part of the naive and terrified last remaining girl in a horror movie.

"Those were not fireworks," Five said, also playing a part. He acted grim, as if he'd received some dire news.

"The cavalry is here, isn't it," Tyler said with a wide grin that looked comical beneath his badly broken nose. "You have no idea who you are messing with."

Now it was Five's turn to smile. "No, that wasn't the cavalry. No one has any idea where you are."

Oh, the looks on their faces. So much fun to watch the privileged experience true disappointment. And this was much worse than not scoring a reservation at a trendy Beverly Hills restaurant or being denied membership at an exclusive VIP-only social club because their assistants had missed the deadline to file the paperwork.

"And from what I hear," Five continued, staring directly at Tyler Schraeder, "the payment for you is not quite working out. I doubt you'll be seeing the sun again."

He turned to the door, then paused and gave Cass a wink over his shoulder.

"But you, my lovely...I like your chances."

As Five bolted the door again, muffling Tyler's cries of rage, he wondered about his future. This was too much fun. Maybe he should be an actor.

CHAPTER 54

Thursday, 6:40 p.m.

MIKE AND NICKY met outside FBI headquarters in Westwood. Mike held up a smoked-turkey wrap from the Corner Bakery, and when Nicky raised her eyebrows quizzically, he smiled and said, "Special K's not the only one who needs good food in her belly." Nicky took the wrap gratefully. She hadn't eaten anything since their hurried breakfast many hours ago.

Nicky noted that Mike's own dinner appeared to be hits from his vape pen, which was why they were standing outside in the warm evening air.

"Who's that financial-crimes guy again?" Mike asked. "Guy who looks like a linebacker?"

"Ross Lindbergh," Nicky said. "Why?"

"We're going to want Lindbergh to nail something down for us," Mike said. "If this is true, then I think this case is about to solve itself."

"You want to tell me first, maybe? You know, before I send out for the champagne?"

Mike smirked. "An old buddy from the narcotics squad hit me up while I was waiting for your wrap. Apparently, he and his buddies saw Randy Schraeder ranting on TV, and the eye-rolling started."

"Why?"

"According to the narcotics guys, these kidnappings are clearly a cartel deal. They're the only ones with the bankroll, the bodies, and the organizational muscle to pull it off."

Nicky could follow the logic, but it didn't feel right. This threat felt homegrown.

"So, what, the cartel is doing a little fundraising by targeting one of the wealthiest people in America?"

"Not targeting. *Working with.*"

"What?"

"The narco boys have long suspected that Old Man Schraeder and one of the most powerful cartels go *way* back. They can't prove any of it—the guy is too slippery for that."

Nicky was only two bites into her turkey wrap, and already she felt like tossing it away. "The same Randolph Schraeder who goes on cable news ranting about wanting to get the border wall built and sending refugees back to wherever they came from?"

"There's a lot of money in hypocrisy," Mike said.

"Okay," Nicky said. "Forget that for now. That's a DEA headache. But in terms of *our* case—"

"I'm right there with you," Mike said. "It's looking more and more like Schraeder had his own family kidnapped."

"He'd collect his own ransom and the insurance on top of that."

"All stage-managed by the cartels and those assholes at Capital." Mike took a long hit of his vape. The pale fumes floated above them for a moment before being swallowed up by the thick evening air over Westwood.

Nicky couldn't stomach another bite of her turkey. The mom in her refused to waste food, so she wrapped it up and tucked it into her jacket pocket despite knowing she'd never return to it.

"Let's see what Lindbergh can find," Nicky said. "We need something real before we go after Schraeder directly."

As they made their way into the building, Mike said, "Promise me you're going to finish that wrap."

"As soon as you promise you'll quit vaping," Nicky replied, "which, by the way, is just as bad as actually smoking."

"You sound just like Special K."

As soon as he mentioned Kaitlin, Nicky's cell phone rang. She answered it eagerly, thinking it was her daughter giving her the obligatory *Hey, Mom, I'm here and safe, now please let me go live my best life* call.

That's not who it was.

CHAPTER 55

"WHO IS THIS?" Nicky asked.

"My name is not important."

Nicky Gordon didn't recognize the number on her cell, although the call appeared to be originating from another country. A standard trick if you were trying to disguise the location of your phone. The caller was also using some kind of voice-distorting software; the tone modulated between masculine and feminine.

"Fine," Nicky said. "Still need to call you something."

"We do not have names. Only numbers."

"So what's your number?"

"My number will mean nothing to you, Agent Gordon. Listen carefully."

She noted the reference to the plotters having numbers, not names, just as their lone witness, Ian Coughlin, had described during his interrogation.

Mike Hardy was straining to hear the other side of the

conversation. Nicky raised her index finger, telling him to hold on. They both stopped short of the security check-in area to focus on the call.

"I'm listening," she said.

"You have a mole on your task force."

She'd already figured that out. "Who?"

The caller ignored her question. "Not only that, but this individual is intimately involved in the kidnapping plot you are investigating."

"Unless you're willing to share a name, I'm not interested."

"Oh, you are very much interested. You are a special agent, skilled at investigations, and I am sure you'll uncover the name. But will you be able to do it in time to save the lives of the Schraeder family?"

"Hold on—"

"Good luck."

The caller disconnected.

Nicky waited until they were through security and at the elevator before she relayed the other end of the conversation to Mike. He smiled and let out a long, slow whistle.

"These people really do love messing with our heads, don't they. Every time we turn around, there's someone telling us that we should be chasing our own tails."

Nicky scanned her card at the elevator. "That doesn't mean they're not telling the truth."

"Next, someone is going to call me and say *you're* behind the whole thing."

Nicky gave him a sardonic smile. "Can't believe it took you this long to figure it out, Detective Hardy."

"Well, save me a piece of that sweet Schraeder billion," Mike said. "I'll help you make your getaway. I know people who know people."

On the ride up, Nicky and Mike quickly reviewed the list of task force members, trying to figure out who could possibly be the mole. The list was short; their task force wasn't that large. It was agreed that Nicky would give the names to someone in the Office of Professional Responsibility, OPR. Pure surveillance and background checks for now.

As they reached their floor, Mike said the uncomfortable thing that nonetheless had to be said: "By the way, add my name to that list."

"Because you used to work with Tim Dowd?"

"Okay, that. And I don't want any doubts getting in the way of..."

"In the way of?" Nicky asked, watching him closely.

"Whatever it is we are," he replied with a boyish smirk.

"Maybe I was going to add you to the list anyway."

"That's because you're a smart woman," he said, then his smirk vanished. "Oh, shit—I just thought of another name for you. Jenna Hetzel."

"Why her?"

"Bunch of years ago, she used to be Dowd's partner."

Nicky nodded. "Consider her added."

Before they reached the office, Nicky's assistant, Hope Alonso, intercepted them with a padded envelope in her hand.

"There's another tape."

CHAPTER 56

"WHY DIDN'T YOU message me immediately?" Nicky asked.

"This was hand-delivered just three minutes ago," Hope said. "It literally just reached your office."

Three minutes ago, Nicky thought. Just as she was held up by the mystery caller. The only way to hand-deliver something to FBI headquarters was to give it to someone at the security station downstairs.

That meant whoever delivered it had passed right by them both.

The first tape-delivery person had turned out to be a true nobody—no priors, no criminal past. Chances were, the second one would be the same, but Nicky sent agents in pursuit of this person anyway. The kidnappers might have slipped up.

The plastic cassette tape was rushed to the Sandbox and prepared for playback while Hope started the chain of calls that would gather the team. The tape could not be played until all members of the task force—the mayor of Los Angeles included—were connected to the Sandbox so they could hear it at the same time. The mayor herself had insisted on this after their first meeting, and Jeff Penney from the SWAT team backed her up. *We all need to work together on this one,* blah-blah-blah. Although Jeff was backing up the mayor not so much because he agreed with her as because he was angling for a promotion in the near future.

The wait was driving Nicky up the wall. In a rapidly evolving situation like this, every second mattered. What if the kidnappers had given time-specific instructions for the drop-off? Clearly they had arranged to have this tape delivered at a specific time.

In the Sandbox, Nicky said, "Alonso, play the tape now."

"Ma'am? Are you sure?"

Even Mike Hardy raised an eyebrow at this one.

"One hundred percent," Nicky said. "Any blowback will be on me. I'm tired of these bastards screwing around with us. If they do have a mole on the task force, I'm sure they'll know about the built-in bureaucratic delay."

Hope glanced over at Mike. *A mole?*

Mike Hardy shook his head slightly. *Not the time.*

Hope pressed play on the thirty-year-old machine. After a minute-long silence, which appeared to be the kidnappers' way of making sure their listeners were paying attention, the tape began.

"Surely Mr. Schraeder has been able to gather the money by now. Yet we are seeing no signs of him being prepared to deliver it."

Hope frowned. "How do they know if Schraeder has the money ready?"

"They're confirming that they have someone on the inside," Nicky said.

After two minutes of additional silence:

"We are growing impatient."

And then an even longer stretch of nothing but magnetic-tape hiss, to the point where Nicky found herself checking her watch to see if time was passing as slowly as it seemed to be.

Finally Mike grunted. "They're not the only ones getting impatient."

"Should I fast-forward it?" Hope asked.

"No," Nicky said. Later, she'd have the tape analyzed for any subliminal or ambient noises in the long silences. For now, they would experience the tape recording as intended.

After what felt like a pocket-size eternity, the same voice spoke again, but in a hushed tone, as if sharing a dirty secret:

"Do we have to *kill* someone to get your attention?"

CHAPTER 57

Thursday, 6:42 p.m.

DINNER CONVERSATION WAS glum. Four tried her best to draw the kids out, but they mostly pushed their food around on their plates, making tiny barricades like mini-forts. Four was a little hurt by that and wished the kids would at least try a small bite.

"This mac and cheese is my little girl's favorite," Four said, as if this would entice them. But when Three shot her a look, she realized she'd have to tell him about her earlier mistake. They weren't supposed to reveal any personal information.

"What's wrong with her?" Finney asked. "Your daughter?"

"Never mind that," Three said. "Eat up before it gets cold."

But Four couldn't sit there and ignore the question. "Three," she said, "it's okay. I already told them."

"You what?"

Four turned back to Finney, rested a hand on her forearm, and squeezed it gently.

"We're doing all we can to help her through it," Three said finally.

He didn't explain that what they were doing right now, at this very moment, was the only option they had left. They were a day into this ordeal. Perhaps after one more day—or sooner—they'd be living in a different world.

"Why don't the doctors help her?" Cal asked.

Four and Three exchanged glances. How many times had they had this conversation with concerned friends? *But I've heard that's very treatable* was the inevitable reply. To which they were forced to respond: *Yes, treatable if you have the money or insurance that covers the treatment.* Mind you, an offer of financial help never followed from these friends. Only sympathetic, sometimes pitying looks.

"It's not the doctors," Four replied. "It's the people who run insurance companies." Seeing Cal's and Finney's confused expressions, she said: "Sometimes adults can be very bad people."

Finney nodded, looked down, then looked up at Four. "But you're not a bad person, are you?"

There was a buzz across the room—the cell phone in Four's handbag. The phone she wasn't supposed to have.

CHAPTER 58

IN THE BEDROOM, Four read the text from her sister:

Can you come here now?

The blood in Four's veins felt like ice water. This was what she had been terrified of. "It's two days, tops, One told us," her husband had assured her. "She'll be fine for two days." Deep inside, however, Four had known something like this would happen.

Four's thumbs trembled as she tried to think of the best way to tell her sister that now was absolutely not a good time.

It's urgent. They're worried about her platelet count. They want to do another transfusion.

Four read the text and was surprised by the gasp that came out of her mouth. Quickly, she thumbed:

Can't you agree to it?

Three blinking dots, and then:

Yes, but... don't you want to be here?

Four typed quickly:

More than anything.

But leaving this house right now would be catastrophic. Four knew that One had watchers all over, keeping tabs on his team. There had to be a watcher here too. Maybe several. And leaving this house was grounds for immediate termination of their contract. One's chilling words were seared into her memory:

The plan must be followed precisely. Not a single change will be permitted. If you ignore a step, you will not be paid. If you improvise, you will not be paid.

But this was her child. Her heart. Her everything.

Four typed quickly:

I'm on my way.

Three intercepted her in the bedroom doorway. She didn't have to say a word; the panic in her eyes said everything. Three knew that nothing was going to stop his wife from going to their daughter right now. He kissed her firmly, then wrapped her in his arms. They went downstairs.

"Where are you going?"

Finney stood up from the kitchen table and stared at Four with a haunted look in her eyes. Cal pushed his chair back from the table, his small hands trembling slightly.

Four hadn't expected Cal and Finney to be upset by her leaving, and the looks of panic on their faces broke her heart. Right now, she was exactly half of the only stability they had in this world.

Four crouched down and wrapped Finney in a hug. A real hug, not the hug of a kidnapper trying to lull her charge into a false sense of security. A hug she wished she could be giving her daughter—and would be, very soon.

Unless One stopped her.

CHAPTER 59

Thursday, 6:54 p.m.

"IT'S CUED UP, Ms. Gordon."

"Let's see it, Hope."

On-screen: Grainy black-and-white footage of Michael Hardy and Tim Dowd sipping coffee in the parking garage of the Beverly Center.

The footage was from more easygoing times, just nine months ago. Both Mike and Tim Dowd had been assigned to the LAPD's follow-home-robbery task force. This was the high-profile initiative that gave Mike his big promotion—and ultimately caused Dowd's career to unravel.

Mike used to tell Nicky funny stories about his long surveillance hours with Tim Dowd. Most of the stories revolved around Dowd's impatience, to the point where he'd be actively *praying* for a couple of thugs to follow some rich lawyer home to Bel Air or Beverly Hills. Dowd craved action; he hated just sitting there staring at rows of fancy cars, eating dry turkey sandwiches, and sipping bitter lukewarm coffee.

Nicky could see that in Dowd's body language. The man was not just fidgety; he seemed to have some kind of internal beat throbbing at all times, and his fingers tapped in rhythm to it. Mike told Nicky this drove him nuts. "Calm the hell down, man," he'd always tell him. "When it happens, it happens."

But that impatience was Dowd's undoing. The way Mike told it, Dowd began to stake out the high-end malls on his own time, hoping to catch one of these thugs in the act. And he did. Dowd followed an ex-con who was following an entertainment lawyer back to her condo on Doheny Drive. Dowd claimed he'd seen the ex-con pull out a blade as he slipped into the building's lobby, which was why he proceeded to tackle the guy into a glass coffee table.

According to Dowd's testimony, he believed the ex-con planned to overpower his victim in the elevator, then force her at knifepoint to let him into her condo (where he would presumably take her belongings and possibly her life). Dowd said he identified himself as a police officer, at which point the ex-con attacked him. Dowd testified that he subdued his suspect, cuffed him, and read him his rights.

But another resident happened to be in the lobby at the time, and he'd captured the encounter on his cell phone. The video revealed a different story.

In the fifty-second clip, the ex-con's back was still to Dowd when the big blond officer tackled him into the table, shattering it spectacularly. Dowd then beat his suspect with his fists until the man was unconscious and bleeding from multiple cuts and lacerations. There were no words spoken, and no knife was visible, nor was one recovered from the crime scene.

The LAPD rank and file thought Dowd was a hero, but the brass dismissed him from the force. Mike had stopped telling Nicky funny stories about Tim Dowd after that. In fact, he didn't mention him at all anymore.

Which was why Nicky had kept him on her short list of dirty cops possibly involved in the Schraeder kidnappings. He had the experience and skills. He had the chip on his shoulder. And, most important, he needed the money.

But that's not what worried Nicky the most.

What worried her was the image now on her screen—Mike and Dowd, in their surveillance car, thick as thieves. Was this still the case?

She remembered words of the anonymous caller:

You have a mole on your task force. Not only that, but this individual is intimately involved in the kidnapping plot you are investigating.

Intimately was the telling word in that sentence. Did Nicky's mystery caller know about her relationship with Mike Hardy? If someone was watching Nicky, even from a distance, it wouldn't be difficult to put it together.

Nicky supposed she could ask Mike directly. Though his answer could potentially break her heart—and she didn't have time for a broken heart right now.

No, it would be better to simply watch him. Closely. If Mike Hardy *was* involved in this, he could be their best lead yet.

CHAPTER 60

Transcript of audio-only conversation (authenticated) between a third-party tip-line operator and an anonymous caller

TIP-LINE OPERATOR: Thank you for calling the Schraeder Investigation tip line. For the purposes of this conversation, you are number 4738.

CALLER 4738: Oh. Do I have to remember that number?

TIP-LINE OPERATOR: No, ma'am. The number is for our internal use only. Can you tell me why you called?

CALLER 4738: Do you need my name?

TIP-LINE OPERATOR: Do you wish to tell me your name?

CALLER 4738: Uh, no, I don't think so. Not right now. I mean, I'm not looking for any reward or anything. There isn't a reward, is there?

TIP-LINE OPERATOR: Why don't you tell me why you called.

CALLER 4738: Okay, okay. It's the house next door. It's been a problem for a while. I mean, I think it's one of those illegal Airbnb units. People are coming and going with luggage all the time. But I can't complain because the place is owned by a cop. I mean, who am I going to call? His buddies?

TIP-LINE OPERATOR: Ma'am, this is a dedicated tip line for the Schraeder kidnappings. Does this house connect to these kidnappings in any way?

CALLER 4738: I'm getting to that! It's been quiet lately, so I'm thinking, okay, maybe this cop sold it or something. Which would be great. But then I see this luxury car pull up. And believe me, this is not a luxury-car neighborhood.

TIP-LINE OPERATOR: Ma'am...

CALLER 4738: The weird thing is, when the cop rents his place out to people, they park on the street and use a keypad thing to let themselves in the front. This guy in the fancy car didn't do that.

TIP-LINE OPERATOR: What did he do?

CALLER 4738: He pulled right into the garage. Which means he must have had a remote control in his own car. Which is weird, right? I mean, what kind of Airbnb guests already have a remote? But I know he doesn't live there. Like I said, a cop owns the place, which is why I'm powerless to do anything.

TIP-LINE OPERATOR: Can you tell me the address of this house?

CALLER 4738: It's thirteen Briar Drive. That's in Culver City.

TIP-LINE OPERATOR [*Tapping keys*]: I can see that. Has this man left the house since he arrived?

CALLER 4738: That's just it! He hasn't left for one minute. I mean, if you're on vacation here, why would you stay all holed up? I saw him pull in yesterday afternoon—

TIP-LINE OPERATOR: Do you remember the time you saw him?

CALLER 4738: I don't know. I think it was two thirty or so? Definitely after *The Talk* but before *Kelly Clarkson*.

TIP-LINE OPERATOR: Did you see anyone else in the car with him?

CALLER 4738: No, why would I? Didn't the kidnapper stuff that poor woman—what's her name, Boo?—didn't he stuff her in the trunk?

TIP-LINE OPERATOR: What did this man look like?

CALLER 4738: Big guy, blond hair. Like a soldier or a cop. Which is why I think it's a friend of the owner...who, by the way, is kind of a dick.

TIP-LINE OPERATOR: Any other details?

CALLER 4738: He looked like he was in an awful hurry to get in the house before anyone saw him.

TIP-LINE OPERATOR: Have you overheard any conversations in that house? Any sounds at all?

CALLER 4738: No, which is also weird. You'd think there'd be something.

TIP-LINE OPERATOR: How long have you been watching the house? Is it possible you could have missed this guest leaving?

CALLER 4738: I watch when I can, but I also pointed my Nest camera at the house and I've been recording this whole time. Because, you know...I'm curious.

TIP-LINE OPERATOR: Ma'am, we are going to send someone out to look.

CALLER 4738: Oh, thank you!

TIP-LINE OPERATOR: Will you give me your name?

CALLER 4738 [*After a pause*]: Do you think Randolph Schraeder is good for the reward money? He seems a little cranky to me.

CHAPTER 61

Transcript of audio-only conversation (authenticated)

SAC NICOLE GORDON: Penney? It's Gordon. We just got something promising on the tip line.

CAPTAIN JEFFREY PENNEY: In my experience, tip lines are full of shit.

GORDON: It's a possible location for where Tim Dowd could be keeping Boo Schraeder.

PENNEY: So I'm supposed to break into yet another house on another wild-goose chase?

GORDON: Not so wild. The tipster saw a man matching Dowd's description pull into a private house in Culver City. It's a relatively short drive from the Beverly Hills salon where Boo was taken.

PENNEY: That's all you've got? What if it's just some bored housewife listening to too many true-crime podcasts? I don't want to roll up on some dipshit tourist who rented out the place for vacation.

GORDON: The house is owned by David Hetzel and his wife.

PENNEY: Wait, wait. I know Dave. He worked Robbery-Homicide in North Hollywood, right? Pretty sure he retired years ago.

GORDON: That's right. And now Hetzel's daughter is on the force.

PENNEY: Yeah, little Jenna. I haven't seen her in forever.

GORDON: Well, little Jenna grew up and became partners with…ex–LAPD officer Tim Dowd.

PENNEY: Oh, shit.

GORDON: Yeah. Oh, shit is right.

PENNEY: Fair enough, Gordon. I'll scramble the team. We're on it.

GORDON: I want to know your every move.

PENNEY: I wouldn't have it any other way.

CHAPTER 62

Thursday, 6:58 p.m.

"YOU *REALLY* DON'T know what you're doing," Boo Schraeder said with a sweet smile.

"Pretty sure I know the usual moves."

Two couldn't help himself—he leaned forward for another kiss. But Boo pressed an index finger against his head to halt his progress. Her smile disappeared.

"I mean it," Boo said. "This is *not* how kidnappers should behave."

Two found himself disappointed when she removed her finger. He was liking this dominant side of her. Then again, it would be difficult for her to be fully dominant with one hand cuffed to the frame of the cot.

"See," Two said, "I thought you'd like where this was heading. As the person who has been abducted, you should be trying hard to get close to your abductor. Get him to let his guard down. And then you'll make your move."

"My move?"

"Yes, your move. The one where you incapacitate me in a moment of personal weakness and make your escape."

"This is what I'm talking about," Boo said. "Instead of being a professional, you're playing out a sexual fantasy. The strapping kidnapper and the helpless wife with the ridiculously wealthy older husband."

As she spoke, Two was slowly tracing his finger along her jaw.

"How does this end in your fantasy?" she asked. "Is this just a..."

Boo eventually gave up, sighed, and even began to close her eyes... then she caught herself. She stared at him sharply for a moment as if to continue her complaints. Just as quickly, however, she seemed to relent, running her free hand up his tight chest. She surprised him by pinching his left nipple—hard—through his shirt.

Two didn't flinch. He kind of liked it. "Is *that* your move?" he asked her.

Boo squeezed harder. "Most kidnappers are sadists, not masochists."

Still, Two did not flinch. "Like you said, maybe I don't know what I'm doing."

Only then did she stop squeezing and finally allow her lips to be kissed again. Two did so eagerly, and soon they were exploring each other. *My God,* Two thought. *What is happening?* Had he lost his mind?

The banter was fun at first and not a bad way to pass the long hours between the abduction and eventual release. But maybe this was something more. Something neither of them expected.

And if all this was so Boo Schraeder could make some kind of move to escape...Two had to admit that he didn't care much. His life had been in free fall for so long that a taste of something this *random,* this *real,* was exhilarating.

Boo's free hand was now on a downward trajectory that led straight to his belt buckle.

Okay, this was actually happening. They were going to have sex.

What are you thinking, what are you thinking, what are you thinking...

She had his belt loosened (so easy for her to pull it from his waist and use it to choke him) and the button of his jeans undone (even easier for her to grab hold of sensitive flesh and twist) before Two realized he needed to respond in kind; he began liberating his captive from some of her clothes.

Two almost had her shirt unbuttoned when a buzz went off in his pants, surprising them both.

Damn. His burner phone.

Boo locked eyes with him. "You should probably..."

"Get that, yeah."

CHAPTER 63

"THIS IS TWO," he said as he'd been instructed.

"Two, this is One."

Oh.

Oh, shit.

Two had not anticipated this call yet. He wasn't supposed to hear from anyone until the ransom had been safely delivered, at which point he would be told to initiate the sequence that would return his captive to freedom. And Two hadn't expected One to be personally delivering the instructions.

One had implied it would most likely take at least forty-eight hours, given the logistics of such a large transfer of money. It wasn't as if Old Man Schraeder had bags of cash just sitting around.

It had been barely a day. This seemed *too* soon.

Now would be one hell of a time to part ways.

"Go ahead, One," Two said.

"We will be reaching our objective soon, Two. The time is coming."

"I understand, One."

"There is a SWAT team en route to this location. You must exit immediately with the package. When you receive word from me, and only me, you will close the account. Do you understand?"

A jolt coursed through Two's nervous system. At that moment, Boo was studying him closely, as if trying puzzle out the other half of the conversation.

If she could, she wouldn't like it very much.

One had told them in their briefing sessions that there were only two possible outcomes. If they were successful and the ransom was safely delivered, the abductors would be told to complete the transaction. If not, the order would be to close the account.

Close the account meant "kill the hostage." Quickly, cleanly, with no preamble or debate. *Done.*

Two fought back the shock. This didn't make any sense. Did it mean the ransom had not been delivered? Was it possible that One's meticulous plans had unraveled so quickly? Or had that cranky old bastard simply refused to even consider a ransom for his wife and children?

Annoyance in his tone, One repeated, "Do you understand, Two?"

Boo was studying him very, *very* closely now.

Two knew he shouldn't ask a question—any question. One discouraged such things. He wanted people to carry out his wishes without pushback or improvisation. But he had to know.

"One, has there been an issue with the . . . transaction?"

There was a lengthy pause. Two felt like he was dangling between the sky and the earth. Boo reached out and touched his arm. Her touch felt like cold death.

Finally, One said for the third time: "Do you understand, Two?"

No. No, he didn't. Not a damn thing about this made sense.

All at once, the hairs on his arms stood on end. Something in the world had just shifted—Two's professional instincts were coming back online. In his former life, he could always tell when a tricky situation was about to go south, usually a few seconds before the rest of the team knew.

"What's wrong?" Boo asked.

Wrong.

Something was about to go very, very wrong.

CHAPTER 64

TWO DID NOT like the sound of any of this. Not One's irritated tone. Not the abrupt change of plans. What the hell was going on? Clearly, *something* had gone wrong, and some part of the plot, if not the whole thing, was collapsing. But all Two could say in this moment were words of total compliance:

"Yes, One, I understand."

One disconnected before Two had the chance to do it himself.

Shit.

Two truly missed the built-in gossip network of the LAPD. Even if your commanding officer wouldn't tell you jack shit, there was always someone you could ask for insight on any given situation. Maybe a fellow cop who'd had one too many after a long shift. Or bored retirees keeping a hand in the mix. Ex-wives. Even somebody else's CI, someone who might want to get one over on their handler.

But with One, there was no network. One was the lone

nexus point for all of them. Two didn't even know the identities of his fellow teammates. (He had some vague ideas, but nothing concrete.) There was no way to know if one of them had screwed up or maybe turned snitch on the rest of them. They were all operating in the dark, except for those times when One deigned to let a little light slip in.

"What is it?" Boo asked.

Two realized his captive had been studying his face and could easily read the complex emotions playing out on his features. There was no time to sugarcoat it for her.

"We have to move," he said. "Right now."

"Where?"

"I'll let you know when we get there."

Boo reached out and grabbed his forearm as if trying to stop him from touching a hot stove. "No. Don't do that. Don't pretend we're right back to the way things started. I can help, you know."

"Help? Help how, exactly?"

"I think best when I'm under pressure. First, tell me why we're leaving in such a hurry."

Two almost blurted it out, but hesitated. This was moving too fast. He suspected he could trust her, but it was far from a certainty. If he told Boo Schraeder what One had just told him—that a SWAT team was en route to this location—she could easily make trouble for him. Even delaying him by thirty seconds could make all the difference.

And then Two would end up in jail, the last place someone in his former profession would want to be. And even if he survived for a while, One would surely offer a reward for his murder. Probably wouldn't even require much of a bounty. A few extra candy bars and cartons of cigarettes from the commissary would do it.

And then there was Boo... something about her touch. Her kiss. The way she spoke to him, even reassured him despite the circumstances.

Two had always trusted his gut. And his gut was telling him this was real. Was this the world's most bizarre meet-cute? Absolutely. But that made it even more special.

"We have to leave because I just received a tip that the police are on their way."

"Here?" she asked. "To this address?"

"Yeah," Two said.

"You didn't have to tell me that," Boo said. "You could have just said it was all part of the plan."

"I know I could have. But I thought you deserved the truth."

Boo considered this. "Either you're the world's worst kidnapper or you're actually a decent human being."

Two shrugged. "Both can be true."

"Did you call your boss Mr. One?"

"I called him One," Two admitted. "We all have code names, like in the *Taking of Pelham One Two Three*."

"I was thinking about the code names from *Reservoir Dogs*."

"Pretty sure Tarantino got that idea from *Pelham*."

Boo laughed. "Well, then, Mr. Number Two, my fate is in your hands."

"Forget all that. Call me Tim."

Boo smiled as if her captor had just shared his deepest, darkest secret. "Is that your real name? Tim?"

"Yes," Two said. "That's my real name."

"Tim what?"

Why not? Two thought. *I might as well tell her everything. And maybe she'll be smart enough to get us out of this place alive.*

"Tim Dowd."

"Well, then, let's go, Tim Dowd."

CHAPTER 65

Thursday, 7:07 p.m.

THE SANDBOX AT FBI headquarters displayed multiple angles on the house in Culver City, some from the sky and some on the ground. A twelve-man SWAT strike force was in position; a strict neighborhood perimeter had been established. If anyone was still in the house, they'd have no way out, barring some unknown drug-cartel-style tunnel running beneath the property. This tip could be nothing—or everything.

"Go," Nicky said.

On the other end of the phone, Jeff Penney gave his team the signal.

There was almost too much action to follow. Team leaders had helmet-mounted cameras transmitting in real time. Nicky tried to keep up with the video feeds and get a sense of the layout of the house, but it felt like playing a dozen first-person-shooter games at once.

Bam! The front door was knocked open. Pistols up, officers fanned out in every direction.

Bam! The back door rocked off its hinges, affording her a glimpse of more strike force members coming in through the side windows.

"Clear!" A two-man team checked every corner of the ground floor; another pair cautiously made their way up the single flight of stairs to do the same on the second.

"Clear!"

"Clear!"

Nicky followed the flurry of action, looking for any clues that Tim Dowd or Boo Schraeder had been here. But the place appeared to be just another Airbnb awaiting its next guest. There were no signs of life.

"Make sure you have people outside the house check for any escape routes," Nicky said.

"All due respect, Gordon," Jeff said, "this is not the first house we've breached."

Nicky ignored that. "And if you find Dowd, you take him alive."

"Last house was a bust," Jeff reminded her. "I don't think Dowd would be stupid enough to hole up so close."

"I need to know you hear me," Nicky said.

"Hey. If it comes down to Dowd or the hostage, and Dowd tries something funny, he's a goner."

"Damn it, Penney, listen to me—"

Her admonition was interrupted by an explosion of shouts and commands. Something was happening on multiple screens. Nicky found the video feeds that displayed the helmet cams of the team heading into a windowless room. Pistols and rifles up, all of them spreading out.

They were here.

CHAPTER 66

Thursday, 7:08 p.m.

NICKY TOOK IN every detail displayed on the camera feeds. The military cot with the pancake-thin mattress and spare bedding. The handcuffs. The gallon jugs of water. The generator. The microwave oven hooked up to the generator. The lantern. The box of industrial paper towels. The open box of MREs. These either belonged to a squatter who happened to be a trained survivalist, or a kidnapper prepared to keep his hostage alive with the bare necessities for the next few days.

"Penney!" Nicky shouted into her mic. "Get some men into the garage to see if there's still a vehicle inside."

"After my men finish clearing the room," Jeff said, sounding more than a little annoyed, mostly because Nicky's wild-card tip had been correct. "They might still be down there."

"Trust me, they're not," Nicky said. "Which is why you also need to get someone next door to talk to the neighbor, see what she heard or saw. I'm sure she's been watching this whole thing play out."

Jeff Penney grumbled but followed her orders and gave the commands. Nicky watched as the garage door was lifted. Flashlights revealed a black Audi very similar to one they'd caught on traffic cams in the area not long after Boo Schraeder's abduction. Beams of light focused on the car's interior; there was no one inside.

Before Nicky even said anything, Hope ran the plate. A few seconds later, she told Nicky that it came up clean. Still, the Audi would be hauled to their garage to see if forensics could find any traces of Boo Schraeder inside.

The conversation with the next-door neighbor was fruitless. No, she hadn't seen anyone leave the house—just the holy hell of the SWAT team interrupting an otherwise quiet night on the block. The noise distracted her from her favorite reality show, in fact, and no amount of reward money would cause her to rest easy now, not with all of this "ruckus." (Never mind that this was the same busybody who'd called in the tip to begin with.)

"Oh, they were definitely here," Jeff said to Nicky. She looked at his personal video feed and saw that Jeff was searching the room for anything Dowd might have left behind by mistake. "And they left not too long ago."

"How do you know?"

"There's food in the microwave. I stuck my finger in it. It's still warm."

"So they left in a hurry."

"Yeah," Jeff said. "Clearly somebody told that asshole Dowd we were on our way. Any idea who that somebody might be?"

Nicky said nothing, because she had a very good idea who that might be. Michael Hardy wasn't in the Sandbox right now, but he had access to everything the task force did, including the anonymous tip-line call. And if Mike had let his ex-partner know about the SWAT team even a few minutes after the command to strike the house was given, Dowd would still have had plenty of time to slip away with his hostage.

"Gordon? You still with me?"

Nicky wasn't about to share her suspicion with Jeff. "Yeah."

"Perimeter is up," Jeff continued, "but there's a chance they've already slipped though. Very likely they made it to the freeway. And this time of night, they can move quick in any direction. Any bright ideas about where Dowd might be headed next?"

Nicky knew this was Jeff needling her, trying to save face. But it wasn't necessary. This would be considered *her* failure—that she hadn't acted on the suggestion from the tip line fast enough. Never mind that it took Jeff Penney longer to gather his team than she thought it should have. *Heavy is the head that wears the crown,* as Nicky's boss John Scoleri liked to say.

"They had to have been on foot, at least at first," Nicky said. "I want all your men scouring the neighborhood, and I'm going to call in reinforcements. We haven't lost them yet."

"You got it, Gordon," Jeff said and hung up. Nicky called up a map of that section of Culver City. Right behind the row of houses on Briar was the campus of Culver City Middle School.

Nicky didn't think Dowd would be foolish enough to hole up in a school, but he might have used the campus as a shortcut over to Sepulveda, in which case there might be footprints on the softball field or even signs of a stolen car on the campus—

"Agent Gordon," said Hope, "I have Virgil Tighe on line one. He insists you're going to want to take his call."

CHAPTER 67

"GOT SOMETHING FOR you, Agent Gordon," Virgil Tighe said. "Something potentially huge."

"Go on," Nicky replied. But she was wary; this could be a fishing expedition. No doubt Virgil had heard about the raid on the Culver City property and wanted the inside track on this part of the investigation. Many Capital operatives were former LAPD or FBI. They had a lot of ears to the ground.

"I've been working with the Federales," Virgil said. "They seem certain they know the identity of the man who kidnapped Tyler Schraeder and his actress girlfriend."

"Okay, I'm listening."

"The name they gave me was Ramiro Flores," Virgil said. "Mexican ex-army. A decorated sergeant, as a matter of fact."

"Why is he no longer with the Mexican army?"

"Officially? Gross insubordination. Unofficially? I'm hearing that Flores beat the living crap out of his superior officer over the choice of music in their Humvee."

The name Flores was new to Nicky, but she had to admit he fit the kidnapper profile she was working up. Like Tim Dowd, a law enforcement or military background. And, most important, a fall from professional grace and a need for cash. If you were to handpick collaborators for a plot like this, you'd need people in that sweet spot: talented enough to get the job done and desperate enough to follow specific orders.

"What else do you know about Flores?"

"Our operatives are compiling an extensive file right now," Virgil said. "But what matters most is that he has a connection with Rubin Padilla."

The name gave Nicky pause. "Wait...Padilla. Is this the suspect your men killed in Las Vegas earlier today?"

"One and the same."

"So what's the connection? Did they serve together?"

"In a manner of speaking..."

Nicky was confused. Was Virgil screwing around with her? "Why don't you just come out and say it instead of wasting everybody's time?"

Virgil laughed and offered an apology. "I'm sorry, Agent Gordon," he said. "What you said struck me as funny. No, Padilla wasn't in the Mexican army. What he and Flores have in common is time served. And a girlfriend. I don't know who dated who first—hell, maybe they're still both banging her. Well, not Padilla. Not anymore. But I'm liking Flores as our guy."

And Nicky was liking him too.

CHAPTER 68

Thursday, 7:09 p.m.

THE STRIKE TEAM'S first order of business: taking out that goddamned box gun hidden on Little Rami's patio.

Plenty of locals had shared rumors about Ramiro's fancy and expensive military toy. They also said Rami had the whole damn place booby-trapped, like some kind of nut. But neither the gun nor the traps were the top priority—the top priority was seizing Rami's captives.

Still, there was some debate over how to take out the box gun. Some suggested a direct hit; others thought that was too risky. What if Rami was holding the abductees on the second floor? Perhaps the best option would be to send someone up there to disable it quietly and slit the throat of anyone guarding it.

But others dismissed this idea. Rami wasn't stupid, and one of the captives was famous. The smart play for him would be to lock them out of sight. Which meant keeping them on the first floor or, ideally, in a panic room. It took a while, but permission to strike was granted.

The cartel had been adding military weaponry to its arsenal for the past two decades, so it was relatively easy to secure a portable, single-shot, recoilless AT4 and position it across the street in the bedroom of a neighbor who was more than happy to accept payment for the inconvenience.

Finally, at 8:13 p.m., when the rest of the strike force was in position, the order to fire was given.

The thunderclap of the AT4 echoed through the neighborhood. Even if Little Rami's four armed guards had understood what they were hearing—and, lacking military experience, they did not—they would not have had the time to do more than lift their weapons before the rocket blasted apart the entire upper floor of the house.

One of Rami's men had been stationed on the balcony, and he disappeared in a haze of fire and smoke and chunks of concrete and body parts.

The remaining three drew their weapons and searched the street for the perpetrator, believing that someone had managed to lob a hand grenade up onto the balcony. They were so focused on the street that they didn't see the half a dozen strike team members approaching from behind the house.

All three were chopped apart by gunfire before they could turn around. They fell to the street and bled out.

Now to the primary objective: ensuring Little Rami's captives were alive and relatively unharmed.

And locating Little Rami.

CHAPTER 69

FIVE INSTANTLY RECOGNIZED the sound of the launch blast as an AT4 and knew the game had just changed.

He had been sipping a Skorpios 1618 Extra Anejo (he dug the red serpent-shaped bottle) when the rocket struck the top floor of the house. Five had been enjoying his tequila just down the hall from his captives, his phone perched on the arm of his chair, waiting for word from One.

But—was *this* word from One?

No. Couldn't be. If the plot had failed, Five would be given the order to kill his captives. If the plot had been successful, Five would be given the order to free his captives. That's the way it was supposed to work.

Five listened to the members of the strike team force their way into the house as he strapped on his body armor. No, this was something else. Someone had snitched. Maybe friends of those cops who'd tried to shake him down or an overly curious neighbor who'd caught the scent of blood and money and had an impulse to help the cartel.

Although—maybe this *was* the wrath of One. He'd warned Five and the rest of the team against using any outside help, and Five's brothers-in-arms certainly qualified as outside help. But no, that didn't make sense. Why would One choose this violent display of force with his valuable hostages in the cross fire? Wrath was one thing; money was another.

But it didn't matter now. Five could sort out the message later.

Let those sons of bitches come down here—they'd be stepping into a cellar of death. Five had all the advantages. His days in the military had taught him to plan ahead.

Any men who were stupid enough to step into this hallway would probably think they had their target pinned down. What they didn't know was that Five had the entire length of the hall rigged with smoke bombs, and if his attackers fired blindly at him, they risked hitting his captives. A desperate kidnapper might use them as human shields. Five was not a desperate man. He was a careful and prepared man.

His attackers would have no choice but to venture into the smoke. Which would also play to Five's advantage. He wouldn't shoot at them. He'd wait until enough of them were in the hall, then he'd go to a hidden wall panel and trigger the series of explosives he had wired along the floor and ceiling. Death from above; death from below—Five's preparation for a doomsday scenario, installed just last year when he thought he might be going to war with the cartel.

And by the time the survivors of this assault team were

scraping body parts off the walls, Five would be hustling the rich boy and his actress girlfriend through a tunnel to an awaiting car that nobody—not even his own brothers—knew about.

Five would miss this house, this neighborhood. But all the money would ease the hurt. And if this *was* One messing with him, Five would mess right back and take the whole billion for himself.

The idea of all the money made Five think of Julia, naturally. *You're gonna be sorry you stuck with that loser Rubin. The best he'll be able to buy you is a $9.95 breakfast buffet in some shitty casino.*

Smoke was filling the hallway now, and Five slipped on his 3M full-face respirator. As he was tightening a strap, he looked down at his left hand and saw something odd.

A *glowing red dot* danced on one of his knuckles.

Before Five had a chance to follow the dot to the laser light that cut through the smoke, the meat of his hand exploded. Detached fingers tumbled down his armored body.

No. No, no, no...

These bastards had infrared laser sights that could find their targets even in all this smoke!

Five turned and stumbled down the hall. One hand was gone; that was fine. He didn't need both hands for what came next. He'd worry about the future later. A billion bucks could buy all the hands he wanted.

The next bullet found Five's right shoulder and spun him around. Where was the control panel? In front of him? Behind him? Another bullet took out his left leg, forcing him to drop to one knee.

Still, this wasn't over. You might take a few hits in battle, but proper preparation always won the war, Five knew. *Get your head together and find that panel.*

He oriented himself and crawled along the ground to the control panel on his one hand and one good knee. Five thought staying low would keep him from much of the gunfire, but the glowing red dots found him anyway. By the time he reached the end of the hall where the trigger panel was located, he'd taken at least a half a dozen more bullets.

At this point, Five looked through the blood-spattered plastic of his mask and saw that he had been mistaken. This wasn't the end of the hall with the trigger panel. In the smoke and confusion, Five had crawled *right to his attackers,* who put two more bullets in his skull and waited for the smoke to clear.

CHAPTER 70

CASSANDRA BART VERY badly wanted someone to yell "Cut" or give some tiny indication that this was a low-budget action movie and not reality.

Right before the door to their informal cell was pried open, Tyler had told her to stay calm. "This is the cavalry arriving, babe. My dad knows people. Serious people."

She couldn't deny that they sounded serious. For the past few minutes—maybe longer?—they'd heard a series of teeth-rattling explosions and ceaseless gunfire that sounded like a popcorn machine running amok. Tyler, God help him, looked *excited*. How was that possible?

Cass had looked at his badly beaten face and said: "What if it's not the cavalry? What if it's somebody worse?"

Even if that was the case, Tyler insisted he'd handle it. "Baby, I can negotiate with anyone." Exactly what an overconfident asshole would say in an action movie right before his head was blown off.

Spoiler alert: Tyler's head wasn't blown off.

But he did not have the chance to negotiate or even say a single charming word. As soon as the door was blasted open, guns were pushed into their faces. Cass could not see the men. There was too much smoke and frenzied activity. And she and Tyler couldn't move because their wrists were still cinched to the bed with hard plastic zip ties.

But not for long. *Snip-snip*—the zip ties were cut away. Hoods were pulled over their heads. Cass heard Tyler groan in pain a second before she felt thick, rough hands on her shoulders forcing her to her knees. And then a boot in the middle of her back sent her flying forward, and her face smashed into the floor.

Stunned, she was barely aware when they lifted her into some kind of stretcher or maybe a blanket—it was hard to tell when she was so disoriented. Then she was being moved, bouncing helplessly as the men hurried her out of the house.

Cass was loaded into what felt like the bed of a pickup truck. She knew this feeling—her first vehicle, back in Odessa, Texas, had been a used pickup, and she and her friends would lie in the back of it, look up at the stars, and talk about their dreams. Later, at state fairs, she'd sing from that same flatbed, accompanied by a boom box playing instrumental Taylor Swift tracks.

Some part of Cass's mind thought this was funny, her life coming full circle—flatbed to flatbed.

The ride was rough. She struggled to use her elbows and heels to steady herself, but the driver of the pickup kept swerving, speeding up, and braking hard. Cass bounced around for what felt like forever. Occasionally she bumped into Tyler, but he must have been unconscious because he didn't speak.

Soon Cass was unconscious too.

When she woke up, the hood was off, and she was sitting up. The lights were way too bright, and her eyes refused to focus. Her wrists and ankles were zip-tied to a sturdy wooden chair. She became aware of all her injuries at once.

When her eyes finally focused, she was surprised to find herself on a film set.

That's what it had to be, right? Granted, Cass didn't see the usual gear; there were no lighting rigs or craft services.

But there *was* a digital camera on a tripod and a crew of bored-looking people standing around and staring at her as if waiting for her to speak her line.

What was her line? What was she supposed to say in this moment? And where was Tyler?

Her eyes found the person who looked most like an authority figure. The director, maybe? "Excuse me, can you tell me what's happening?"

The authority figure glared at her. That's because he was speaking to someone on the phone—the real authority, it turned out—and she had rudely interrupted him. "Blindfold them," he told a minion.

And then he returned to his phone conversation. "We have the two of them," he said. "One hundred percent."

CHAPTER 71

Thursday, 8:47 p.m.

SIX BLENDED IN perfectly with the civilians. Which was why One had hired her for this assignment. Six had a certain look.

Or non-look.

If you happened to glance at Six, you'd instantly dismiss her, regardless of your generation. If you were a Gen Z or Millennial, you'd think she was a factory-model Karen, ready to manage a youth soccer team or complain to the manager at any moment. If you were Gen X, which happened to be Six's generation, you'd also ignore her, because there were plenty of people who looked like Six already populating your feed, and why the hell did you need one more? Everybody that age had gone to college with dozens of women who now looked like Six.

And Boomers? They'd view Six as another one of the sheep,

blindly following whatever was trending. They would not consider her worthy of their attention.

Six was, for all practical purposes, invisible.

Which was why she was perfect to float among the shoppers and tourists at the Grove. She'd spent the past two days patiently waiting for this moment. She felt like the surprise guest star late in the season of a streaming series. The audience didn't know how important you'd be or to what degree you'd alter the storyline—but *you* knew, and as you waited, you got to watch all the pieces falling slowly into place, knowing that your role was the most vital one of all.

Six strolled past the synchronized fountain, where a couple of kids up way past their bedtime were trying to predict where the bursts and streams would jet out of the concrete. She made her way to the AMC Grove 14 ticket booth and purchased a ticket to a movie she'd never see.

Well, maybe Six would catch it later, after this was over. But not tonight.

Tonight was all about her part in the grand plan.

Six took her ticket and walked into the lobby. The ticket taker scanned the ticket. Six tucked it in her pocket. *For tax purposes,* she thought, and almost laughed. Then she walked to the concession booth and stood there pretending to study the digital menu.

She was not going to order food, however. She was waiting for someone.

And here she was...

CHAPTER 72

RIGHT AT THE incredibly tense midpoint of the movie, Kaitlin Gordon's cell phone buzzed twice. Without reading the text, she knew who it was from and what it said.

"My mom wants me to call her," she whispered to her friend Callie. "Be right back."

It wasn't like she had a choice. Kaitlin's mom's cell was the only number that could bypass the do-not-disturb feature on her smartphone—"I want to be able to reach you when I need to reach you," she'd said. Kaitlin had been pretty much forced to agree with her mother's "request" when they'd bought the device; it was that or she'd have had to settle for an embarrassing flip phone or something basic like that.

Which was a bummer at the moment, because after a long slow burn, the movie was *finally* picking up. On the screen, a killer crawled down the hallway toward his helpless victim, a severe agoraphobic who'd rather die than leave her apartment.

She'd better get her shrink on the phone quick, or that's exactly what will happen, Kaitlin thought.

This had better be important, Mom.

Kaitlin wound her way through the near dark to the exit. She didn't even bother to read the text because her mother always left the same message: Call me please.

As she walked to the lobby, Kaitlin felt the presence of someone keeping pace directly behind her. Growing up in LA made you hyperaware of any breach of personal space. But when the woman behind her spoke, Kaitlin realized this wasn't some rando with boundary issues.

"Kaitlin," said a very soccer-mom voice, quiet yet confident, "I need you to come with me right now."

Kaitlin turned to face her. "Are you talking to me?"

"You're Kaitlin Gordon, aren't you?"

Okay, that was creepy. "What, did you read that off my debit card while I was buying a ticket? Leave me alone, lady."

"Your mother sent me. Now, please, we don't have a lot of time!"

Kaitlin didn't know what was going on, but she knew her mother had *not* sent this tight-ass weirdo. Forget growing up in LA; growing up with an FBI agent for a mother, Kaitlin had learned every possible safety precaution from the time she was old enough to read a board book, and one of the earliest rules was never to go anywhere with someone who claimed that a parent had sent them.

Kaitlin checked out the woman. She was maybe a little younger than her mom, but much more tired around the eyes.

(And if you knew her mom, that was saying a lot.) But Kaitlin didn't recognize her, not even a little. She wasn't an FBI agent. There was something... *off* about her.

"I don't know you," Kaitlin said.

"Your mother is Agent Nicky Gordon," the woman said quickly and quietly. "She's currently working on a task force with Mike Hardy. I think you know what case they're working, so you should understand the urgency. *It's not safe for you out here.*"

"Sorry, I'm not buying it."

"Didn't you check your phone? Your mother just sent you a message."

"There are quite a few people in this lobby," Kaitlin said calmly. "I can scream."

"That would be an awful idea. You have no idea who's around. Who might be watching."

And then the stranger proceeded to tell Kaitlin the exact floor where her mother worked at FBI headquarters in Westwood and the exact location of her office. Her mother was there now.

How could this woman possibly know that?

Because her associate was in the same office. And if she did not call that person within the next few minutes...

Okay, that worked. Kaitlin felt her blood chill.

So she bolted.

CHAPTER 73

KAITLIN RAN OUT of the movie theater and darted through the middle of the Grove shopping center, which was starting to look like a ghost town at this hour. The retail stores were closing for the night, leaving only the AMC and one lone Asian boîte with a pricey cocktail lounge open. Was there not a single security guard around? Seriously?

She could hear the stranger behind her, running just as fast as Kaitlin. This crazy bitch might be tired, but she was also quick and athletic. That was not good.

Kaitlin was wary about running up to another stranger out here, because who knew? This psycho could have an accomplice. Kidnappers usually worked in teams.

You have no idea who's around. Who might be watching.

Kaitlin decided that the massive parking structure was her best bet. She might find someone in there with a tin badge and a Taser. And if not, she could hide behind cars and eventually lose this weirdo.

But as she ran toward the garage, a better plan came to mind: She could run back into the theater and leap over the entrance barrier, which would, hopefully, cause a theater employee to call the police.

Hold on. Why wait? She could call the police herself right now. And then do some fancy fake-out end run around her pursuer, make her way back to the AMC, and wait for the po-po to arrive.

Kaitlin looked down at her phone and finally glanced at the text from her mom. To her surprise, it didn't say Call me please. In fact, it was nothing Kaitlin would have expected in a million years.

Kaitlin stopped running, and so did her pursuer. The woman pulled a phone out of her purse, pressed a number, and said:

"One hundred percent."

CHAPTER 74

Thursday, 9:58 p.m.

FOUR'S BURNER PHONE went off at the worst possible moment. She considered not answering, but if One was on the other end, ignoring it would be very close to suicide.

She tapped the button to accept the call and braced herself. What if he'd somehow discovered that Four had strayed from the strict letter of the plan and left the kids alone with Three? What would One do? Would he punish them as he'd threatened to?

"Hello," Four said quietly, stepping out into the hall. She had to be mindful of her surroundings at this late hour, but she didn't want to stray too far.

A raspy female voice asked, "Is this Four speaking?" This voice did not belong to One.

"Who is this?"

"This is Six. I need you to listen to me very carefully."

"Hold on," said Four, still in a near whisper. "Who are you? How do I know this is real?"

"Do you have many prank callers who know your secret code number?"

"Look, even if it *is* real, we're not supposed to be talking to each other."

"You're free to hang up," said the woman claiming to be Six. "You and Three can take your chances. But if you don't listen to what I have to say, there's a good possibility that both of you will be dead within the next twelve hours."

Four didn't know how to respond. Clearly this Six had some kind of inside information. Otherwise, how could she know that Three and Four were working together? Or, like she'd said, even know the number to this burner phone?

"I'm listening," Four said.

"You need to get out right now. One is going to double-cross you and your husband. It's part of the plan. It's *always* been part of the plan."

The warning would have been easy to ignore if Four hadn't secretly believed all along that this would be the outcome. Of course One was going to double-cross them. She and her husband were nobodies. Someone smart enough to plan this kind of audacious triple kidnapping would also be smart enough to keep all the ransom money for himself.

Still...

"How do you know?" Four asked. "Maybe this is some kind of test. Maybe you're working on One's behalf as a kind of... quality control."

The person claiming to be Six said, "Maybe I am. You want

quality control? Just wait a few hours and find out for yourself. By then, it'll be too late to complain to the manager."

"I don't understand what you're saying. What are we supposed to do with—" Four caught herself before she said *the children*. There was still a chance, a good one, that this was some kind of trick or test. One had said he had eyes everywhere. Maybe he had ears too. Best to reveal as little as possible.

But Six knew what Four had almost said. "With the children? Leave them where they are. They won't be alone for very long."

"Do you know what you're asking me to do? On nothing more than your *word*?"

"You'd better hurry," Six said. "It might be too late already."

Four hung up and returned to the hospital bed. Her daughter was ten years old and suffering from a rare blood cancer that wasn't responding to chemotherapy. All this time in the hospital, all the expensive treatments, and the experts had only slowed the progression of the cancer. There was no cure, no hope of one. Except...

Except for an experimental drug trial down in Central America. It was already showing excellent results but had a price tag of two million dollars. Impossible for people in their financial state. Until One showed them a way it *could* be possible.

"Who was that?" her daughter asked.

"Nobody important."

"That sounded really important."

"Honey," Four said, "I hate to say this, because I know how awful you're feeling, but..."

Her daughter nodded. "We have to go, right?"

Yes, it appeared that they had to go right now, again at the worst possible time. Four's daughter's platelet count was perilously low, even after several platelet transfusions. Four's sister had said earlier that the medical team was very concerned.

So was Four.

CHAPTER 75

Thursday, 10:22 p.m.

THE SANDBOX WAS still bustling with activity. For most members of the task force, going home tonight was not an option—not with their best suspect, former cop Tim Dowd, and his possible captive still in the wind. There were also unconfirmed reports of a fierce gun battle in Tijuana that might or might not be linked to the Tyler Schraeder kidnapping. And finally, there were absolutely no leads on the Schraeder children, which was particularly heartbreaking to Nicky Gordon.

And there had been no word from her own child in a while. Kaitlin's movie had ended half an hour ago, and she should have texted her mother to check in by now, even if it was only a sarcastic and annoyed *Got your message, I'm home now and not dead, k thx bye.*

Nicky kept her head in the evolving case, but she was

hyperconscious of every minute that ticked by without word from Kaitlin.

She felt a warm hand on her shoulder. "Nick—can I borrow you for a sec?"

Nicky turned around to see Mike Hardy, although he didn't look like himself. There was usually an amused quality to his resting expression, as if life were one big joke and he was the guy hired to police it. But now Hardy looked gravely serious.

"What is it?"

"Let's duck into somewhere quiet."

"Mike, come on. We don't have time for somewhere quiet. Just spit it out." Nicky saw everyone in the Sandbox looking at them and regretted her insistence on staying here. Zero chance of privacy now.

"You hear from Special K tonight?"

"No—why?"

Mike looked as if he'd tasted something sour. "A detective of mine just called—some kids at the Grove reported their friend missing. The last name rang a bell with her, which was why she called me right away. Now, I don't know what this means, but..."

"Kaitlin is missing?"

"All we know for sure is that a couple of teenagers say their friend Kaitlin Gordon went missing from a movie theater at the Grove just a little while ago."

The entire task force fell silent. All eyes were on Nicky.

"Look, I think I speak for everyone here," Mike said. "If you need to go, we'll understand."

"No," Nicky said. "I'm staying."

Mike's expression was a blend of empathy and confusion. *Why doesn't she want to leave? Yeah, there's being strong in front of your team. But this is her kid.*

Mike leaned in close and whispered, "You *really* don't need to be here right now."

But there was no way Nicky was leaving the Sandbox. Not now—not at the most crucial part of this investigation. Everything was in flux, and she believed the kidnappers had engineered it that way.

She turned to her assistant, Hope. "Has there been any communication from the kidnappers? Any suggestion that these same people have taken my daughter?"

Hope shook her head. "This is the first we're all hearing of it."

"Then maybe it's nothing, and Kaitlin left the movie early for a good reason," Nicky said. "Or if they did take her, it's meant to be a distraction. And I'm not going to let it become one."

What Nicky Gordon didn't want to say out loud:

The very idea of her daughter in the hands of a well-financed, highly organized band of criminals terrified her to her core. As it would any mother.

But Nicky knew that that same band of criminals had a mole on her task force, and that individual was most likely sitting in the room right now. If she left or showed any kind of weakness, that person could effectively steer the investigation any way the kidnappers wished.

And that definitely was not going to happen.

"Hardy, keep me posted on what your detective learns," Nicky said. "Everyone else, back to work. Let's find these sons of bitches."

CHAPTER 76

Thursday, 10:29 p.m.

THREE HAD JUST proposed one final round of Mastermind (and he meant it this time, even though the children were refusing to go to bed until Four was back home) when there was a frenzied *knock-knock-knock* at the door.

At first, relief flooded Three's veins, because he thought Four had finally returned. But why on earth would his wife knock on the door of their secret kidnapping hideout?

Cal and Finney Schraeder were obviously thinking the same thing. Both eyed the door nervously. Who could be visiting at this late hour? And then the two of them exchanged glances. Maybe it was the police coming to rescue them. But…what would that mean for Three?

"Stay right here, guys," Three said, and he moved slowly toward the door. He almost wished he were the kind of professional criminal who carried a firearm. He'd actually never held a gun, and they'd dumped their only weapon, the Taser, not long after they'd scooped up Cal and Finney. So he was defenseless against whoever had decided it was cool to show up late at night.

Maybe he should duck back into the kitchen and look for a butcher knife...but what good would that do? Was Three supposed to get into a knife fight with a professional who was here to kill him and his wife?

Because that's where Three's mind was going now. Someone had been watching them. Someone saw Four leave. Someone called One and told him that Three and Four had broken the rules. One then called someone else, maybe one of the other numbers, maybe someone outside their little group, and told that person to kill whoever answered the door and then take the children.

Then it came again, even more rapid this time: *knock-knock-knock-knock.*

Would professional killers do this? Wasn't their whole thing slipping inside undetected and using guns with silencers to murder their sleeping victims? They didn't usually roll up, knock on the door, and announce, *Hit men here! Open up!*

Three was relieved but confused when he opened the door to find his trembling wife.

"We have to leave," Four said. "Right now."

"And go where, exactly? What happened? How's our girl?"

"She's outside in the car waiting for us."

Three's eyes widened in shock. "She's *where*? You gotta be kidding."

Four quickly recapped the call from the woman claiming to

be Six, a supposed coconspirator. The most important part of that brief conversation was the revelation that One had intended to double-cross them all along. Three shook his head furiously, not believing it.

"Doesn't make sense," he said. "There's no way One would risk losing all that money. I mean, what's to stop us from taking the kids with us?"

"What's to stop him from killing us the moment Cal and Finney are gone? One knows everything about us. We know nothing about him!"

"Honey, it just doesn't add up."

"Sure it does. And maybe Six just found out the hard way. Maybe she kidnapped some other member of the Schraeder family and learned the truth about One at the last minute, right before he could kill her. Maybe she's spreading the word so the rest of us don't end up on a slab somewhere."

Three rubbed his eyes. It was late, he was bone-weary, and he knew there was zero chance of sleep anytime soon. And now his wife was spinning around with crazy what-ifs and half-baked conclusions right when they had literally everything on the line.

"Sweetheart, you need to bring our girl back to the hospital," he said. "You know we can't care for her on our own. We don't have the equipment."

"She'll be okay until morning," Four said, rather unconvincingly.

"That can't be right. Did you clear it with her nurse?"

Four shot him a withering look that made him realize how stupid this question was. There was no way the oncology team would have let their daughter leave. Either Four had taken their daughter out of the hospital against medical advice or she had sneaked her out. Returning her to the hospital might not even be an option.

"Even if we left," Three said, "don't you think One would find us? You know what kind of resources the man has."

"All I know," Four said, "is that if we run right now, we still have a chance."

CHAPTER 77

THREE KNEW HIS wife was right. She usually was. Only a fool would patiently wait for someone to walk up, place the barrel of a gun on his forehead, and pull the trigger.

But running meant destroying any hope of their daughter surviving.

Wasn't that why they had agreed to this outrageous plan in the first place? There had been no other option. Oh, Three and Four had convinced themselves that no one would get hurt aside from some wildly rich jerk. Parents were supposed to sacrifice everything for their kids—even their souls, if need be.

That's what they'd told themselves when One approached them with his take-it-or-leave-it-right-now offer. Three knew that if they turned down One, they'd regret it forever.

But wait...was there a way to do both? Keep themselves safe and yet still honor their agreement—the spirit of it, at least, if not the letter?

"We can make this work," Three said, "if we bring Cal and Finney with us."

Four shook her head. "No. I thought about that while I was driving back here. If we break One's rules by taking them out of this house, we're done."

"So we tell One that we *had* to move. Maybe we noticed a local cop car drive past too many times. Maybe we didn't want to risk getting caught before the ransom was delivered—"

"Don't forget, One will double-cross us no matter what. *There won't be any money.*"

"Which is all the more reason to take the kids," Three said. "They're our leverage. He needs them for this plan to work. We can set some rules of our own!"

Four paused to consider that, and Three continued to press his case.

"And we can't leave these kids here alone to fend for themselves. They'll run first chance they get, and then what? You really want them wandering around this city at this hour?"

Four nodded. Her mind had been on their daughter and *her* needs.

"How about we keep them for now," Three said, "and maybe when we hear the ransom has been paid, we negotiate with the mysterious Mr. One. If he wants these kids back, he's going to have to honor our agreement."

"So where will we go?" Four asked. "We never came up with an option B for a hideout."

Three smiled. "We can have that conversation in the car, right?"

Which reminded him of who was sitting in the car right now—the most important human being in the world to both of them. Three could see her silhouette in the back seat, where she waited patiently for her parents to finish their debate.

Their precious girl had no idea what her parents had actually been up to over the past few days. She'd been told they'd taken a very lucrative house-rehab job somewhere in the San Gabriel Valley, a two-day gig they absolutely could *not* turn down. The real estate business her mom worked for (their daughter called it her "fancy-mansion side hustle") sometimes hired her father, a skilled handyman. Their brave girl understood that you didn't turn down money, and besides, she'd get to spend some quality time with her auntie Shannon.

But what would their daughter do when Mom and Dad came out of this house—which was clearly *not* being rehabbed, by the way—with two white kids not much younger than herself and said that they had to go on the run?

How were they going to explain *that* to her?

CHAPTER 78

Thursday, 11:02 p.m.

AT TWO MINUTES after eleven, the ransom directions were finally delivered to Nicky Gordon's task force.

This time, the communication was not on an audiocassette. It was also not delivered to the field office by an unhoused person pressed into service. These directions appeared digitally, and simultaneously, on every screen and handheld device in the Sandbox.

Each member of the task force looked around, wondering how this was possible. Their internal chat system, built along the lines of a Slack platform, was highly encrypted and absolutely walled off from the outside world.

Nicky, though, knew exactly how: the mole. Wouldn't take much to push a message to every available screen in the house *if you were already in the house.*

"Are we all seeing this?" Jeff Penney asked. "Holy God."

Almost everyone had their eyes fixed on their screens, but Nicky resisted the urge and instead studied the people in the Sandbox, the diehards of the task force who remained here at this very late hour:

Mike Hardy, LAPD chief of detectives and her sometime lover
Hope Alonso, Nicky's personal assistant
Jeff Penney, head of SWAT
Ross Lindbergh, FBI financial-crimes specialist
John Scoleri, Nicky's boss, who wasn't in this room but was on the floor (Long ago, Nicky had realized that the man had no life outside the office, especially during high-profile cases.)

In all likelihood, *one of them was the mole.*

Nicky examined their faces while a flurry of excited voices bounced around the Sandbox.

"They want more than a third of the ransom in cash and the remainder in precious metals or jewelry. They're giving specific breakdowns, down to the types of pallets and cases to use."

"Is someone relaying this to Virgil Tighe's team at Capital in real time?"

"I'm on it, and they're alerting the Schraeder team in Omaha. Private jet is on the tarmac and waiting. They didn't want to leave in case the kidnappers decided they wanted the handoff to happen somewhere in Nebraska."

"Okay, good thing, because it looks like they want their takeout delivery at the Santa Monica Airport."

"Huh. The Pacific is right next door. Maybe the plan is to get the money out into international waters."

"What, where they're sitting ducks for the Coast Guard and air teams? No, that doesn't make sense. They gotta have another exit strategy."

Nicky watched their faces while also processing the kidnappers' demands. The text on her screen was dense and loaded with absurdly specific details, as if the kidnappers were particularly cruel micromanagers.

Ultimately, Nicky knew, the details weren't important. The ransom delivery would surely maximize the kidnappers' advantage (stealth) and minimize the task force's greatest strength (manpower). There was a reason the instructions had been issued so late at night. It guaranteed there would be fewer agents on the case, and those that were there would most likely be exhausted.

But if Nicky could somehow read minds and knew beyond the shadow of a doubt who the mole in this room was, this could all be over in five minutes, following a brief but tense interrogation.

She glanced at Mike as he joined the others in the discussion. She hated herself for this, but she had to ask: Was that genuine surprise on his face or was he just acting out a role, one that he and his former partner Tim Dowd had practiced for months on end? Nicky didn't want to believe Mike Hardy could be capable of this level of betrayal. But a share of a billion dollars could make a man capable of almost anything.

"Hold on," said Mike, rising from his seat. "What is this?"

Jeff Penney slammed the table with his fist. "What the hell is going on?"

As Nicky watched the screen, the ransom directions simply vanished, as if the sender had access to a global Undo button.

A moment later, a new message appeared. This one was only two sentences long.

"'Ignore previous instructions,'" Nicky read out loud. "'Revised delivery protocol to follow.'"

CHAPTER 79

MIKE HARDY LOOKED up from the screen, where new instructions had just appeared. "Anybody seeing this insanity? Is anyone actually in charge over there at Kidnappers Inc.?"

"Now they want delivery near San Clemente," Jeff Penney said. "That's damn near halfway to Mexico. Maybe that's their plan?"

"Who are we liaising with down there, Gordon?" Mike asked. "Maybe they've got a team in TJ waiting for the handoff."

"Handoff?" Jeff said. "This isn't a football, Hardy. This is a *billion dollars*. They're not going to shove the money down the front of their pants and take a stroll over the San Ysidro crossing."

"It's a long border, genius. I'm not suggesting we guard it. I'm saying we get our Mexican pals to hunt for the team on *their* side. You know, look for suspicious transport vehicles, anything out of the ordinary—"

The usually reserved Ross Lindbergh, who had volunteered

to stay in touch with Schraeder's team, was becoming increasingly agitated.

"Quiet, quiet! I'm on with Omaha. They're preparing to load the bags onto the jet. Do I tell them to proceed?"

They all looked over at Nicky Gordon. She was still considering the sudden change of delivery instructions, trying to see the bigger game. Moving something as monumental as a billion dollars—ten tons in paper money—would be a logistical challenge on an ordinary day. And damn near impossible to change on impulse. So all this noise was just that. Noise and disinformation. *Of course the kidnappers know their plan, right down to the smallest detail.* "They just haven't given it to us yet," Nicky mumbled.

"What's that?" Mike asked.

She turned to Ross. "Tell Omaha to stand by. Delivery instructions aren't complete yet." And then, to the others gathered: "Nobody respond unless I say so. Let's let them finish clearing their throat, and maybe they'll get around to giving us the real instructions."

Nicky's hunch was correct. For the next half hour, the delivery details continued to shift like beach sand. From San Clemente, the drop-off was switched to nearby John Wayne Airport, then to an absurd number of closed roads in the immediate vicinity, none of which gave them any indication of where the billion might be moving after the drop-off.

After sending what seemed to be the final version of these instructions, the kidnappers demanded the task force acknowledge their receipt, and they wanted separate confirmation from the Schraeder team via Capital.

"What do we say?" Ross asked.

"Nothing," Nicky Gordon responded.

"Come on," Jeff said. "At the very least, we have to let Schraeder's team know what's going on. The last thing we told them was Santa Monica. They might be preparing a flight plan. Hell, they might be in the air as we speak!"

"No," Nicky said. "Not yet."

In this moment, she was multitasking like crazy: Considering the shape of the kidnappers' ultimate plan. Checking the faces of her fellow task force members to see if anyone displayed a nervous tell or was trying to urge a specific course of action.

And of course, her thoughts were on Kaitlin. Where she might be. What was going through her daughter's mind.

"Hey."

This was Mike, who had rolled his chair over next to hers. He leaned in close and flashed her a warm smile. "Real talk. You doing okay?"

Nicky nodded, trying not to betray any emotion on her face. *Are you asking for me, Mike, or are you asking because you're the mole?*

"What I mean is, are you still okay doing this?"

This meaning "the job." Nicky didn't know if she should be touched by his concern or insulted by the implication that she could no longer head up the task force.

"I'm good," she replied. "But I would appreciate it if you could follow up with your detective friend about Kaitlin."

"We're in constant contact," Mike said. "We'll find her, Nick. Don't worry."

"I know she's in good hands."

Ross Lindbergh slammed his fist on the table, which was an extremely un–Ross Lindbergh–like thing to do. He was the quiet man of their team, the patient and methodical money expert.

"I can't *believe* these assholes!" he shouted.

That was because, abruptly, an entirely new set of ransom instructions had been delivered to their internal chat service. This one focused on the Santa Anita racetrack and involved an entire fleet of police helicopters. Which meant they had to start the process all over again.

CHAPTER 80

Thursday, 11:03 p.m.

THEY WERE TALKING excitedly to someone over the speakerphone, but Cassandra Bart didn't know enough Spanish to keep up. The single course she'd taken in her sophomore year of high school wouldn't be helpful unless she needed to ask her kidnappers for directions to the bathroom: *¿Para baño?*

But that was also not an option; she was still bound to the chair and blindfolded. Tyler was also bound and seated to her right. She could hear his annoyed grunts and snorts. And then, a mumbled question: "Hey, Cass. You there?"

She swallowed, wondering what she'd have been doing right now if she hadn't foolishly agreed to this midweek getaway with Tyler Schraeder.

"Yeah. I'm here."

"Do you understand a damn thing they're saying?"

"A little."

Which was true. Certain words jumped out at her, like *actriz* and *dinero* (which, granted, didn't require advanced degrees to translate). But little phrases alarmed her, like something that translated to "taking them out." Did that mean taking them out of this place and moving them elsewhere? Or did that mean... *taking them out*?

"Something about us and money," she said quietly.

"That means the old bastard is paying up," Tyler said. She heard him exhale as if he'd just received the best news of his career. "We'll be going home soon."

"How can you be so sure?"

"My father must know these people," he said. "I'll bet he arranged all this to get us out of the hands of that idiot who grabbed us."

Do you mean the idiot who beat the living hell out of you, Tyler?

Cass wanted Tyler to shut up so she could focus on the words. She also fervently hoped he was right and that this would all be over soon. She tried to think of it as an interesting anecdote to tell on a press junket someday. *How did I prepare for this Martin Scorsese film? Well, I was once held for ransom by a violent Mexican cartel, and let me tell you...*

But there wouldn't be any more press junkets, Cass was certain. Not for her, anyway. Everybody in the world wanted to be famous; people would do anything for their share of the spotlight. But why? So you could be famous enough to be used as a pawn in a massive kidnapping plot?

Now the excited conversation stopped; the conference call was over, important cartel business tabled for the moment. Cass thought it sounded like a decision had been made.

Footsteps approached. A gruff voice asked them both: *"¿Encendido o apagado?"*

"What are they asking?" Tyler asked.

"'On or off,'" Cass translated, not understanding what they meant by that.

"Oh, shit," Tyler said. "The blindfolds. They're asking us if... listen, tell them we want to keep them on. We absolutely do *not* want to see their faces! Tell them, Cass!"

Cass, however, wanted very much to have this gross, scratchy rag removed from her eyes. She'd spent enough time in the dark.

"If we see their faces, they'll have to kill us!" Tyler said.

Was that true? Cass didn't know what to think anymore. Even if they were going to kill them both, she didn't want to die blind. She wanted one last glimpse of this strange world before it was snatched away from her.

"Listen to me," Tyler told their captors. "Leave the blindfolds on. You will be rewarded handsomely! You know who my father is, don't you?"

A quiet voice whispered in Cass's ear, "Miss, on or off?"

"Take it off, please," she said.

"Cass, *no*! You don't *understand*!"

Immediately her blindfold was removed, and the harsh warehouse lighting stabbed her eyes. When her vision finally cleared, she saw that one of their captors was holding a pistol to Tyler's forehead as he continued to writhe in his chair and plead for them to leave his blindfold on.

He'd get his wish.

CHAPTER 81

Thursday, 11:49 p.m.

“WHERE ARE WE going, exactly?”

“We are looking for a car.”

“Something wrong with the one we’re currently using?”

“Sooner or later the owner is going to notice it’s missing. Won’t take long before they realize it was taken within walking distance of—”

“Your top secret hideout?” Boo Schraeder asked, smiling.

God, that smile. It absolutely melted him.

This woman was funny, smart, beautiful, and worth a billion dollars. (Okay, that price tag included her adult stepson and two grade-school stepchildren, but still.) How on earth did a disgraced bruiser ex-cop like Tim Dowd—currently the kidnapper known as Two—wind up with his life hitched to hers?

Two said, “Let’s find something that’s more *us*.”

"Oh, *we* have a specific type of car now, do we?"

"Yes. Something luxurious that runs insanely fast."

Boo laughed. "That sounds about right."

Two suggested stopping at one of those long-term parking lots near LAX or maybe in nearby El Segundo to do a little car shopping. But Boo countered with posh Manhattan Beach, just a few more miles down the 405.

"The richer the people," she explained, "the better the selection."

How could he argue with that? They were far enough away from their near capture in Culver City that Two could breathe a little easier. Also, he could stop thinking of himself as Two; he'd already told Boo his real name. Things would be different from now on. He could just be Tim Dowd again. A man with a future. Possibly one with the most amazing woman he'd ever met.

Boo steered him down Valley Drive and into a quiet, palm-tree-studded neighborhood. The hour was late, so there wasn't a soul in sight.

"How about that one?" Boo nodded at a 2024 BMW X3. "You know how to boost a Beemer?"

Dowd laughed. "I worked TRAP for years. We had, like, a ninety percent recovery rate."

"TRAP?"

"The Task Force for Regional Auto Theft Prevention."

"Everything has an acronym, doesn't it?" Boo asked. "Did *Two* stand for something? Maybe 'The Wild One'?"

Dowd felt his cheeks flush. She was funny and knew how to make him feel like a shy high-school dork. "The BMW looks fancy enough. But does it have the muscle we need?"

"How about muscle that goes a hundred and eighty miles an hour?" Boo asked with an amused smile. "Plus, it's an SUV. Which, you know, is practical. All leather too. Okay, that's not so practical. But it also has puncture-resistant tires and a panoramic sunroof."

"You know a lot about luxury cars."

"I do a lot of online shopping."

"Why do we need a sunroof?"

"To see this great land of ours as we cross it."

"What are you talking about?"

"I think once we change cars, we should just keep driving. You wanted a fresh start, right?"

Dowd stared at her. Was she saying what he thought she was saying?

CHAPTER 82

OKAY, TIME TO pull over, hijack this Beemer, and hit the road again. For Dowd, stealing the BMW was stupid-easy. His time with TRAP had given him access to an assortment of override microchips that worked on any vehicle with a computerized ignition system. Which was pretty much all of them. This was how he had been able to quickly change cars yesterday.

Good thing Boo hadn't suggested they boost a '72 Dodge Challenger because Dowd would have been screwed.

Dowd opened the passenger door of the BMW for Boo as if they were on a date. And who knew? Maybe they were now. She touched his hand as she lowered herself into the seat, nodded thanks, then gracefully pulled her legs into the car. As he walked around to the driver's side, the cell phone in his pocket buzzed.

There was only one person in the world who could be calling. And it was pretty much the last person Dowd wanted to hear from right now.

But Dowd reminded himself he was still very much Two, at least for the moment. He answered the phone with "This is Two."

Boo smirked at him. She crossed her eyes and stuck out her tongue as if they were on a playground instead of committing grand theft auto.

"I understand you and your hostage are in the wind," One said.

"Yes, thanks to your warning," Dowd replied. "We were on the road before SWAT was on the scene."

"Just *two minutes* before the police arrived," One said in the tone of a chiding schoolteacher. "You received your warning *five minutes* before that."

Dowd glanced over at Boo, who was running a finger along the leather dashboard, tracing a slow, lazy line toward the glove box. She was either bored or flirting. Perhaps both.

"Five minutes isn't very long," Dowd said, trying to keep his annoyance in check. "There were certain . . . logistics to consider."

"You cut it way too close."

"I understand."

"Do you have your hostage under control? We're at the end-game now. There can be no slipups."

"You don't have to worry about that."

"I know I don't."

CHAPTER 83

"THAT SOUNDED TENSE," Boo said after a moment of silence, possibly out of respect for Dowd's bruised ego. She hadn't had to hear both sides of the conversation to know he'd just had his ass handed to him.

"Doesn't matter," Dowd replied.

They were back on Valley Drive. The immediate plan was to navigate to the 405 and then head south toward San Diego. From there, they'd have to have a serious conversation. How had he put it to One? *There were certain... logistics to consider.*

Was this beautiful woman serious about ditching their lives and driving across the country together? A true fresh start? Dowd had next to nothing in his bank accounts, even if he could access them without being immediately tracked. But maybe Boo had some mad money socked away, maybe in some account in the Caymans. Smart women married to billionaires would think of something like that.

"Wait," Boo said. "One last request before we leave the beach."

"Nothing's open this time of night," Dowd replied. "It'll be dawn in a few hours. We can grab breakfast then."

"No, I'm not hungry," she said. "I just want to wave goodbye to the Pacific. We're probably not going to see it again for a while."

Holy shit. She *was* serious about running away together.

"The Manhattan Beach Pier is right down the hill."

"Perfect."

Dowd steered their stolen BMW down Manhattan Beach Boulevard, then turned left toward an empty municipal parking lot. The gates were chained shut, but he figured idling here for a minute or two wouldn't hurt.

Boo had opened the glove box and was reaching inside.

Dowd smirked. "Wondering who we ripped off?"

"No," she replied. "I know exactly who this car belongs to."

And with that, she removed a Smith and Wesson CSX micro-compact nine-millimeter pistol from the glove box and emptied it into Dowd's chest. The shots rocked the car and filled the interior with the bitter scent of cordite.

In that moment, Tim Dowd assumed this was an elaborate prank that would end with both of them laughing their heads off before they drove off into the dawn. Not until the life was draining out of his body did Dowd realize that this was indeed a joke, the biggest joke of all, but the joke was on him.

Dowd would have asked why, but he couldn't breathe, let alone speak.

"I'm sorry, Tim, but..." Boo started. Maybe she finished the sentence, but Dowd would never know, because that was when the lights went out forever.

DAY THREE

CHAPTER 84

Transcript of audio-only conversation (recovered from private Macao-based server)

ONE: I hope you have a very good reason for calling this number. You are not supposed to contact me unless it is a dire emergency.

SIX: I believe you'll consider this dire.

ONE: What is it?

SIX: Gordon's daughter is gone.

ONE: What do you mean, *gone*? How did this happen? Did she have some kind of weapon on her? You were supposed to know about these things!

SIX: No. She had no weapon.

ONE: Then why are you wasting time with a phone call? Chase that kid down and hold her until further notice. She's a vital part of our plan.

SIX: It's too late for that, One.

ONE: There is no such thing as too late. You find her right now, before she can contact her mother, or the consequences will be severe.

SIX: Why would I try to find her? I'm the one who let her go.

ONE: What?

SIX: You've gone too far, One. This has stopped being about the money. Now you're just a murderer.

ONE: No one is dead.

SIX: So you're a murderer and a liar?

ONE: No one...important.

[*There is a lengthy pause.*]

SIX [*Quietly*]: I'm going to enjoy watching this house of cards fall all around you. You're not going to see a penny of that billion dollars.

ONE: And you're not going to live to see the sun rise. You think I'm a murderer? Guess what, Six—you're next on my hit list.

SIX: You'll never find me. Or the girl.

ONE: After all this time, all this preparation...you don't believe I have eyes everywhere?

SIX: It's too late, Mr. One. We're both in the wind. I just wanted to give you fair warning. I'm giving the others fair warning too.

ONE: You're a dead woman, Ms. Parker.

[*Call ends.*]

CHAPTER 85

Friday, 12:02 a.m.

"I HAVE… *THEM*…on line one," Hope Alonso said.

Here it was, at long last. The first direct communication between Nicky's task force and their adversaries. Seven minutes before, the kidnappers had again hijacked the FBI's internal messaging service with instructions to call a WhatsApp number at exactly midnight. Using WhatsApp meant the communication would be encrypted and untraceable, even for the FBI.

Nicky scanned the faces of the people in the Sandbox. *Which one of you knew this call would be happening right now? And how do you plan on helping from the inside?*

"Okay, gather everyone who's awake."

Ross Lindbergh immediately patched in the team from Capital; a younger operative had been standing by the phone all night. Virgil Tighe was temporarily unavailable, so his boss,

James Haller, was pulled away from a dinner party to listen in. The slightly tipsy lawyer insisted on conferencing in Randolph Schraeder as well.

"I know he'll want to be on this call," James insisted. "This simply isn't happening without him."

"Cool, but can you keep your client muzzled?" Mike asked. "We don't need him antagonizing these guys."

"Hardy, this is a *billion fucking dollars,*" James Haller practically snarled. "My client can antagonize whomever he wants whenever he wants."

"Well, I don't know, *Jimmy.* Does your client understand that his entitled mouth could get his own children killed?"

At this point, Nicky had had enough. "You two want to keep trading punches or are you ready for this call?"

"The mayor's office is on the line," Hope said. She had spent the past few minutes struggling to reach the mayor's chief of staff so that he could keep his boss updated, but he was unreachable. Hope diligently worked down the line until she roused the director of LA's Chamber of Commerce from a dead sleep. Not ideal, but it would cover their asses politically.

"Are we all here?" Nicky asked.

James Haller confirmed that yes, his client Randolph Schraeder had joined the call. They saw Schraeder's face on a screen, but the man did not speak. Perhaps Haller had been smart enough to preemptively mute him.

"Everyone who's awake is on the line," Mike replied.

"Okay," Nicky said. "Let's hear what they have to say."

CHAPTER 86

"THIS IS AGENT Gordon," Nicky said. "To whom am I speaking?"

"Who I am is not important," a modulated voice said. It sounded similar to the voice on the cassette tapes, only this version was crystal clear and obviously spoken live.

"What should I call you, then?"

"You may call me One."

"Thank you, One. Are you prepared to guarantee the safe return of the Schraeder family?"

"First, we need to discuss the money. Do you have it gathered as per our specifications?"

"We were waiting for your *final* delivery instructions," Nicky said. "Are you ready to share them?"

There was silence on the line. The word *final,* of course, was pointed. Nicky knew One was playing games. One knew that he was playing games. It was time to end the games and get down to business.

"Yes," One finally said. "We will be sending coordinates once we know the payment is ready for delivery. But first we will require visual proof of the ransom and accountant-verified documentation."

Nicky had anticipated something like this. She knew they would be wary of a ringer package, perhaps counterfeit paper and Hollywood-style costume jewelry that would pass a visual test.

"And we require similar proof," Nicky said. "We want to see Boo Schraeder alive and well. And Tyler Schraeder. And, most of all, Cal and Finney Schraeder. Otherwise, there will be no ransom delivery."

"Unacceptable," the synthesized voice of One said, and he disconnected.

Huh.

After a moment of stunned silence, Mike Hardy exhaled. "Well, that was interesting."

"What did you people do?" bellowed Randolph Schraeder, who clearly had not been muted by James Haller. "If my family *suffers* because of your *bungling*—"

"This is give-and-take, Mr. Schraeder," Nicky said calmly. "We need to make it clear that this is a negotiation, not a one-way street. This is for the safety of your family."

"Are you seriously trying to school *me* on how to negotiate, Agent Gordon? I've been closing multimillion-dollar deals since before you were a gleam in your daddy's eye. Hell, before your daddy was in *diapers*."

Nicky had expected Schraeder to say something like this—to throw his age and so-called experience in her face. She nodded to Hope Alonso, who had the power to mute Randolph Schraeder during any future communication with the kidnappers. The nod meant *Be ready*. Hope sat with her finger ready to click the mute button on the call software. She had been tasked with managing the communication among the parties if things went south.

"Agent Gordon," James Haller said, "I hope you're doing everything in your power to get the mysterious Mr. One back on the line."

Hope nodded at Nicky, who said: "We're trying him again right now."

"You'd better pray he responds," Schraeder said, "or I swear to God, I will destroy all your careers. You will spend the rest of your miserable lives in courtrooms being deposed."

Mike Hardy made a gesture with his right hand indicating self-pleasure. Nicky shot him a glare: *Funny, but not the right time.*

"The kidnappers will respond, Mr. Schraeder," Nicky said. "They don't want your family. They want your money."

"They had better respond, Agent Gordon."

But Hope shook her head—no response yet. Nicky remembered the long stretches of silence on the two previous tapes and realized they might be in for a long wait. These kidnappers took a sadistic pleasure in keeping their targets twisting in the wind.

"While we wait to reconnect," Nicky said, "we're going to

need those photographs of the ransom. Can you forward them to us?"

"My team just sent everything you need."

And so they had. Hope opened the dozen images and pushed them to the Sandbox's largest overhead screens.

So *that* was what a billion dollars looked like.

CHAPTER 87

THE FIRST FEW images from Capital showed four tightly wrapped pallets, each as big as an industrial-size washing machine. The next focused on a much smaller vessel: a black polycarbonate container.

"Whoa," Mike Hardy said with the awe of a car enthusiast checking out a high-end sports car. "What are we looking at here, Haller?"

"We will forward copies of the itemized lists, along with serial numbers and requisite paperwork, within the hour," James Haller replied.

"Walk us through it now," Nicky said. "The more we know about the ransom, the better we'll understand how the kidnappers might move it."

Randolph Schraeder said in his gruff voice, "Go on and tell them, Jim."

"Of course, Mr. Schraeder," Haller said, sounding as if he'd been smacked on the nose with a rolled-up newspaper.

The pallets were stacks of cash, Haller explained, all in hundred-dollar bills, each pallet containing one hundred million dollars.

"There was no way to make the stacks more compact, since the US government no longer circulates anything larger than a hundred-dollar bill," he continued. "These four pallets add up to four hundred million, forty percent of the ransom."

"How much does each pallet weigh?" Nicky asked.

"A little north of two thousand pounds."

So the handoff would require a pallet jack or power stacker. A good operator could transfer the pallets from one vehicle to another in short order. But it wouldn't be instantaneous, meaning they'd have a little bit of time on their side, Nicky thought. "Nonsequential numbers?"

"Naturally, because they'll ask. But each bill has been scanned and recorded."

"What's in the little guy?" Mike asked.

The "little guy" was the polycarbonate container. It held the other 60 percent of the ransom.

"Assorted jewels," Haller said.

Randolph Schraeder snorted, clearly offended by the terse summary. The man was strangely proud of what he'd been able to gather, and he began to detail the contents of the container.

"That single case," Schraeder said, "holds a number of one-hundred-carat diamond rings worth nearly twelve million each. Also, a collection of rare Colombian emeralds, the largest collection of its kind *anywhere* in the world, and they run about seven million for each fifty-carat gem. There are also rubies, padparadscha sapphires, paraiba tourmalines..."

All of which added up to six hundred million dollars—and not a penny more, according to Schraeder, who had insisted on having a certified gemologist assist Virgil Tighe in gathering the ransom.

The next series of photos sent by Capital showcased those precious gems. If you were into fine jewelry, the images were borderline pornographic. To Nicky, it looked like someone had smashed the front windows of a fancy jewelry boutique on Rodeo Drive and cleaned out the displays. Just *one* of those gems would take care of Kaitlin's educational needs forever. All that value depended on eons of geological formation—and all of it was set to change hands in a couple of days. *Human beings,* Nicky thought, *are absurd creatures.*

"As soon as we have the delivery point," James Haller said, "we'll have the cash and jewels in the air. My associate Virgil Tighe will accompany the ransom the entire way."

"They're gonna ask about tracking devices," Jeff Penney said.

"I'm sure they will," Haller responded.

Nicky frowned. "Anything you need to tell us?"

An awkward silence descended. Randolph Schraeder started to say something, then apparently thought better of it.

"That won't be a problem," Haller said. Which was not a denial that there would be tracking devices.

"One is back on the line," Hope said.

CHAPTER 88

“ARE YOU PREPARED to take this transaction seriously?” One asked.

“We are forwarding visual confirmation of the ransom,” Nicky said. “The documentation will follow shortly. Now we’d like proof of life for the hostages.”

“No.”

“You can’t seriously believe that we’ll release the money without some indication that you are holding up your end of the deal.”

“That’s exactly what I believe, Agent Gordon. What choice do you have?”

“At least show us the children. You’ll get everything you’ve asked for.”

One sighed. Processed through the voice-disguising synthesizer, it sounded like a computer glitch. “Do you wish to end this discussion now?”

“I just want to bring the Schraeder family home safe.”

"Your words are guaranteeing the opposite. But maybe the failure is on my end. Maybe I haven't convinced you that I am capable of following through. Fair enough, Agent Gordon. So pick one."

"I'm sorry?"

"Pick one of the children."

Everyone in the Sandbox wore an expression of pure terror. Nicky could have sworn she saw James Haller's soul leave his body.

She tried to salvage the moment. "If I pick one of the children, you'll show them alive and unharmed?"

"No," One said in a tone of gleeful malice. "I want you to pick one of the children so that when that child's face is destroyed with a shotgun blast, you'll know I'm serious."

Out of the corner of her eye, Nicky saw Randolph Schraeder try to contain his rage and fail. Spectacularly.

"Stop antagonizing him, you stupid bitch!" Schraeder bellowed from his screen. Then he leaned forward as if to speak directly to the kidnapper. "Listen to me, *whoever* you are," he said, this time without the thunder in his voice. "This is Randolph Schraeder. Ignore the feds. I oversee this operation. And I am prepared to pay you right now, no questions asked. Just tell me where to send my plane."

One ignored him. "So who will it be, Agent Gordon? Brave little Cal? Or sweet young Finney? Would you find it useful to hear them cry first?"

"She doesn't speak for me!" Schraeder shouted. "Didn't you hear me tell you to ignore her? Do not touch one hair on the heads of my children! I'll give you anything you want!"

But One heard exactly none of that, because Nicky had given Hope the signal to mute Randolph a split second before he called her a stupid bitch. The billionaire was, for all intents and purposes, screaming into the void.

James Haller must have realized this, because he hurried outside the Sandbox to call his client directly in a kind of sidebar. On-screen, Randolph looked furious when one of his assistants pushed a phone in his face, insisting he take it. He refused at first but eventually gave in and took the call, turning his back to his computer camera.

Well, that's one good thing about having Haller here, Nicky thought. Wrangling Randolph must be a full-time job.

"There's no reason to do that," Nicky said to One with as much calm as she could summon. One had to know she wouldn't flinch, no matter how horrifying the threat.

One had to understand that *Nicky Gordon* was the only obstacle between him and the billion dollars.

There was a great and terrible silence on the line. Nicky scanned the faces of everyone in the Sandbox: Mike Hardy. Jeff Penney. Hope Alonso. Ross Lindbergh. If one of them was the mole, she couldn't tell; none of the faces betrayed a thing. Randolph Schraeder turned back to the screen as James Haller rushed into the room.

As if One were waiting for the return of the entire party, his synthesized voice finally spoke again.

"Here is what will happen. The billion will be delivered to a former military airstrip in the Antelope Valley, about an hour north of Los Angeles. The billion will be placed on the tarmac no later than three a.m., otherwise Schraeder's wife and children *die*. The billion will be left unattended, otherwise the wife and children *die*. If I detect police presence anywhere near the airstrip, the wife and children *die*. If anyone tries to follow the pickup aircraft, the wife and children *die*. If there are tracking devices on the ransom, they *die*. If these conditions are met to my satisfaction, the hostages will be released and their locations shared with Mr. Schraeder.

"Do you understand these instructions and agree to follow them?"

Now it was Nicky Gordon's turn to be quiet, because this was not her money. There was only one person in this room who could agree to these terms.

Randolph Schraeder said: "Pay the sons of bitches."

CHAPTER 89

Friday, 2:57 a.m.

RANDOLPH SCHRAEDER'S PRIVATE plane arrived at Sargent Field just before the three a.m. deadline.

It was a minor miracle that the plane had made it on time, even in the middle of the night, when air traffic was quieter. But One must have known precisely how long it would take. They had considered every detail, every possible factor.

Kidnappers usually planned these things down to the second.

Sargent Field was a decommissioned World War II–era airstrip on the outskirts of Palmdale, California. The site had been intended for use as postwar housing until developers realized that there wasn't exactly a demand for homes in the high desert so far away from Los Angeles. All that remained now was a ghostly grid of almost-streets and a few sample bungalows that had been taken over by desert squatters.

This was where Jeff Penney and a small elite unit of SWAT

officers holed up, about three phantom blocks away from the airstrip. Nicky prayed none of One's spotters had watched them move into position.

The moment the location was given, all available FBI and LAPD forces gathered around that dusty scrap of an airstrip. In the bright light of day, the airstrip looked like it had been made by a bored giant scraping a fingernail along the desert floor. At night, it was barely noticeable. You had to know it was there.

Yes, Nicky Gordon was well aware that One had warned them not to watch the handoff. But One had to know they would be watching anyway. Nobody just drops a billion dollars in the desert, shrugs, and walks away.

Nicky had stayed back in the Sandbox with Mike Hardy, Ross Lindbergh, and Hope Alonso, who were busy gathering all possible eyes on that tiny strip of desert. LAPD air support, the National Guard—whoever was available at this ungodly hour. But when Schraeder's private plane landed, all they had was Jeff Penney's SWAT video feed from three blocks away.

"I need more eyes online," Nicky told Hope.

"We're working on it," she said. "There's just not much out there."

One most definitely knew that too. And the wide-open desert spaces meant that it would be easy to spot any law hanging around. His choice of a handoff location was brilliant, Nicky had to admit.

"How about some eyes inside Schraeder's plane?" Nicky asked. "Even a FaceTime from Virgil Tighe's cell phone would be useful. Hope, can you get him on the line? And where the hell did Haller go?"

"He said he was taking some time in the conference room to regroup," Hardy said. "I know, I know. I'm also pretty bummed he didn't kiss us good night."

"Are you still trying Tighe, Hope?"

"He's not answering his phone," Hope said.

Keeping his eyes fixed on all those pallets of cash, no doubt.

Virgil Tighe remained unreachable right up until the plane landed, when he sent a terse message to the task force: We're here.

Touchdown was a lot rougher than anyone had anticipated. Nicky watched as the plane skittered down the tarmac like a wobbly stone across the surface of a pond. She didn't realize how nervous she was until she released her grip on the arms of her chair.

The plane braked to a complete stop mere seconds before the deadline.

Virgil and three Capital employees made quick work of unloading the four pallets and single jewelry case. The cargo door, unfortunately, was on the opposite side of the video feed, so Nicky didn't lay eyes on the ransom until Virgil and the others returned to the plane and took flight once again.

Leaving a *billion dollars* on the dusty tarmac in the middle of the high desert.

How easy would it be, Nicky thought, to just speed in with an ATV and scoop up that jewelry container? More than half a billion dollars for a tank of gas and about a hundred and twenty seconds of effort.

Was this part of One's plan? Scoop up the gems and leave behind the cash as if it were pocket change, a sick kind of gratuity?

She wouldn't know until the kidnappers finally showed up to collect their prize.

CHAPTER 90

"YOU KNOW, THIS is my favorite part of police work," Mike Hardy said. "Up late, belly full of candy bars and coffee, waiting for absolutely nothing to happen."

Nicky gave him a tiny smile. "We won't have to wait too long. I don't think these guys are going to leave an obscene amount of money just sitting there on the tarmac."

"I don't know, Nick," he replied. "I'm not sure I'd drive all the way to Palmdale even for a billion dollars."

"I'm surprised I can convince you to spend the night in Koreatown with me."

"You're right. You might as well be in the real Korea."

This was about as much humor as they would allow themselves under the circumstances. Though maybe *humor* was too generous. Both had spent the past twenty-four hours wide awake and stressed to the breaking point—pretty much *anything* would be funny at this moment. Anything to ease the tension of Nicky's secret fear that Mike was somehow involved with One. That *he* was their mole in the task force.

Because it's the charming ones you need to watch out for.

"I'm surprised you didn't want to be out in the field for this one," Nicky said. "You usually like to be in the center of the action."

"Didn't I just tell you how much I hate Palmdale?"

"But you'd have the thrill of the stakeout and all, just like in the good old days."

Mike grinned and nodded slowly, understanding Nicky's not-so-subtle dig. "The good old days with my pal Tim Dowd, you mean?"

Here it was, finally out in the open.

"Is that why you stayed behind, Mike? To keep an eye on our little task force?"

"Yeah, Nick. That's *exactly* why I stayed behind. My job in this whole thing is to make sure you don't get too close to my employers. Who are totally the kidnappers. If I start to think you're onto them, I have instructions to take you out." Mike made a gun with his fingers and pulled the trigger.

"But you wouldn't have to kill me," Nicky said. "It would be enough to let One know everything happening here in the Sandbox. And you could have given your accomplices access to our chat program."

"Which would be incredibly clever, if I knew how to do such a thing, which I don't," Mike replied. Then he stared at Nicky, all humor drained from his face.

"What is it?" Nicky asked. "You ready to confess?"

Thing was, Nicky wasn't sure if she was kidding right now.

Maybe it was the lack of sleep or the general undercurrent of paranoia. But it would be very Mike Hardy to laugh and joke until the moment he admitted the ugly truth.

"It's funny," Hardy said. "When you asked me for help uncovering the mole, you know who I thought about straightaway?"

"Who?"

"You."

Nicky returned Mike's intense stare. "You're going to have to walk me through that one."

"Think about it," Mike said. "You had this sudden promotion to lead this *specific* task force, and that's after you've spent months investigating a smaller group of kidnappers. Why didn't you bust them? Why haven't you shared a single suspect's name? Maybe you're protecting them because you've joined forces with them. Maybe you thought they were thinking too small. Maybe it's all about the billion-dollar score."

Nicky held Mike's eyes for a long time before finally saying, "Well, Kaitlin *will* be starting college in a few years."

Mike cracked a smile. "Okay, so we've established that neither of us is the mole?"

Nicky twisted her face into a grin. "We've established no such thing."

Mike's cell phone buzzed, rattling the desktop. "Hold on," he said. "Must be my evil overlord One, calling to give me my next set of instructions."

Nicky stared at him as he answered his cell.

"Tell me you've got something good for me," Mike said. He nodded and stood up from his chair. "Put her on." Then he handed his cell to Nicky.

"Mom?"

"Kaitlin, honey! Are you okay?"

"I'm fine, don't freak out, everything's good!"

"Where are you right now?"

"Surrounded by about a dozen dumpy old cops, thanks to you."

"I'm sorry," Nicky said. "I truly am. Listen, ask one of them to find you a place to crash for a while, preferably not the drunk tank. I'll come get you as soon as I can."

"Come on, Mom. The people in the drunk tank have the best stories!"

"I'll see you soon. I love you."

Kaitlin told her mother she loved her too, which gave Nicky the strength to deal with what lay ahead. She would need it.

Nicky handed the phone back to Mike, who was grinning wide.

"And *that* is why I stayed behind," he said. "I was waiting for word from my crew. They picked up your girl outside the Grove, not far from where she disappeared."

"Okay, so maybe you're not the mole," Nicky allowed.

"But you haven't cleared yourself yet," Mike said. "I mean, Special K is kind of a genius. You may need that billion dollars to cover the tuition for all the advanced degrees she'll earn someday."

"So let's keep our eyes on her college fund."

CHAPTER 91

Friday, 4:02 a.m.

THE FIRST SIGN of the kidnappers: the sound of whirring blades cutting through the calm of the desert.

"Everybody, quiet!" Jeff Penney said over the comms. "You hear that, Gordon? They're arriving an hour after they told us to be here. They're screwing with us!"

"Yeah, I hear that."

The chopper emerged from the dark, speeding toward Sargent Field. But it was hard to make out details, at least from where Nicky was sitting in the Sandbox. It looked like a blur in the night sky. Maybe the digital image quality wasn't the best. Or maybe this helicopter was built for stealth so it would be tricky to follow.

That wouldn't be a problem, since the task force had access to long-range radar. Now that the chopper had made itself known, the flight tracker revealed that it had been following a path that originated in Nevada.

Nicky wondered if the kidnappers were actually based in Las Vegas or if they simply wanted the task force to think so.

The former was a good possibility, considering dead ex-con Rubin Padilla's ties to their suspects.

But they wouldn't know anything for certain until the kidnappers picked up the ransom, flew back to their home base, stripped naked, and started rolling around in those four pallets of cash or engaging in whatever kind of celebration they had in mind. They'd do that right up until the task force showed up and slapped handcuffs on every last one of them.

You can't just grab a billion dollars and expect to disappear off the face of the Earth.

Although One planned on doing precisely that.

The chopper drifted closer to the airstrip. The pilot didn't seem to know anyone was down there watching; Jeff Penney and his team were doing a good job of staying out of sight.

"The bogey has all lights off," Jeff said. "This guy is good."

"Anybody know the make of that chopper?" Mike asked over his mic. "Hard to tell in the dark, and I'm no expert."

"Looks like a Bell 407," Jeff said over the comms. "We had those until air support started cycling in the AS350s."

The helicopter turned on its lights as it began descending to the airstrip, illuminating the four pallets of money and case of jewels below. The image reminded Nicky of a dozen bad science fiction movies where a UFO beams something up into its cargo hold.

"This guy is probably a former military pilot," Jeff said. "He knows what he's doing."

The Bell 407 lowered itself to the tarmac swiftly and efficiently, touching down within a few yards of the ransom. All the kidnappers had to do was load the money and jewels, and Randolph's billion would be theirs.

CHAPTER 92

WHAT WORRIED NICKY Gordon most was the lack of guarantees about the safety of the kidnap victims.

There had been zero signs of life since the family members had been taken a day and a half ago. The children seemed to vanish into thin air. There wasn't even visual evidence that Tyler Schraeder and Cassandra Bart had been taken; Nicky and her team were relying on the word of Mexican police. And the only clues that Boo Schraeder might still be alive were her personal effects found at Tim Dowd's borrowed hideout, and that was highly circumstantial.

Those personal effects could easily have been taken from her corpse.

Nicky wondered if this entire plot was even about the money. Perhaps it was about hitting Old Man Schraeder right where it would hurt him the most: his family and his fortune. The captives might have been killed immediately. The kidnappers might set the money on fire and upload a video of it to YouTube;

the jewelry might be destroyed or dumped into the Pacific. Schraeder had made plenty of enemies over the decades.

But deep down, Nicky knew the truth.

Of course this was about the money.

"What's going on out there, Penney?" Mike asked. "We can't see a damn thing."

"The chopper is blocking our visuals too," Jeff said. "I can't risk sending anyone out for a look. And it's tough to hear anything over the engines."

"No," Nicky said. "Nobody move. Just watch them."

They didn't have to watch long. Soon the Bell 407 ascended into the night air, leaving behind on the airstrip... absolutely nothing.

The chopper went dark and sped toward the San Gabriels.

CHAPTER 93

THE MYSTERIOUS BELL 407 departed from Sargent Field ten thousand pounds heavier and a billion dollars richer than when it landed.

Now the real chase would begin.

Unless this thing truly had some sort of unknown cloaking technology, Nicky knew it would not be too difficult to track it in real time as it carried the cash and jewels away. It was not easy to hide in the air. Which was precisely what troubled Nicky most.

How do these guys think they'll get away with a billion dollars?

They could try to transfer all or part of the ransom to another aircraft midflight. They could try to elude and outmaneuver any task force choppers following in pursuit. They could hold on to one or all of the kidnap victims until they achieved a safe distance. But ultimately there was no such thing as a safe distance. The trail would never go cold. They would eventually be tracked down.

If Nicky knew this, the kidnappers obviously knew it too. They'd thought of everything so far.

If these conditions are met to my satisfaction, the hostages will be released and their locations shared with Mr. Schraeder.

So what was their escape route? How would this end?

"Nicky!" Mike cried. "Are you seeing this?"

"And there goes another one!" said Ross Lindbergh. "Can you see it? What the hell are they doing?" The financial-crimes expert sounded personally insulted.

They were all pointing at the oversize screen, tracing an arc from the chopper to the mountains. The high-res video feed from Jeff Penney's team was enhanced as much as possible.

"What *was* that?" Nicky asked. "They're not all jumping out of that chopper, are they?"

"That was a money pallet," Ross said, unable to hide his astonishment. In this job he'd seen pretty much everything, but he'd never seen anything like this before.

"That was the *second* one," Mike said. "I watched them heave the first one overboard. What the hell are they doing?"

"And there goes the third," Ross said.

Nicky's mind raced. Okay, what was *this* play? Smart bank robbers often stashed their loot not far from the scene of the crime so it could be recovered later, sometimes weeks later, after the heat had died down. But that depended on the law not knowing the stash's location. Why would the kidnappers do this in plain sight?

"Penney," Nicky said, "tell me you can track the location of those bags."

"We're about ten miles away from the chopper," Jeff said.

"But we're in pursuit from the north. I'm going to need blockades on the south side of the mountain range."

"Are there any parachutes on those things?" Mike asked over the comms.

"Not seeing anything resembling a chute," Jeff replied.

"There's *gotta* be chutes on them," Mike said. "Those pallets smack into the side of Mount Baldy from that height, cash will be sprayed all down the canyon!"

"There goes the fourth and final pallet," Lindbergh said. Nicky pulled her attention away from the screen and saw that the flight path of the Bell 407 had radically changed—it was swerving to the northeast, picking up altitude and speed.

"Did they chuck the jewels too?" Mike asked over the comms.

"One of my guys said he saw something before they dumped the first pallet," said Jeff.

"We've got to get to that fucking drop site," Mike said.

CHAPTER 94

THE DROP SITE turned out to be somewhere in the wilds of the San Gabriel Mountains, a few miles west of Mount Baldy. This was *not* a move that Nicky Gordon had seen coming.

None of them had.

Was this the plan or was it some kind of accident? Why go through all this preparation and expense and trouble just to essentially *throw away a billion dollars*?

Depending on where the bags had landed, they might be located quickly or months from now or never. Even experienced hikers could get lost in the San Gabriels and not found until there was nothing of them left but bones, belts, and shoes.

Nicky *knew* this had to be on purpose. They must have attached tracking devices to the bags so they could recover them quickly and make their getaway at ground level before the task force could catch up with them.

"I want to know *exactly* where those bags fell," Nicky said. "Hardy, who do you have out there?"

"Nobody, Agent Gordon. That's way outside city limits. Hell, I'm not even sure that's Los Angeles County. The money could have been dumped in friggin' *San Bernardino*."

"I'm getting both sheriff's departments on the line," Hope Alonso said.

"I'll reach out to San Bernardino," Mike said. "Former colleague of mine runs their detective division. Give me three minutes and I'll have black-and-whites crawling up the side of the mountain."

"You know anybody with the LA County sheriff?" Nicky asked.

"Do I know anybody?" Mike asked as he thumbed a number into his cell. "Sure. But do I know anybody who would bother to piss on me if I were on fire? Not exactly."

"I'll contact them," Hope said with a trace of disgust in her otherwise unflappable demeanor. Hardy frequently offended her, and Nicky kind of loved her for it.

Into this Sandbox frenzy walked James Haller. His eyes looked wild, and his gait was unsteady. Nicky assumed he had been fortifying himself with something stronger than coffee from the machine in the conference room.

"What the hell is going on?" Haller said. "I've got Schraeder on the line telling me the kidnappers threw all his money out of the goddamned helicopter?"

Exactly *how* Randolph Schraeder knew that was beside the point. He most likely had an eager informant or two on Jeff Penney's SWAT team who'd fed him or friends at Capital text updates as the chopper came and went with the ransom. No, the troubling thing about Schraeder knowing was that he would be second-guessing her every move from here on out. Maybe even to the detriment of his own family.

"We're tracking the money right now," Nicky told Haller. "If you have any friends or pull with LA County sheriff, we could use your help."

Haller came to his senses enough to agree, then told Schraeder he'd call him back with an update. Of course he knew people who worked for the LA County sheriff; lots of disgraced deputies from there washed up on Capital's shores.

From the multiple video feeds in the Sandbox, Nicky followed the hunt for the fallen money on three fronts:

Jeff Penney and his team were speeding east on the 138 through Llano and then down toward Phelan, where they could catch the 2 and head south up into the mountains.

Sheriff deputies from San Bernardino were gunning toward the same route but approaching from I-15 and then speeding west on the 138.

And finally, sheriff deputies from LA County were making their way up the 39 from Azusa.

Now it was simply a matter of who would reach the suspected drop site first—and whether they could find the fallen pallets of cash in the thousands of acres of wilderness surrounding Mount Baldy.

Nicky was aware of James Haller following the hunt on the screens as well. He took frequent breaks to tap on his cell phone and mutter a few brief updates to his number one client, Randolph Schraeder: *Nothing yet. No, sir. No response. I am trying.*

"You planted a tracking device somewhere in the ransom," Nicky said.

"Of course we did," Haller replied. "In the jewelry case. My associate Virgil saw to it personally. The device is inside one of the emeralds."

"But it's not working right now, is it?"

"No," Haller said quietly. "Care to join me for a drink, Agent Gordon?"

An excited shout came over the comms. "We've got company out here!"

Company? Nicky thought. *On dark mountain roads two hours before dawn?*

But the LA County deputies who were close to the estimated drop site reported the same thing. They passed one late-model Jeep Wrangler and then, a mile up the road, a second, near-identical Jeep Wrangler. And then a third.

"We just passed two Jeep Wranglers as well," Jeff said. "What the hell is going on? Someone else here we should know about? You guys call in Homeland Security?"

Air support was able to confirm there were a total of eight Jeep Wranglers moving away from the top of the mountain. They weren't in any kind of formation or pattern; they were just ordinary vehicles headed down the sides of the same mountain.

Maybe it was a coincidence they were all the same make and model.

Maybe—if you were a complete fool.

"Turn around and stop them all!" Nicky shouted into her mic. "That is our only priority now!"

Goddamn, they were getting away with it.

CHAPTER 95

Friday, 4:19 a.m.

CASSANDRA BART'S SPANISH was just good enough for her to translate the words of an underling (she assumed he was an underling, based on his cautious tone) to his boss: *"Ellos pagaron el dinero."*

They paid the money.

Oh, thank God, she thought. Maybe this would all be over soon. She couldn't wait to be back home in her apartment, where she would shower for two days straight and then call her manager and instruct him never to say the name Tyler Schraeder to her ever again.

Or maybe she wouldn't spend another night in LA. Her sleepy Texas hometown sounded pretty great right now. If someone had told her that the road to Hollywood involved forcible detention, torture, gunfire, and mass explosions, she would have happily stayed in the bed of that truck watching the stars in the sky.

"What did they say?" she heard Tyler whisper. She couldn't see him because they'd blindfolded her again. "Cass?"

"I don't know," she lied.

"They paid the ransom, right? I heard the word *dinero*."

"Shh," she replied. "Let me listen."

"I knew my father wouldn't leave me dangling," Tyler said, relief in his voice. "I mean, I'm never going to hear the end of it, but whatever. The important thing is that we're going to be back home and safe very soon."

Their captors were chattering even more excitedly now; something was happening. Cass tried hard to tune out Tyler's nervous patter so she could focus on their words, but she was able to pick up only snatches of conversation. Sounded as if their captors were arguing.

No, I want to do it. It should be me. You promised this to me.

I promised you part *of the money. Not this.*

I'm better at this. What if you screw it up?

You can see to the girl.

Oh, I like the girl.

Or something along those lines. Why on earth would they be arguing if they'd just received their share of ransom? Their cut, it seemed, was something like a million *dinero*.

"Stay with me, Cass," Tyler said. "This will all be over s—"

Then came the thundering explosions that nearly knocked Cass out of her chair.

Blam!

Blam!

Blam!

She could smell smoke and pennies. She couldn't see a thing because of the blindfold, and now her hearing was gone too, thanks to the three explosions. Deep down, she knew why Tyler had just stopped talking. But Cass refused to accept it. This was not how it went in the movies, and movies reflected real life, or were supposed to. Hence, this could not be happening.

But Tyler did not say another word.

Nor would he, ever.

Cass stayed in this dark cocoon of denial for a long time, even as they untied her wrists and ankles and carried her to another chair, which turned out to be the passenger seat of a vehicle. A safety belt crossed her chest and clicked down near her hip. The blindfold was removed, but Cass didn't dare open her eyes even when the vehicle began to move and she felt fresh air on her cheeks. Eventually, someone began speaking to her in English.

"Miss Bart, please open your eyes," a man's voice said. "We are almost there."

No, thank you. Opening her eyes meant accepting what had just happened, and she was not ready for that yet.

"I assure you, Miss Bart, you are in no danger," the man continued. His accent was heavy. "I am just a driver. I am here to take you home."

Home. That was the magic word that unlocked her paralysis. Did she have a prayer of seeing home again?

Cass opened her eyes and saw dawn beginning to creep over

the horizon. She was on a Mexican highway, approaching the Cross Border Xpress pedestrian bridge. Her driver hadn't been lying—on the other side was home. Or San Diego, anyway.

"I have all of your papers right here," the driver said. "Your passport and entry permit from the Instituto Nacional de Migración. It has been already filled out, for your convenience."

Cass remembered this border crossing. In happier, more carefree times, she loved to come down with fellow actors to Rosarito Beach, where nobody recognized them (or were polite enough to pretend they didn't) and they could drink salted margaritas, act as stupid as they wanted, and make fun of the other tourists doing the same thing.

"I am sorry I cannot escort you across," the driver said. "I would very much have liked to spend time with you, maybe ride the trolley up to the city. Today is going to be a beautiful day and...well, this is embarrassing to admit, but I'm a very huge fan."

CHAPTER 96

Friday, 4:32 a.m.

THREE HEARD THE scream of police sirens and worried it was the LAPD or FBI trying to locate them. Maybe One had already sold them out.

But the sirens faded into the distance, and both Three and Four breathed a quiet sigh of relief. They were safe. For the moment, anyway.

Now the question was: Where in Los Angeles could they possibly leave these children in the middle of the night?

Police stations were open, but Three and Four weren't going anywhere near one of those. Way too risky. Malls were closed. Restaurants were too. Even if they found a twenty-four-hour diner somewhere, they couldn't just put Cal and Finney in the hands of strangers.

"What about a fire station?" their daughter asked. She'd overheard them talking, even though they'd been quiet—they were all in the same car, after all. Keeping secrets was just not possible. And their daughter was very sharp.

Three and Four looked at each other and grinned. Once again, saved by their super-brilliant kid. A fire station. Yes! That would be perfect. By the time the firefighters dragged the story out of the children and the local cops were summoned, the three of them would have put a comfortable distance between themselves and the station. They could make it to the 210 and head east as fast as possible.

They found a station a few minutes away, Arcadia Station 106. Three suggested just letting the kids out and telling them to walk up to the entrance, giving the three of them the maximum time to get away.

Four told him no way, they couldn't do that to these poor children. "What if they were our own kids?"

So they told their daughter to hang tight for a quick moment while they said their goodbyes. Three got out of the car but refused to get any closer to the fire station; Four was fine with that. As long as she was able to give them hugs.

"Don't worry," Cal said. "We won't tell anyone who you are."

"You tell them the truth," Four said. "About anything and everything. I'm just happy you'll be going home again."

"Will your daughter be okay?" Finney asked.

"She will," Three said, though he didn't sound terribly convinced. He knelt down to Finney's level and gave her a tight squeeze. Her return squeeze was even tighter.

Cal received a manly handshake from him. "Guess we'll have to wait for that Mastermind rematch, huh?" Three said.

"You really enjoy losing, don't you?" Cal replied, and Three couldn't help laughing. He patted Cal on the head. *Hell of a kid.*

Four wrapped both children up in a hug for so long that Three started to get nervous.

"I'm very sorry to have put you both through all this," Four said. "I hope you believe me when I tell you that we really had no choice."

"You are nice people," Cal said. "But you are also lousy kidnappers."

"Agreed, little man," Three said.

Then it was time to part ways. Three climbed behind the wheel of the car; Four waited to get in until they were at the door and knocking. Which, truth be told, drove Three out of his mind a little. But he understood. That was his wife for you.

The moment she climbed into the back, Three hit the gas. The screech of tires almost frightened him. *Way to not draw attention to your vehicle, dumbass.* "Sorry," he said.

Three didn't speak again until they took the Huntington Drive on-ramp to the 210.

"Where do we go now?" he asked. "Mexico?"

That was the cliché, wasn't it? A daring escape to the closest foreign country, where they would magically discover a kindly old doctor who knew how to cure their daughter of her blood cancer and where they'd somehow make enough money doing odd jobs to rebuild their lives, complete with a modest house on the beach and nothing but sunsets and one another.

But that wasn't reality, and Three was filled with the stark terror of knowing that their troubles were nowhere near over, and perhaps the worst still lay ahead.

"I'm calling my sister," Four said. "At the very least, it's somewhere we can stay for a day or two."

"But you said Aunt Shannon hates it when you stay with her," their daughter reminded her helpfully.

"She's going to hate me even more when I call her at four thirty in the morning."

Three fought back a laugh, which felt nice. You could almost be fooled into thinking this was just another family outing, full of in-jokes and spilling tea about various relatives. But he heard no phone call being made, and after a few seconds, Three glanced into the rearview mirror. Four was staring at her phone, mouth open slightly.

"Mom?" their daughter asked. "Are you okay?"

"Honey?" Three said. "What's wrong?"

"Nothing. Nothing at all. I just received a text from you-know-who."

Three felt his stomach turn into a block of ice. Clearly, One must have discovered they had betrayed him. Of course he knew; he had eyes everywhere. And now they were living on borrowed time...

"It says 'Release the children. Payment has been issued.'"

"What? Was that really him?"

"I'm logging onto our bank app right now," Four said.

Three checked the rearview again and saw his wife's astonished face. When she looked up and locked eyes with him, he knew everything was going to be okay. He couldn't believe it. They could finally go home.

CHAPTER 97

Friday, 4:46 a.m.

THE GOOD NEWS was that there were relatively few roads coming down from the mountain. Blockades were easily set up on the northern and southern routes. And the eight Jeep Wranglers were pulled over to the side of the road without a fight.

The bad news: The drivers were completely baffled about *why* they'd been pulled over.

All of them were rideshare drivers. Sure, it was a little weird to receive a notice to pick up someone in the mountains at four in the morning. But this was LA, so weird was kind of the norm. Plus, the person who'd booked each ride promised them triple their rate. The long drive was more than worth it, especially when the streets were pretty much dead.

And okay, sure, it was super-weird that someone had summoned eight of the same vehicles to trek up to Wrightwood to pick up the same passenger—"Randy Schraeder," according to the profile on the rideshare app—but again, this was LA. It could be part of some reality show. Who knew?

So they'd all driven here, but there was no Randy Schraeder in Wrightwood. Each driver tried calling the phone of the person who'd summoned them, and in each case, there was no reply. Weird, but who cared as long as the credit card charges went through?

But being pulled over by an assortment of LA and San Bernardino sheriff's deputies and members of an LAPD SWAT team, shotguns and revolvers drawn, lights flashing, threats shouted, and not-so-polite orders to eat gravel and lock your fingers behind your head—now, *that* was weird.

The drivers knew nothing about money or pallets of money.

They'd found nothing at the site but a closed mountain lodge, and there was no one to pick up.

Back in the Sandbox, Nicky wanted to scream. But you're not allowed to do that when you're the person in charge of the task force. This failure was on her alone.

"One," she said. "He's always a step ahead."

"He faked us out," Hardy said. "I'm so sorry, Nick. But this isn't exactly a win for him. Maybe he kept the jewels somehow, but that idiot just threw away four hundred million dollars that hikers are going to be collecting over the next decade. If the bears don't eat it first."

"The money's not up there," Nicky said quietly.

"We saw it fall out of the chopper," Hardy said.

"We saw what One wanted us to see. Sure, he might have thrown something out of the chopper. But it wasn't the money."

"So we keep following the chopper."

"Which dropped off the radar, literally, while we were chasing the phantom money on that mountain."

CHAPTER 98

Friday, 6:05 a.m.

TIM DOWD'S BODY was discovered beneath the Manhattan Beach pier just after sunrise by a couple of surfers on the dawn patrol.

Tyler Schraeder was still considered a captive, but security cameras at the San Diego border crossing picked up the image of a woman who strongly resembled his girlfriend, actress Cassandra Bart. A local FBI team was dispatched to pick her up and see what she might know about the missing heir to the Schraeder fortune. Maybe she'd talk. Maybe she'd lawyer up.

Boo Schraeder was discovered hitchhiking back to Beverly Hills. At first, she refused the ride in an LAPD squad car, saying that she just wanted to breathe fresh air and not feel like a captive anymore. The car crawled alongside her until she finally relented; she was rushed to Cedars-Sinai for medical evaluation.

Cal and Finney Schraeder had walked into an LA fire station, apparently unharmed.

A search team was dispatched to the San Gabriel Mountains to look for the money, but Nicky knew it wouldn't be there.

And there was no further word or demands from One, who seemed to have vanished into thin air along with the rest of the kidnappers.

ONE MONTH LATER

CHAPTER 99

Friday, 3:00 a.m.

JEFF PENNEY'S PHONE trilled at precisely three a.m., but he was already wide awake.

He'd been looking forward to this day for a long time. His whole *life*, actually.

His bags were already packed—one carry-on, one stowable hard case—and waiting by the door. Everything Jeff wanted from his former life was inside those bags. The personal items he didn't want to save had already been burned or dumped. Everything else he owned would be left to rot, and good riddance. He was done with LA. He didn't even want to shower one last time in this crappy overpriced place.

Jeff Penney would rather rinse the last remnants of this ugly, gross city off his body when he was resting comfortably in paradise. Or at least when he was on his way there.

He pulled on his leather jacket, slung the strap of the

carry-on over his shoulder, grabbed the hard case, and left his apartment. He didn't bother locking the door behind him; he didn't even close it. *Have at it, squatters.* That would make the forensics unit's job a little messier.

His carmine-red Porsche 911, his beautiful baby girl, was waiting under a tarp in the garage beneath his apartment complex. Of all the things he was leaving behind, the Porsche was what he'd miss most. Jeff hadn't taken her out as often as he would have liked; he was forever worried that some jerk would key her body in a parking lot somewhere out of sheer jealousy.

Now it's time for one last ride, baby.

Jeff threw aside the tarp, stuffed his bags in the small trunk, and fired up the 911. He raced through the garage and was annoyed by how long the exit gate took to crank itself open.

Once outside, he roared down Angeleno toward the I-5 on-ramp, headed north. *Goodbye, job. Goodbye, Burbank. Goodbye, lousy post-divorce crash pad. Goodbye to all the drama, professional and otherwise.*

The best thing about driving through LA at three in the morning was that you pretty much had the city to yourself. Jeff drove fast but not too fast; he didn't need to be pulled over by some bored rookie on a last-out shift. From now until the moment he landed at his final destination, he couldn't leave any traces.

Jeff glanced in his rearview and saw another car—a black Dodge Durango—about half a football field behind him. The Durango seemed to be keeping pace with him. Maybe it was some idiot coming home late from a party or some poor sap reporting for his construction job at stupid o'clock in the morning. But maybe...

Maybe it was something else.

The Durango never got any closer, which was a little worrying. Cars almost never stayed in lockstep with each other on LA freeways; somebody was *always* trying to overtake you. But just as Jeff started to wonder if he should hop off the freeway and shake the guy, the Durango took the Osborne Street exit and disappeared into the hinterlands of the San Fernando Valley.

Okay, Penney, take a deep breath. This was no time to succumb to paranoia. All his dreams were about to come true.

Jeff's 911 blasted up the I-5. He turned on his CD player to see what he'd left inside the last time he'd driven his baby. Turned out to be an Eagles album, *The Long Run,* with Joe Walsh whining away about being "In the City." He wanted to laugh.

Not for long, Joe.

Jeff Penney was going to a magical land far, far away from the cesspool of El Lay. And he'd be traveling there with enough money to...

Well, to do absolutely *anything* he wanted.

CHAPTER 100

WHEN BOO SCHRAEDER and Virgil Tighe arrived at the desert meeting spot, Jeff Penney was already there, leaning against his Porsche with his arms crossed.

Before Virgil even killed the Peterbilt's rumbling engine, Boo was climbing out of the cab. She hurried across the airstrip, squealed excitedly, and wrapped Jeff in a tight hug, practically knocking him off his feet.

"Hey," Jeff said, laughing. "Good to see you too."

"It's been way too long," Boo said. "Do you know how many times I wanted to call you and just laugh my head off?"

"Tell me about it," Jeff said. "You look great, by the way."

Jeff had been tight with Boo back in the Seventy-Fifth Ranger Regiment. He was a few years older than Boo and immediately took her under his wing to serve as her mentor—with benefits, he'd hoped, although Boo had declined Penney's overtures.

"You know, I wasn't sure I'd be seeing you," Jeff said.

Boo playfully pushed him away. "Like I'd miss this part?"

"Couldn't have been easy escaping your fancy Bel Air fortress," Jeff said. "I heard that your husband went a little nuts with the cameras and armed patrols after...you know. Everything."

"Wouldn't *you* if your whole family had been kidnapped?"

"See, this is why I don't have a family. Still, ol' Randy must be watching you like a hawk."

"Maybe I escaped because I'm just that good," Boo said. "Or maybe he's in Nebraska tonight."

"Ahh. Nicely done."

"And maybe it helped that all of these fancy security upgrades were overseen by a certain Mr. Virgil Tighe."

Jeff Penney burst out laughing.

By this time, Virgil had climbed out of the Peterbilt and stretched his back. He ambled over to his coconspirators.

"What's so funny?" he asked, his face breaking into a wide grin.

Boo had met Virgil thanks to her soon-to-be ex-husband. Randolph and James Haller, Virgil's boss, were practically joined at the hip, spending hours puffing on Cubans and downing tumblers of Pappy Van Winkle 23 while discussing plans for global domination (or whatever). That left Virgil to entertain Mrs. Schraeder Number Five. They became friendly. Very friendly. Most men, from ex-cops to billionaires, couldn't help but fall for Boo. It was her superpower.

And the unlikely trio were now gathered at Sargent Field, where you could still see the grooves in the ground left by the Bell 407 a month ago. They stood in the desert dark, the sun not even a glimmer on the horizon, giddy with anticipation.

"Boo was just paying you a very nice compliment," Jeff said. "She told me she was able to slip away from the old man thanks to you."

"She's the one who deserves the praise," Virgil said. "I could do only so much with the cameras. But Boo slipped out of that rambling pile like a ballet dancer."

Boo felt herself blush. "Before we get too busy giving each other high fives, we have one last bit of business to attend to, right?"

The three conspirators hadn't spoken to one another since the events of last month. This was part of the plan. The investigations of the kidnappings, the midflight money dump, and the savage murders of producer Tyler Schraeder and ex-cop Tim Dowd were the most intense in California history. Nobody was above suspicion. Everybody and her grandmother had a theory. And as it turned out...

Absolutely none of those theories were correct.

Nobody suspected that Jeff Penney had played the role of One.

Nobody suspected that Virgil Tighe, who had just stepped down from his position as second in command at Capital for "family reasons," had played the role of One when Penney was otherwise engaged.

And absolutely *nobody* had guessed that Boo Schraeder, the fifth and current wife of target Randolph Schraeder, had planned the whole thing.

Yeah, Randolph had thought he'd dump her on the sidewalk like garbage while scheduling auditions for Mrs. Schraeder Number Six. Boo hatched the plot the same day she received the call from Randolph's fancy Century City lawyers offering her an absolute insult of alimony.

She didn't have every last detail figured out on day one, but she knew the perfect coconspirators: Jeff and Virgil. She'd come up with the broad strokes: The triple kidnapping. The code numbers. The evolving ransom instructions. Eliminating Tyler, Randolph's oldest child, had been Virgil's idea. But the coup de grâce—the final touch that had brought them here to the desert at four in the morning—that was all Jeff Penney.

"Boo's right," Jeff said. "The sun will be up before we know it and we've got a lot of miles to cover."

"Shall we collect our reward?" Virgil asked.

Boo smiled at them. "Let's see you boys work those muscles."

CHAPTER 101

JEFF PENNEY AND Virgil Tighe crouched down and used their hands to clear away enough sand to reveal a set of buried chains. They each gathered up a thick length of chain.

"Ready?" Jeff asked.

"Hold up," Virgil said. "Why don't we use the power lifter in the truck on this thing?"

"Because we don't need the power lifter," Jeff said. "What, did working in Capital's executive suite make you soft?"

"That's the whole point of being an executive, my friend," Virgil replied, grinning and patting his ample belly. "You get nice and soft while everyone else does the grunt work."

"Even people at the top," Boo said, "need to get their hands dirty once in a while."

"Come on, let's do this," Jeff said. "One... two..."

On *three,* they pulled on the chains that were welded to a large steel plate; it did not move easily. Soon the two men were sweating, even in the desert cold. The plate seemed to move only a fraction of an inch at a time.

After they'd pulled for several minutes, the steel plate shifted, revealing a good-sized hole in the ground. The men dropped their chains to look. Boo joined them and used the flashlight app on her phone to illuminate the contents of the hole.

Four heavy pallets of cash.

And a box containing six hundred million dollars' worth of rare and precious gems.

The billion dollars in ransom had never left the airstrip.

"I can't believe this worked," Boo said quietly, sounding almost reverent. "I'll admit it, boys, I had my doubts."

"I learned this trick from bank robbers we chased over the years," Jeff said. "The smart bandits hid their loot in the last places most cops would look. You know, like the trunk of an abandoned car parked a few blocks from the bank. Hell, this one heist team I knew stashed their booty inside a medical-waste facility. Dirty needles and bandages and everything."

"Stashing money in a dumpster is one thing," Boo said. "But leaving a billion dollars in cash and jewels out here in the middle of nowhere?"

"Genius, right?" Jeff asked.

"I still don't know how you managed to make the switch with everyone on the task force watching," Boo said.

"That's just it," Jeff said. "There was only one set of eyes on this airstrip. *My* eyes. Once the chopper landed, it blocked the team's view of the hole, and Virgil did his thing."

"Just a simple billion-dollar sleight of hand?" Boo asked.

"Wasn't too hard, really," Virgil said. "I had a couple of Schraeder's warehouse guys with me. They both have records, so they're not going to say jack shit unless they want a one-way ticket back to Leavenworth. Once they pulled the plate off the hole, I used the power lifter to take out the fake pallets and case. Put the real ones in the hole. Loaded the ringers onto the Bell. Took a couple of minutes, tops."

"And then you dumped the ringers somewhere near Mount Baldy," Boo said. "What happened to the helicopter?"

"Stripped and set on fire in the Mojave," Virgil said. "So it hasn't been recovered?"

"If it had been," Jeff said, "I would have heard about it."

The three conspirators stared down at their treasure.

"Well, boys," Boo said, "congrats on pulling off the crime of the century."

The former second in command at Capital allowed himself a tiny smile.

"Look at me, forgetting the champagne."

CHAPTER 102

"I'LL GET THE power lifter," Jeff Penney said and started off toward the dry van hitched to the Peterbilt.

Boo and Virgil had driven that monstrosity from a construction site in West Hollywood all the way up to Palmdale. But the rambling drive was the easy part. Jeff lowered the lifter off the truck, and Virgil jumped down into the hole and handed the case containing six hundred million dollars' worth of gemstones up to Boo.

"Don't spend it all in one place," Virgil said.

"I won't," she responded. "I'm going to spend it in a *lot* of places."

The jewels were her cut. Yes, the largest portion of the billion. But this had been Boo's idea, and she'd had to suffer throughout her marriage to Randolph Schraeder. The others agreed that she deserved every penny.

She was also getting Jeff Penney's beloved Porsche 911. Not that she'd have it long; she would take it only as far as a private airport in nearby Agua Dulce, where a chartered Gulfstream was fueled and waiting for her.

And from there, she'd be off to Europe to visit the black-market jewelry dealers she'd been flirting with online for the past couple of weeks.

"Hey," Boo called to Jeff, "I'm going to need those keys."

Jeff, who had just gotten the power lifter out of the truck, frowned. Then he dug into his jeans pocket, pulled out the keys, and tossed them to Boo, who caught them one-handed.

"Thanks," she said.

"Treat her nice. Don't go punching the snot out of her."

"I'll be gentle," Boo replied.

And she would. Right up until she turned the Porsche over to a chop shop in Lancaster so that it could disappear forever.

Jeff and Virgil would handle the cash. Each had his own preferred money launderer (Jeff had a connection in Russia; Virgil used a crew working out of Macao). They would drive the four pallets down to San Pedro, where a container ship waited to take them overseas.

Where—like Jeff Penney's beloved Porsche—they would disappear forever.

CHAPTER 103

Friday, 3:30 a.m.

NICKY INSISTED ON driving, and Mike Hardy was smart enough not to argue with her. Not at this ungodly hour.

"We should have stopped for coffee first," he said.

"No time for coffee," Nicky replied. "Because if we'd stopped for coffee, sooner or later you'd want to stop to pee."

"I could have used my empty coffee cup."

"Not in *my* car. Also—gross."

Mike rubbed his eyes. "Am I even awake? Or am I just dreaming about work again?"

"Take some deep breaths and clear your head," Nicky said. "We're almost in Palmdale."

For the past twenty minutes they'd been following a GPS tracker one of Nicky's agents had slipped into Jeff Penney's Porsche.

Their day had begun at ten past three with an urgent phone

call. One of Nicky's agents had spotted Jeff leaving his place in an awful hurry, in the Porsche he almost never drove. Nicky had nudged Mike, who was dead to the world. "Penney's on the move," she'd said.

Maybe now, after all these weeks, he felt safe enough to recover the ransom money.

Mike had groaned, and Nicky pushed him until he was practically falling out of her bed. Within two minutes, both had pulled on their clothes and strapped on their weapons. Nicky left Kaitlin a note, and they were on the road sixty seconds later, speeding toward the I-5.

Nicky refused to let Jeff Penney and the missing billion in ransom money slip through her fingers.

Jeff had been her favorite suspect from the start. She'd had zero hard evidence, but her informant on the Big Sur kidnapping (the million-dollar ransom for the comedian and his wife) said they bragged about having someone high up in the LAPD working for them. Someone with military training. Someone, the informant said, who rubbed *everybody* the wrong way.

So Nicky had put eyes on Jeff Penney 24/7.

He was *good*. He went about his normal routine, pretending to be just as frustrated and pissed as the rest of the task force. He tracked down leads and volunteered to help search the Mount Baldy drop site. And why wouldn't he? Jeff had no life outside of work. At home, all he ever did was drink a few craft brews and watch some wrestling or MMA on TV before falling asleep on the couch. Nicky was beginning to think maybe she'd been wrong about him.

And then came the call just a few minutes ago, Nicky's source telling her Jeff Penney was speeding out of town like his ass was on fire.

That same agent had stayed on Jeff's tail for a while but pulled off the freeway when he started to worry that he'd been made. But that was okay, because they'd slipped that GPS tracker into his Porsche 911 weeks ago.

"Where is he now?"

Mike checked Nicky's phone, which was mounted on the dash. "Looks like he's headed into the desert. But why? You think he's taking the long way to Mount Baldy?"

"No idea, but Penney's leading this dance," Nicky said. "All we can do is follow."

"Want me to call the sheriff's department, at least? Get a little backup out here?"

"We don't even know what this is yet," Nicky said. "Penney could be taking a drive to nowhere to see if anyone's following him."

"Or he could be out for a late-night drive to relax."

"Exactly."

Mike frowned. "You don't really believe that, do you?"

Nicky glanced over, then shook her head. "No."

They continued down the empty desert highway—the 138—in silence. Soon they were speeding by the ruins of Llano del Rio. Nicky had brought Kaitlin up here to tour the failed utopian commune from a century ago.

"Gee, Mom," she'd said. "I guess people have always been trying to escape LA."

All that remained of that social experiment were a few retaining walls of the meetinghouse and a massive fireplace from the former hotel.

But soon, even those ruins seemed like a metropolis. There was absolutely *nothing* out here but an endless expanse of scrub and sand and a desert wind that whipped everything into a frenzy now and again.

Dark thoughts crept into Nicky's mind. Maybe Jeff *knew* they were following him. Maybe he'd done a sweep of Porsche, found their GPS tag, and was leading them into a trap...

"Nick," Mike said.

"What?"

"Our pal Penney just stopped."

"Where?"

"Middle of freakin' nowhere is where. This doesn't make sense. Unless he stopped to take a leak."

"Guess he didn't have a coffee cup with him. How far away is he?"

"Oh, shit," Mike said. "I know *exactly* where he is."

As soon as Nicky glanced over at the screen, she knew too.

CHAPTER 104

JEFF PENNEY AND Virgil Tighe had two of the money pallets loaded onto the back of the Peterbilt and were about to lift the third out of the hole when Boo spoke.

"Uh, guys... what the hell is *that*?"

She was referring to a set of bright, bouncing headlights on the dim horizon. Lights that grew in size. This vehicle was gunning straight for them.

The three of them exchanged worried looks. Nobody should be out here this early in the morning. Or any time of the day, for that matter. This was a former airstrip used by no one, not even the military. There was nothing to do out here. Nothing to see. No reason for this vehicle to be approaching.

Unless it was coming for *them*.

"We got two pallets on the truck and two in the ground," Virgil said. "How do you want to handle this?"

"We don't know who they are," Boo said. "Could be nobody."

"We could leave right now," Virgil said, "split off in different directions. They might catch up with the truck, but the Porsche can definitely outrun 'em."

"Come on, man!" Jeff shouted. "We're not just gonna leave two hundred million dollars in the ground! Are you out of your mind?"

Virgil squinted into the predawn dark. "Better than staying put, getting caught, and losing it all. Maybe we can cover it up fast and come back for it later."

"That's *two* dumb ideas. We stay to hide it, we're as good as caught."

Boo watched both men closely. Virgil was the cold, analytical one. He would gather the facts and select the option that maximized reward and minimized risk, even if meant leaving behind a sizable fortune. Jeff, however, was more of a street fighter. Never admit defeat, never surrender—and never, ever walk away from that much money.

And who did Boo side with? Most days she was all about minimizing risk. But the idea of going through all this planning and sweat and drama just to leave two hundred million behind for Scrooge McDuck to shovel back into his vault? Hell no.

Boo caught Jeff's eye. He nodded.

Virgil sighed and shook his head—he'd read the conversation as it floated through the air. "Oh, no," he said. "No, no, no. I refuse to die in the Antelope Valley, of all places. If we're going to leave, we do it now."

"We're not leaving," Boo said.

Jeff pulled out the Glock strapped to his waist. "It's just one car. We're both experienced marksmen. I like our odds."

"I agree with you in theory," Virgil replied. "But think this through. We take out whoever's approaching, we've got to deal with another body. Possibly more, depending on who's in that car."

"I think it's an Escalade," Boo said. Her vision had always been sharp.

"So what?" Jeff said. "We've got a giant hole right here that's big enough for an Escalade."

Virgil just stared at him.

The vehicle was racing into view, and Boo had been right.

CHAPTER 105

THE ESCALADE GROUND to a skidding halt about twenty yards away. Its doors spread open like wings, and out of each side emerged a cop with a gun drawn.

Wait.

Boo Schraeder *knew* these cops.

They were the leaders of the task force investigating Boo's own abduction. Special Agent Nicole Gordon and Detective Michael Hardy.

Both had grilled her pretty hard over the past few weeks. Especially the fed, Gordon. She'd forced Boo to repeat certain details of her abduction over and over again, perhaps hoping to catch her in a lie. Boo was too prepared and polished to fall for an old trick like that, but it became clear that Gordon was the kind of relentless investigator who could not be discouraged, reasoned with, or even bribed.

Knowing this, Boo felt a heaviness fall over her. This could end only one way: with Gordon and Hardy dead and buried.

"Hey, how did you two know we were out here?" Virgil called to them, arms spread wide as if to say *See, I'm not a threat. We're all still on the same side.*

"Lace your fingers behind your head!" Gordon shouted. "You and Mrs. Schraeder both."

"Hold on," Virgil said. "You are seriously misunderstanding the situation. We're here at Mr. Schraeder's request. We're hoping to recover some of the ransom money you all lost."

"Hands behind your heads and get down on your knees!"

"We're not going to do that," Virgil said calmly. "Listen to me. I want you two to lower your weapons and talk to us sensibly."

"We're not misunderstanding a thing," Gordon said. "We know you were behind the kidnappings. You two along with Jeff Penney."

"Isn't Jeff Penney one of yours?" Virgil asked.

"Apparently not," Gordon said, keeping her aim steady.

"Oh, and for the record, Virgil?" Detective Hardy said. "You're an asshole."

"I've been called worse by better men than you, Hardy."

Boo frowned. She appreciated Virgil's valiant efforts but knew talk would not work. Not with these two. They were way too stubborn. They didn't want money; they wanted the *win*.

"You're right," Boo said. "Congrats. The money's been here the entire time. I'm tired of running. Tired of lying. It's right there in that hole. See for yourselves."

She wasn't lying. There was still two hundred million in that excavated rectangle in the earth.

But Penney was down there too. He'd jumped in just before Gordon and Hardy arrived.

So go on, Boo thought. *Take a good look.*

Gordon looked at Hardy, who nodded. He approached the hole carefully, gun still trained on Virgil, who shot Boo a quick look that meant *Be ready for anything.* Boo swallowed and nodded slightly. Gordon watched them both closely.

Hardy was only a few feet from the hole. "You might as well climb on out of there, Penney," he called. "Isn't this your Porsche up here?"

So that's how they found us, Boo thought. *Jeff was the weak link. He led them straight here.*

Boo had known this would end with killing—and now so did everyone else.

Jeff, in the hole, fired first, squeezing off a shot meant for the center of Detective Hardy's head. But the bullet missed its mark, and Hardy instantly returned fire; he shot twice, and both bullets found their target. Boo couldn't see where Jeff had been hit, but she heard his astonished yelp. Virgil pulled his sidearm, took a shot at Hardy, and caught him in the right shoulder, spinning him like a top.

Agent Gordon fired twice. Part of Virgil's head turned into wet mist. He twitched like a marionette and dropped to the ground.

Down in the hole, Jeff Penney choked on his own blood.

Gordon raced to check on her fallen partner.

Boo, who held no weapon, had watched this six-second gunfight with a strange detachment, as if it were nothing more than the climax of some action movie she was streaming and not her actual life.

Then she remembered herself and the keys in her hand.

Boo bolted for the Porsche. She had already stowed the six hundred million dollars' worth of precious jewels in the trunk (thank God). As she strapped herself into the driver's seat, she did some hard calculations. Was her escape plan still viable?

Signs pointed to *yes*. The FBI knew about this meeting place thanks to Jeff, but there was no way they could know about the Gulfstream. No one knew about that except her and Virgil Tighe. And Virgil wouldn't be talking anytime soon.

This can still work, she told herself. *But only if you get the hell out of this desert right now.*

CHAPTER 106

NICKY WAS APPLYING pressure to Mike's torn-up shoulder as the Porsche 911 blasted away from the airstrip. It skidded in the dirt and nearly clipped Virgil Tighe's corpse on the way out.

"Go get her, Nick," Mike said. "I'll be okay."

"No. I have no idea how bad this is—there's blood everywhere."

"You can't let her get away. And by the way, *ow*."

"Shut up and stop being so noble. We've got a tracker in the Porsche, remember? I'll call it in and have someone scoop her up."

"You think they'll get her before she has the chance to stash the jewels and lawyer up? Come on. Boo Schraeder was smart enough to kidnap herself and fool everybody, including her billionaire husband. You think she hasn't thought out her escape in absurd detail? That bitch has enough money to relocate to Mars if she wants to. You *know* this is our only shot at her."

Nicky sighed. "God, I hate it when you're right."

"And I haven't even had my coffee yet," Mike said. "Just come back for me after, okay?"

"Keep pressure on it. Can you still use your hand to call this in?"

"Go already!"

So Nicky went.

The Escalade roared across the wildly uneven desert floor. They had laid asphalt down on some of the planned neighborhood but not nearly enough. This was rough ground, and Nicky's vehicle bounced so hard, her teeth hurt.

But Boo Schraeder was blazing the same path. Nicky could still follow the Porsche's movements on her dash-mounted phone. Boo was about a mile ahead. Nicky needed to close that gap. She gritted her teeth and stomped down on the accelerator. The speedometer climbed to eighty and then beyond. The Escalade was rocking so hard on the terrain, she felt like it was about to achieve liftoff.

At least the Escalade was a sturdy vehicle built for abuse; the Porsche was a far more delicate piece of machinery.

Nicky could see it now, just ahead of her, bouncing along the tightly packed sand and through the gnarled scrub, its driver fighting hard to stay in control and make it back to the 138.

But if Boo did reach the smooth asphalt of the highway with her car intact, Nicky's Escalade would have no chance of catching up to her. Boo truly would vanish forever.

Nicky pressed the accelerator to the floor, stressing the Escalade's shocks and suspension system to the breaking point.

She also hit the power window button and steered slightly closer toward the Porsche. The speedometer struggled up past one hundred. Nicky pulled her gun, aimed it out the open window, and emptied her entire clip.

Boom went one of the Porsche's tires, and now Boo's car was spinning out of control.

The sand and dust that had been kicked up obscured Nicky's view. She braked hard and fast when she reached the crash site to avoid adding the Escalade to the wreckage.

The Porsche had plowed into one of the retaining walls of the old Llano del Rio commune meetinghouse. The front was destroyed, the windshield blown out.

But Boo Schraeder was struggling to free herself from the driver's seat, pulling on the seat belt, which was jammed.

Nicky approached, gun in hand. It was empty, but hopefully Boo hadn't been counting bullets.

"Hands on the wheel where I can see them, Mrs. Schraeder," Nicky said. "I'm going to call you an ambulance."

"I suppose you wouldn't be interested in a hundred million dollars' worth of rare gemstones, would you?"

"No."

"I didn't think so."

Nicky took a few steps closer. She could see Boo Schraeder was dazed, blood trickling from her forehead.

"He's a monster, you know," said Boo quietly, not turning to face Nicky. "He thinks he can do whatever he wants."

"I can see that," Nicky said. "I've met your husband."

Now Boo turned and locked eyes with Nicky. "He's not even living in our reality anymore. He's used his billions to build a nice safe bubble, and he thinks the world is his sandbox, that he can move people around like toys. I needed to teach him a lesson."

"I'm not sure he's the kind who will ever learn."

"Boy, did you nail it." A laugh escaped from Boo's throat—one that was utterly devoid of humor. "How did you catch us, anyway? Did you realize Jeff was the mole?"

"That was part of it."

"What was the other part?"

"I had a mole of my own," Nicky Gordon said.

SIX MONTHS LATER

CHAPTER 107

Partial transcript of US House Committee on Oversight and Accountability hearing

MR. ROACHE, CHAIR [*Heated*]: Isn't it true, Agent Gordon, that you ignored Bureau protocol just so you could advance your precious career?

SAC GORDON: No, Mr. Chairman.

ROACHE: Then why did you ignore protocol with the Schraeder family kidnappings, putting dozens of lives at risk? The American people demand to know!

GORDON: [*Inaudible*]

ROACHE: Let the record reflect that the special agent has muttered something profane under her breath.

MR. ASHENBRENNER, RANKING MEMBER: Come on, Howard. Gordon was merely clearing her throat.

ROACHE: She's avoiding the question!

ASHENBRENNER: And you're attacking the witness!

GORDON: Apologies, Mr. Chairman. I was indeed clearing my throat. It's been a long morning.

[*Broad laughter in the House Chamber.*]

GORDON: Let me start from the beginning. I noticed a disturbing pattern of kidnappings and believed the individuals responsible were gearing up for a much larger crime.

ROACHE: Do you have psychic powers, Agent Gordon?

GORDON: No. But I had a suspect, Rubin Padilla, who I believed was part of this kidnapping ring. I asked an agent with a deep background in undercover work to approach and befriend him as a potential accomplice.

ROACHE: Did you receive official authorization for this operation?

GORDON: Mr. Chairman, that would defeat the purpose of placing an operative in the kidnappers' organization. Especially since I had good reason to believe the kidnappers had a member of law enforcement in their ranks.

[*Laughter.*]

ROACHE: So you took it upon yourself to act unilaterally.

GORDON: I took it upon myself to apprehend the kidnappers with the tools at my disposal.

ROACHE: Who is this undercover operative?

GORDON: Her name is Cynthia Parker. We came up together as trainees at Quantico.

ASHENBRENNER: How did this work, Agent Gordon? And please be specific.

GORDON: Of course. Agent Parker spent a year working her way into the ring. First, she gained Padilla's sympathy with a hard-luck story, and he told her about an easy way to make some cash. This was how she met Ramiro Flores, who was later known as Five.

ROACHE: I'm sorry—Five?

GORDON: All the kidnappers were assigned code numbers, Mr. Chairman. No real names were used. The leader of the ring identified himself as One. So as the Schraeder plot came together, Agent Parker stuck close to Five and was able to share certain details. The kidnapper known as Three met Five in prison. Three was apparently a family man, doing all this for a sick daughter. When Three's wife was brought into the plot, she became known as Four. They seemed like the perfect pair to take the Schraeder children.

ROACHE: All of these numbers, and I forgot to bring my calculator.

[*Scant polite laughter.*]

ASHENBRENNER: Please continue, Agent Gordon.

GORDON: Another kidnapper, Two, was rumored to be ex-LAPD, but nobody except One knew his real identity as former LAPD officer Tim Dowd. Agent Parker proved herself so helpful to Five that he mentioned her to One, who thought she'd be useful for a side element to the main kidnapping plot. Agent Parker became Six.

ROACHE: And what was Six's task?

GORDON: To kidnap my daughter.

[*Astonished gasps.*]

ROACHE [*Banging on desk*]: That's enough of that!

GORDON: The idea was that my daughter would be taken at just the right moment to hobble the task force and distract me.

ROACHE: But your daughter was never in any real danger.

GORDON: No. But my daughter didn't know that until later that night. [*Pause.*] She's still pretty sore at me.

[*Warm laughter.*]

GORDON: There was no other way to play it. It had to look real to the mole in the task force. To my daughter. And, most important, to One.

ASHENBRENNER: Apologies, but I'm trying to keep track here. We know the dual identities of One—Captain Jeffrey Penney and Mr. Virgil Tighe, both deceased. We also know the true identities of Two, Five, and, now, Six. But what about the kidnappers known as Three and Four? I've read your reports very carefully, but I don't see any names.

GORDON: Unfortunately, we have not identified them yet.

ROACHE: That's mighty tough for me to swallow. What about the Schraeder children? Uh...[*Flips through pages.*] Calvin and Finnegan? Didn't they give you a detailed description of the perpetrators?

GORDON: The children were vague about their captors. We consulted with the top child psychologists at UCLA, and they believe the shock of the kidnapping made it difficult for them to remember specifics.

ROACHE: As I said, Agent Gordon, I find that very difficult to swallow.

GORDON: Do you have children, Mr. Chairman? No? Maybe if you did, you'd have an easier time understanding.

CHAPTER 108

Friday, 5:07 p.m.

SEBASTIÁN FROZE WHEN he heard the sirens in the distance.

They didn't sound *quite* like the police sirens from back home, and at first, he thought it might be an ambulance or fire engine. But as the wailing sirens grew louder, he realized that, no, this was the sound of the law. When they'd moved to Costa Rica, Sebastián had watched a YouTube video showing local cops—the Fuerza Pública—in action, just so he'd know what to expect. This was *definitely* the police.

And the sirens were getting closer.

All Sebastián could think was *If the police come, what will we do about dinner?*

Sebastián used to be a kidnapper with the code name Three. He and his wife, Four, had finally stopped thinking about themselves as numbers a while ago. They'd also stopped using their birth names when they arrived in Costa Rica and purchased new identities. The names and backgrounds were solid, but they didn't *feel* like Sebastián, Valeria, and Sofía.

The door behind Sebastián slid open. He spun around to see Valeria holding a tray of carne. She immediately knew something was wrong.

"Do you hear that?" Sebastián asked. "I think they're getting closer."

"Hear what?"

"There are more of them now..."

They listened, and, yes—there were clearly *multiple* police sirens.

"That could be anything," Valeria said. "We live in a busy neighborhood."

"Sounds like they're coming right for us. Where's Sofía?"

"She's inside reading."

Sebastián looked around their humble but beautiful home. The idea that they'd have to abandon this place and go on the run again terrified Sebastián. Where could they go? Was there *any* safe place for them?

An experimental drug had lured them to Costa Rica, which had a robust medical system and offered health care at a fraction of what it cost back home. Sofía was expected to make a full recovery after her most recent round of infusions. They almost couldn't believe their luck.

But now Sebastián felt the blood in his veins turn to ice. What would it mean if Sofía was forced to skip her final treatment? Would she relapse?

Now that the sirens sounded like they were right outside

their front door, even Valeria looked panicked. She carefully placed the tray of meat on a little folding table.

"I still have our go bags in the hall closet."

"I'll have to get the car and come back for you."

"We can cut across a few yards, hope they don't see us—"

But then the sirens seemed to fade a little, the Doppler effect bouncing off the sides of all the houses on their block.

When the sirens finally receded into another part of the city, Sebastián and Valeria realized they had been holding their breath.

Now here came Sofía, squinting in the sun, book tucked under her arm.

"Make sure you don't grill the meat too long," she said in Spanish. "Carne is supposed to be tender, not as rubbery as a car tire."

Sebastián looked at his daughter, exhaled, and smiled.

Valeria reached over and squeezed Sebastián's upper arm. Both knew they were going to have minor heart attacks like this the rest of their lives. But it was worth it. For her.

The family settled in for their evening meal at the small folding table out back, mismatched chairs and all. Dinner was good, although the carne *was* a bit overdone. As the sun set, father and daughter squared off for another round of Mastermind, the new family favorite. As usual, the daughter kicked the father's ass.

ABOUT THE AUTHORS

James Patterson is the most popular storyteller of our time. He is the creator of unforgettable characters and series, including Alex Cross, the Women's Murder Club, Jane Smith, and Maximum Ride, and of breathtaking true stories about the Kennedys, John Lennon, and Tiger Woods, as well as our military heroes, police officers, and ER nurses. Patterson has coauthored #1 bestselling novels with Bill Clinton, Dolly Parton, and Michael Crichton. He has told the story of his own life in *James Patterson by James Patterson* and received an Edgar Award, ten Emmy Awards, the Literarian Award from the National Book Foundation, and the National Humanities Medal.

Duane Swierczynski is the two-time Edgar-nominated author of ten novels—including *Revolver, Canary,* and the graphic novel *Breakneck*—many of which are in development for film or TV. Most recently, Duane co-scripted James Patterson's *The Guilty,* an Audible Original starring John Lithgow and Bryce Dallas Howard. He lives in Southern California with his family.

For a complete list of books by

JAMES PATTERSON

VISIT
JamesPatterson.com

Follow James Patterson on Facebook
JamesPatterson

Follow James Patterson on X
@JP_Books

Follow James Patterson on Instagram
@jamespattersonbooks

Follow James Patterson on Substack
jamespatterson.substack.com

Scan here to visit JamesPatterson.com
and learn about giveaways, sneak peeks,
new releases, and more.